W9-CUH-014

The Master
AND OTHER STORIES

SUE KAUFMAN

The Master

AND OTHER STORIES

DOUBLEDAY & COMPANY, INC.
GARDEN CITY, NEW YORK
1976

C. 3 RP

All of the characters in this book
are fictitious, and any resemblance
to actual persons, living or dead,
is purely coincidental.

"The Pride of the Morning" and "Mary Pride" first appeared in *The
Atlantic Monthly*, copyright © 1963 by The Atlantic Monthly Company.

"The Master," "Accomplice," "Under the Trees," and "Without Mistletoe"
were first published in *Mademoiselle*.

"In the Woods of Truro" and "The Rescue" first appeared in *The Southern
Review*.

"Tea at Le Gord" first appeared in *The Paris Review*.

"Icarus" first appeared in *Redbook*.

Library of Congress Cataloging in Publication Data

Kaufman, Sue.
    The master, and other stories.

    CONTENTS: Here: Mary Pride. Summer librarian.
Under the trees. The pride of the morning. Without
mistletoe. An injection. [etc.]
    I. Title.
PZ4.K21294Mas [PS3561.A863]   813'.5'4
ISBN 0-385-12048-6
Library of Congress Catalog Card Number 75–44523

For Jerry and Jim

Contents

Here

Mary Pride

He had been dressed and waiting for twenty minutes, and was sitting on the end of his carefully remade bed in the darkness, thinking that the whole thing was really quite funny, like a cartoon about an elopement, when the whistle finally came. Round, low, warble-pure on the first note, it lightly switched to a clean bobwhite cutoff—a startling sound for a girl to make, especially that one. He picked up the little canvas airline bag that held his swimming trunks and a towel, quickly stole down the uncarpeted stairs, and went out the door, managing to close it behind him without so much as a click. She stood under the streetlight, straddling a boy's bicycle, her brother's, he supposed. With one long look at her, dressed in worn jeans, a shirt, sneakers, a bandanna around her head, he stopped thinking there was anything funny. She wouldn't look that way for anyone else, he thought angrily, irrationally, and padded noiselessly up the driveway to the garage.

Blindly entering the gassy darkness, he groped past rusted garden furniture, a lawn mower, a stack of old M.D. license plates until his fingers closed over the cold handlebars. Carefully he edged the bike out past the coupe's left fender and wheeled it to the front of the house. As he came up, she reached into a brown paper shopping bag hanging off her handlebars and took out a lumpy towel. "It keeps smacking my knees when I pedal," she explained loudly, ignoring the fact that it was just a little past five in the morning and everyone on the block was sleeping. "Can I put it in your basket?" He nodded, then inexplicably dropped the towel; it exploded on the damp sidewalk, a red bathing suit, a cap of pudgy red rubber flowers, a container of Toujours Moi talcum rolling out. She dropped her bike with a tinny clatter and stooped to pick up her swimming things, flipping them all back into the towel, jelly-roll fashion, then jamming it into his basket atop the canvas bag. "We'll use my shopping bags for the flowers. I brought four," she said, louder than ever, and went and re-mounted the boy's bicycle with movements that made him blink.

"Where are we going?" he asked, doggedly whispering.

"The bay. Dodie Finch and Greely Smith are meeting us there," she called, and set off. As he followed, David glanced uneasily up and down the block of ugly-tidy houses, certain that curious eyes were peeping from behind the pulled shades and billowing curtains, and equally certain she had intentionally, perversely wished to draw them. She's really crazy, he thought, knowing very well she had insisted on picking him up because she was ashamed of her own street, her own house; too dumb not to guess that he, just like every other boy in the three top grades of Willett High School, knew exactly where she lived. In fact he, like many others, often purposely used that rundown little street on his way into the village to run an errand for his mother, just to be able to pass the dingy stucco house where she lived with her mother, younger brother, and hopeless drunk of a father, and to let his mind, for soothing seconds, make the plunge from glaring daylight to suave soft dark.

As they turned onto the deserted boulevard, the sky above the streetlamps seemed a lighter gray. It was five-fifteen on what promised to be a fine clear day in June, ground mist aside. Which meant the bunting-trimmed tables could be set up on the school lawn, under the dipping willows, and mothers in straw and flower hats, fathers in light suits could pleasantly mill about, drinking orange punch out of paper cups and exchanging mutual congratulations.

It was the dawn of Willett's graduation day, the day on which he, David Thorne, and by some miracle she, Mary Pride, would graduate from Willett High School. Though no one quite knew why or when they had originated, an elaborate set of traditions had become attached to the events of this day. Always, for as long as anyone could remember, an escutcheon had stood on the auditorium platform where the graduating class sat trembling and perspiring in their white dresses and dark suits, a shield fashioned from flowers, bearing a blue W and the class numerals in cornflowers on a white ground of daisies. Strangely enough, it was the particular job of the graduating class to rise before dawn (on this one day they ought to have been allowed the sleep of the just) and, on bicycles (cars were taboo), to forage in the empty fields and back lots of Willett for the flowers used in the shield.

Since hundreds of flowers were needed, the absolute minimum was one bag of flowers per senior; two were hoped for. Once found, the flowers were carried back to the school and dumped on the grass in back of the gymnasium, a place where the more artistic members of the junior class sat waiting, ready to begin weaving them into a wire frame. Released, the seniors slowly convened at Jim's Diner in the village. After eating a large breakfast, and after waiting out a short token interval for digestion, they proceeded to a small bathing beach on the inlet. There, in lockers still dank with winter, they changed into bathing suits; giggling, covered with goose bumps, they then ventured out onto the dock and, after much shoving and hanging back, plunged shrieking and howling into the still chilly waters of the bay, unwillingly performing the ritual which had become a sort of baptism for the graduation that afternoon.

David, who had decided long in advance that the whole set of customs was stupid and childish, was now angrily certain of it as he cycled down an asphalt road slick as tar from mist and dew. Though for the first time in his life he was alone with Mary Pride

—a situation he had efficiently dealt with many times in his imagination—he couldn't think of anything but how cold he was without a sweater, how queasy he felt without breakfast, and how frightened he suddenly was; riding along, he found he couldn't remember one word of the valedictory address he had to give that afternoon. At the moment it would have soothed him to see the work of a practical joker in his being given Mary Pride as a partner, but he knew very well that poor old Mr. Buckley had done the pairing, and knew, better than anyone, that even had one of his classmates done it, there was just no joke. True, Mary Pride was what she was and, true, he was the valedictorian, one of the most brilliant students Willett High School had seen in many years, but he was not by a long shot the classic grind, the pimply bespectacled scapegoat who is terrified of girls and is the constant butt of his schoolmates' jokes. He didn't have pimples, he didn't wear glasses. He was tall, went out for sports, and was attractive enough to have always had all the friends and girls he could want. If he didn't want many, if he carefully limited the number of these, it was not out of any bookish sense of superiority but out of an almost neurotic hypersensitivity about his father. Oh, he was the doctor's son all right, but with a difference. Like Mary Pride's father, his father drank, but unlike Mary Pride's father, who had started out as a bartender, his father had destroyed a practice which had once encompassed five counties, had disgraced a noble profession, to say nothing of what he had done to his wife, his son. Yet, strangely, David could not hate him. He was just horribly ashamed, in a coldly intellectualized way, of such massive human failure, and now, as he rode along behind Mary Pride, he could not help being struck by the irony of it all, bitterly thinking: If nothing else, we have *them* in common.

With a sudden mechanical click the streetlights went off, leaving the morning hanging shades lighter about them. Everything was coated with moisture; there was a steady *drip-a-drip* from the thick tangles of foliage clumped on either side of the road and from the tall old maples and elms that branched out over the street. His English bike was well over six years old, but David had taken care of it, just as he took care of all the personal possessions that so rarely came his way, and it was good as new. He rode easily, almost effortlessly, while up ahead Mary Pride was almost doubled over with the job of pedaling her brother's old balloon-tire bike. He had seen she was grimly determined to stay in the lead, and he let her, accepting the fact that she resented being paired off with him and didn't even want to ride alongside him. This was not because there was someone else she would rather have been with, or ought to have been with—a girl like that didn't have steady boyfriends; no one wanted the doubtful honor of it—but simply because she disliked him intensely, having mistaken his reluctance to venture even a casual "hi" or "good morning" for pure priggish snobbery.

If she only knew, thought David, suddenly relaxed enough to let his mind drift in this direction. As he had ridden along, his speech had completely come back to him, and he was so relieved he almost began to enjoy the predawn dampness, the strangeness of being out at that unlikely hour. Against his will he found himself staring at Mary Pride's back, unable to keep from noticing the way the thin strained shirting clearly outlined the straps and band of her brassiere, the suggestive way the worn brown leather seat fitted her full bottom. And then, in spite of everything—the hour, the surroundings—he felt it all beginning, the sludgy thickening of throat and tongue, the tensing of muscles in calves and forearms, the strange fumy lechery rising, burning in his chest. Like many sluttish girls—or, at least, girls with sluttish reputations—she roused frighteningly powerful and conflicting emotions: a pure, almost uncontainable lust, along with the brutal need to inflict humiliation, pain. It was this that had kept David away from her, had kept him from making his try like the others. Though, like the others, he despised her, it was just because he despised her that he could not take advantage of what she was. Concerned for her, he was even more concerned for himself; he just didn't think he'd be able to handle the crushing load of self-loathing that was bound to come later, when he had finished with her, in whatever way.

As a result, he steered clear of her in the flesh and let himself meet her only in his mind, constructing lurid little daydreams from what he had heard stated as facts. For the stories about the poor girl were endless, and though David doubted that they were all true, they had the same powerful ability to goad and rouse that her person did, and just by saying some of them over to oneself one could experience a certain intense pleasure—without guilt. And so David let himself go now as he bicycled along in the raw morning air, let his mind swarm and fill with violent images while he softly repeated, like some profane litany, key phrases and words from the things he had heard.

Suddenly, without warning, Mary Pride pulled over to the side of the road, and he shot past her, braking his bike with a grinding squeak. When he turned he saw that she had already left her bicycle on the curbstone and had started on tiptoe across someone's lawn, her target a large flower bed which began on the left side of the house's front steps and ended against a tall privet hedge. Like the rule which forbade the use of cars, another stated that no one, under any circumstances, was to pick flowers from the private gardens in the town. Honor-bound honor student that he was, David smoldered with disgust and hatred as he watched her trample through the bed and greedily pick the flowers, and he began to glance almost hopefully up at the lead-framed windows where the blinds remained tightly closed. She finally came to dump the wet blue flowers into his wicker bicycle basket and smiled up into his furious face. He blushed, almost choking on his anger, and said hoarsely, "There are laws against trespassing."

"Oh, laws," she said with a scornful little laugh, and, her pale eyes full of contempt for all the laws she had knowingly, willfully, gladly broken, she went and remounted her bicycle.

Murder in his heart, David fell in behind her once again. Soon, with an abrupt turnoff, they left the main boulevard, and, passing through an open wooden gate, entered the intricate network of back roads that eventually led, like a maze, to the bay. Here asphalt gave way to dirt; trees arched and tangled in thick meshes overhead; houses, larger, statelier, sat far back on gently graded slopes, half hidden by tall ivy-covered walls or high hedges, reached by long winding gravel drives. As he followed her sure lead, David smiled to himself, taking a sanctimonious pleasure in noting the way she knew each devious turnoff, each new rutted road, until they suddenly passed an ugly yellow stucco wall, higher than the rest, topped with crude iron spikes, and his nasty smile vanished. In fact, he almost squirmed on his bicycle seat as he remembered being parked against that wall, remembered the glare of the flashlight that had thrust through the rolled-down window of his father's coupe and mercilessly exposed him, lipstick-smirched, struggling upward on the seat (the unbuttoned girl wisely stayed down), while a harsh Scottish-caretaker voice ordered him to get a move on before the cops were called. With a roar of the motor and a scrunch of tires on loose dirt, he *had* gotten a move on and had not been back in the two months since. But now, forced to let up on Mary Pride, unable to take cover in self-righteous deceit, David began to use her, found he could not keep from wondering what it would be like when she was beside one in a car parked under fragrant maples, the *tick-a-crick* of leaves, the soft chirrup of crickets, and the slow turning of bodies the only sounds in the dark.

Under a dazzling impact of red-gold light his mind stopped short. Dead ahead the sun was rising over the water, a red ball which burned through thinning mists; to the left and right of the road low grassy hills rolled away and glistened, covered with such a profusion of buttercups, daisies, dandelions, and cornflowers that David's heart began to race. The sun cast a heavy orange-yellow glaze on everything, thickly coating the crude little shacks that stood down near the water, ugly lean-tos which the fishermen used for their equipment. Between the shacks, rowboats lay on their sides in the sand, looking like big exhausted fish washed up by the tide. Not another living soul was about.

Mary Pride had already pulled her bike up into the grass on the right side of the road and sat in the roadbed unlacing her red sneakers. She set them carefully by the bicycle, rose, and without so much as a glance back at him, slipped the shopping bags off the handlebars and waded barefoot into the deep tangled grasses. When she got as far as a large oak halfway up the slope, she unceremoniously sat down on the grassless patch under its boughs, took a pack of cigarettes from her shirt pocket, and lit one. To his great annoyance, her utter indifference stung him, made him feel foolish. He left his bike on the grass near hers and resentfully plunged into the high wet grass, hating the way the bottoms of his khaki pants immediately became drenched and stuck to his ankles. When he reached the place where she sat, lordly as Robin Hood, under the spreading tree, she turned up her pale-blue eyes and for an unnerving moment just stared at him. Then, wordlessly, she held out the pack of cigarettes, with a book of matches neatly tucked down into the cellophane wrapper. After he lit one, he awkwardly dropped down into the dirt at her side. For several minutes they sat in almost hostile silence while twin elastic threads of smoke rose tautly to the boughs overhead, then broke into curly tangles when they hit the leaves. "Why'nt you roll up your pants?" she said suddenly. "And take off your sneakers. They'll only get all wet and sloshy."

Shrugging (but also maddeningly flushing), he rolled the soggy pants halfway up his calves but left his sneakers on; he had always been secretly ashamed of his long, bony, bumpy-toed feet. "Where do you suppose the others are?" he asked, not because he cared, but because he knew she did.

To his surprise she looked bored. "The easiest way to get here is from around the other side," she said, irritating him by her assumption that he would not know this part of town. She stood up. "I think we each ought to get one of a kind," she said as she handed him two paper bags. "One daisy and one cornflower apiece—don't you?"

He nodded and swallowed hard, forced to look away from the face suspended above him: several yellow snails of pinned-flat curls had worked their way out of the edges of her Paisley scarf; without its usual frame of carefully streaked hair, without the color lent by lipstick and powder, her face seemed strange—larger, pale, almost plain—and yet a blunted look of honesty and health and cleanliness shone out of those flat freckled planes, a look that took him unawares and deeply moved him, coming from where it did. Confused, he watched her stride purposefully away up the slope, then suddenly stop and begin to snatch at daisies, and he wondered if it was the cigarette that made him feel so lightheaded. He reluctantly rose and ambled out onto the hill. He veered off at an angle to the place where she worked and kept his distance from clumps of shiny three-pronged leaves he thought might be poison ivy. The thatchy abundance of flowers excited him, and soon he was wholly absorbed in the mechanics of picking the white flowers with furry gold centers, liking the way the hollow tubes of stems broke cleanly between his fingers, even liking the sticky milky substance they left. Methodically, as rhythmically as a field hand, he bent and picked, bent and picked, and he slowly filled one of the bags, astonished when he finally found himself on the crown of the hill, the sun suddenly hot and strong on his back and hands.

"Hey. How're you doing?" she called from somewhere close in back of him. He turned and found her less than twenty feet away, her face red and perspired, her ankles and wrists stuck with bits of wet leaves and grasses. For a long minute they stared warily at each other above the heads of the flowers. Then, simultaneously, they burst into laughter. "Both mine are filled," she said, coming to peer into the one bag he had almost finished. "Lord, but you're slow. I'll help you do the cornflowers. It's getting too hot."

Side by side, they slowly worked their way back down the hill, filling his second bag with the last of the cornflowers. Their grasping hands made rippy-plucky sounds as they closed quickly, almost in unison, over the brittle stems of the blue-starred flowers, which had a faint iodoform smell that David liked. By the time they were near the bicycles the bag was brimming. Mary Pride was left with a fistful of flowers and no place to put them. "Use my bicycle basket," David began, then stopped, perplexed by the look of horror that was slowly puckering her face. Holding her hand straight out in front of her, she slowly uncurled her fingers one by one; together they looked into the glistening, leaf-stained palm, where, mangled among the tangled stems, a large furry yellow and black bumblebee writhed and buzzed in agony. "Oh, no," she whispered, with a sharp little insuck of breath. "Please," she repeated, turning her back. "*You* step on it, David. I'm barefoot." For the span of a second, David listened to the tortured buzzing. Then he took one heavy step forward and savagely ground his rubber heel into the dirt. He felt sick to his stomach. "Okay," he said.

She turned back, paler than ever. "I didn't mean to," she said like a child.

"It could have stung you," he said stupidly, feeling something terrible happening in his chest.

"No. I don't think bumbles do."

He didn't correct her. He just stood there, all hands and feet and neck, suddenly helplessly in love with her. "My sneakers are sloshy," he finally said.

"Take them off," she said simply.

Without a thought for his bumpy bony feet, he did. Setting the sneakers at the roadside to dry out in the sun, he looked at his wristwatch. It was six-thirty, and though there was still no sign of the others, he was reluctant even to mention them. "How would you like to take a ride in one of those boats?"

"Do you think we could?"

"I don't see why not," said her, the observer of rules, the guardian of private property. "Nobody's around. And it's not as if we were stealing it—"

Though she saw their earlier roles reversed, she permitted herself only a faint mischievous smile. She held out her hand, and he took it, pleased by the innocent way her fingers lightly curled in his, by the feeling of sun-warmed dirt under his bare soles. As they drew near the water, a gummy salt smell, thick as broth, rose from the broken shells littering the sand. The sun, climbing rapidly, had burned away the mist. When they walked out onto the sand, a big gull flapped from behind one of the weathered shacks and lit on the still water, sending out concentric rings of ripples.

Unable to bear the heat, David stripped off his damp shirt and laid it out on one of the boats, completely unself-conscious until he turned and saw that Mary Pride was staring at him, frankly curious—and surprised. He almost laughed aloud. Instead, acutely aware of himself, proud of his flat-muscled hairless chest, he quietly asked her to give him a hand with one of the boats. Together they easily turned and lifted one of the old shells, carrying it down and setting it in the shallow water, leaving one corner still resting on the sand. David picked up the oars that had fallen out and, fitting them into the rusted locks, handed her in. When she was seated, he shoved them off with a thrust of one long leg, and the boat slid out along the glassy top of the water. He decided to let it glide by itself, and drew in the oars, folding them across each other in back of him like big wooden grasshopper wings. The sun, shining directly down and reflecting off the slick water top, blinded them. But slowly, as though to oblige them, the boat eased around all by itself, and the sun was no longer in their eyes. It was then that they saw them—six of them—scattered across a grassy rise a quarter of a mile down the curving shore; on the road just below, the hood of a blue sedan iridescently glittered.

Going cold, David dully stared at the car, which belonged to Greely Smith's father, and he wondered about his own tenacity—stupidity, really: everyone else broke rules and got away with it; why did he feel so compelled to obey them?

He did not want to look directly at Mary Pride, did not want to see her reaction. But suddenly one of the figures on the hill straightened up, and after staring intently out at them began waving, calling, "—ary? —ary?, and David had to look at her. She sat very still, neat nostrils flaring. When the call came again she swore softly, and turning away, reached into her shirt pocket for the pack of cigarettes. Wordlessly shaking out two, she lit one for David and handed it to him. He put it, warm and moist from her pale mouth, into his own, but nothing in him stirred; like the mists, all his dank thoughts had burned away, dried up in the sun. Shifting so that he could no longer see the others on the shore, he stared at her. Her kerchief had come so loose she had finally snatched it off; she sat peacefully, unvain, faintly squinting, almost ugly with the light harshly striking her face and Medusa curls snaking all over her head.

"Are you happy about college? About getting in where you wanted?" she asked, breaking the long silence, shyly turning away to trail a finger in the water.

"Yes," he said flatly.

"Are you going to be a doctor too?" she went on innocently, but all the same he blushed, feeling the deep touchy ache that any mention, direct or indirect, of his father brought.

"No. Not a doctor."

"Well, what then?" she persisted clumsily.

"I don't know," he said, sounding curt and irritable, but actually just wanting to end this conversation which could only lead them to her own plans, to her future without college, which at best would contain a job in some village store and a marriage, if she was lucky, to some local fireman or policeman or gas-station attendant.

"I'm going to secretarial school," she announced, as though having read his mind. She looked almost angry, her face red, lips primly compressed. "A good one. In New York."

"That's fine," he said, too loudly. "Good secretarial jobs can lead to all sorts of things. You start that way—and who knows?"

"Yes. Who knows?" she said, her eyes like blue enamel buttons. Then, with a teasing smile, she gripped the gunwale to her right and slipped agilely over the side of the boat, leaving it gently drumming from side to side. She had somehow managed to do this without wetting her head. She laughed up at him as he peered down with stupefaction; then turned and gave several ploppy paddle strokes which carried her a few feet away. "What d'you think you're doing? You crazy?" he demanded, but, ignoring him, she splashed about in a listless circle, finally coming back to the boat. "'S cold," she gasped breathlessly, laughing still.

"What did you expect?" he muttered, furious at her for making him furious. Stonily he watched while she gave a sudden puzzled grimace and went under, then swore aloud. She was willing to play games even at the expense of her hair, carefully washed and put up for the graduation and the dance that night. Almost beginning to hate her all over again, he watched her head break through the stirred-up water. "'S a cramp," she spluttered, rolling forward like a seal, and through the clear green water he could see her, right under the surface, frantically doing something to one of her legs. For an eternal moment David, a fair swimmer, sat and unwillingly considered the lucid, icy water. Then he sprang to life, dropping prayerfully to his knees in the center of the boat. When she surfaced he leaned far out, grabbing hold of a cold and slippery wrist, and the boat gave a violent tipping lurch. "Steady," he said, more to the boat than to her, and drawing her in close, got hold of the other arm. Locked in a chill and viselike embrace, limbs working together, as synchronized as lovers', they slowly, between them, managed to ease her into the boat.

Eyes closed, she sank back into the bow of the boat. David stared disbelievingly at her heaving chest, quickly, guiltily looking away as she opened her eyes. "Felt like tangled rubber bands," she explained between breaths and experimentally moved her right leg. "Thank you."

Remembering his reluctance to jump into the water after her, he couldn't speak.

"I said, thank you, David," she repeated, louder now that her breathing was less labored, and, sitting up straight, stared challengingly into his eyes.

"For what?" he mumbled, hot-faced, and reached around in back of him to fit the oars into the locks.

When the boat gritted into the sandy shore the others were waiting. For a moment they just stood there, the girls tittering and shifting, the boys silent, tensely staring; the wet shirt clung to Mary Pride's torso, defining her deep breasts as explicitly as classic drapery in a museum. Incurious eyes flickered over David, helping her out; someone finally came forward with a shielding towel. At once, like nubile handmaidens, the girls closed ranks about Mary Pride, making hushing little gull sounds. From the boys there came low rumblings: "Bike on the car—" "Scratch the hood—" "I'll ride it to her house—" Dazed, David beached the boat, helped by Greely Smith, whom he heartily loathed, and who softly said, "Hey," winking as David buttoned his shirt back on over his bare chest.

The boys dispersed, one heading for Mary Pride's bicycle, the other two starting toward the shiny blue car. The girls were leading Mary Pride toward the road when she suddenly stopped in her tracks and, shaking herself free of them, turned. "David?" she called clearly, imperiously. "David Thorne!"

He blushed as he paused in the roadbed.

"You all right?" she asked; behind her, two of the girls exchanged a poking nudge.

"Sure," he said.

"I am too," she said, softer, as though they were suddenly alone. "I'm only going home to change into dry clothes. I'll be at the diner. Will you?"

Blinking, but not from the sunlight, David stared. For in her eyes was the whole summer ahead, the summer before he left for school, the last summer he ever intended to spend in this town. A summer of leaf-scented lanes, warm night sands, soft damp grasses, a glad and limitless giving of which he couldn't partake.

He stared, appalled, at his future, at himself, met much too soon, longing to cry out and protest at what he saw. Oh, what kind of cripple *was* a person, so bound by honor and tied by self-esteem they could not move, could neither take in hatred nor love since each asked too high a price.

"David?" she said, uncertain, growing hurt, the girls behind her grinning now.

"Sure, I'll be there," he said lightly, committed. "Hurry and change—I'll save you a seat."

Summer Librarian

The little library was set back in a grove of beech and maple, so old, so dense, the tightly meshed leaves gave anyone inside the building the illusion of being in the heart of a forest, rather than just off the main thoroughfare of a busy village. Made of brown shingle, it possessed all the whimsies of a more romantic period in architecture—dormers, porticoes, eaves, gables, dovecotes—and the rumor ran that it had once been the caretaker's cottage on a huge estate. Whatever its original function, it had been the Community Library for over forty years, and in that prospering, burgeoning town was one of the sole remnants of another way of life, now almost extinct.

Cruel Time, Obsolescence, Everything Passes (the Old Order above all)—of such was Mrs. Foss's obsession, and on the dark humid July morning she and her daughter Maria drove through the village in their old gray sedan she held forth, glaring out at chrome-and-glass storefronts and silvery new parking meters, filling the little car with her smoldering comments. Maria, a mildly pretty, unobsessed girl of twenty, who had heard all this too many times, merely nodded as her mother ranted, and with relief finally pulled the car up to the curb fronting the Woman's Exchange. ". . . heaven only knows what next!" concluded Mrs. Foss, getting out and slamming the door for emphasis, but then leaned down and added through the rolled-down window, "I'll be in front of Humbert's at five. Unless, of course, you want to join us for lunch."

"Five," said Maria, answering the luncheon invitation with a vague negative nod, and sat waiting to see if her mother, who was becoming alarmingly absent-minded, had her keys. With detachment she watched the small wiry woman cross the sidewalk, wryly noting how the pastel golf dress, calcimined gumsoles, and visored piqué cap made her look like a clubwoman off for the greens— precisely the desired effect. When she reached the door Mrs. Foss groped for a moment in a purse shaped like a horse's feedbag, but she finally came up with a bunchy key ring and Maria drove off. She proceeded along the still-deserted street for another block and a half, then turned into what seemed a private driveway, but after a few feet opened onto a vast free parking lot neatly bedded with raked gravel and marked off by spanking whitewashed partitions. Neither the lot nor the supermarket which had generously (shrewdly, claimed Mrs. Foss) built it had been there when Maria had been home from college at Christmastime. Because, unlike her mother, Maria loved progress, particularly when it changed the face of this town she had lived in all her life, she ignored her mother's instructions and left the sedan unlocked—one of those small futile gestures that still symbolize so much.

As she hurried out of the lot through another exit, and started down the long block to the library, massed bluegray clouds, already rumbling and shifting with thunder, were heavily pressing down. It had also rained the day before, and when Maria unlocked the glass-paned door she was almost overpowered by the fusty smell of yesterday's dampness, trapped in old boards, moldings, bindings. She rushed about, banging and tugging at all the warped sashes of the windows in the front room. Aside from the new chintz covering the window-seat cushions, and several additional layers of bright blue enamel encrusting the tiny ladder-back chairs, it was a room that had not changed at all since the days Maria had first come there as a child. The four large wicker armchairs and the rack filled with adult magazines were mere tokens, for grownups never lingered here. This front room had always been considered a children's reading room, and each time she came in Maria would look at the two long low tables (pocked and incised by two generations of furiously restless little hands), the bookcases crammed with brilliantly colored picture books and primary readers, and she would shiver, briefly haunted by the vision of herself, raptly curled in one of the window seats, lost, lost in a book.

After hanging her raincoat in a closet-bathroom off the back stacks, she came out to the big desk bearing Miss Leonard's brass nameplate. Though Maria was an old favorite of Miss Leonard's, the librarian had made plain her wish to have this part of herself kept intact while she vacationed. So each day Maria was forced to work on a surface cluttered with a heart-shaped faïence penholder from Quimper (stuck with blue and yellow quills), three china bowls of paper clips in three sizes, two jars of rubber bands in two sizes, a family of Doulton scotties, a Lalique bud-vase, and a fistful of jabbing pencils in a Toby mug. Sighing, Maria took a metal file-box and a pack of postcards, mimeographed "Dear _____, Your book is overdue!" from a drawer. As she began fingering through the cards in the little file-box, she saw that all the titles were those of current best-sellers, the names of the renters ones she had never seen before, and she knew that her mother would have pounced on this, claiming it as a further piece of circumstantial evidence against the newcomers, who (Mrs. Foss stated) were coarse and vulgar and had no taste. But it only made Maria consider the fate of the books during the heat of the last two weeks—she could see them, lying forsaken, left splayed open on a towel under the shade of an umbrella, or dropped onto the baking sands of one of the new beach clubs—and she sighed again, heavily, with pure envy this time, and dipping her pen into red ink, began.

By eleven, though the rain had still not started, only five people had been in and out of the library. One, a pale lumpish fourteen-year-old named Carol Danziger, had remained, settling herself in one of the wicker armchairs to read her newest selection (Elizabeth Goudge's *City of Bells*) with much noisy turning of pages and sucking of jujubes. In the week and a half Maria had taken over the library the girl had been in five times, clearly protecting herself from something at home by maintaining a careful distance from it, solacing herself with books and a new, instantaneous attachment to Maria she seemed to think secret. Though Maria felt sorry for the poor child—she was so overwhelmingly unattractive—she was more irritated than flattered by all her admiration, and today the creak of that indolent body in straw, the asthmatic breathing and wet sucking noises so set her teeth on edge she was about to do something drastic, when leaf-muffled shouts suddenly came from the front lawn, drowning out the exasperating girl. "Okay, Rourke, okay for *you!*" called someone just beyond the rhododendron bushes screening the front windows, and this was immediately followed by a shrill scream of girlish pain or delight—it was hard to tell which.

With a gritty clomp Carol Danziger brought her size seven-and-a-half moccasins to the floor. "Please, Miss Foss. Won't you tell them to go away?"

"Why?" asked Maria, staring with undisguised dislike into the gray eyes swimming behind lenses.

"Because. Because they're not *supposed* to play here. Miss Leonard always makes them go away."

Frowning, but knowing it would be simpler in the long run, Maria rose and went out on the front porch. Four boys in jeans and a ponytailed girl in tight cotton slacks were ranged out under the roof of leaves, the boys throwing an unraveled baseball back and forth in a magnificently casual game of catch, arcing it tauntingly high and slow while the girl scurried and leapt between them, hopelessly trying to intercept. Delight, thought Maria, diagnosing the girl's screams, and reluctantly started across the spongy lawn; one of the boys caught then held the ball, five pairs of eyes watched her approach—a small long-haired girl in a

chambray dress trying to look stern and imposing, but only succeeding in looking what she felt: foolish. Someone gave a long
low whistle. Her face burning, looking to neither side, Maria
picked the tallest boy, the seeming leader, a grinning rawboned
redhead, and marched straight up to him. Politely, but firmly, she
asked would he and his friends mind playing ball somewhere else,
people in the library were trying to read. In the following silence
she heard suppressed sniggers, from the corner of an eye she saw
the ponytailed girl sidle up to one of the other boys and meaning-
fully nudge him in the ribs.

"Ur. Well now, Miss . . . ah Miss? Well. We thought it being
vacation and like that nobody studied in there." The redhead's
yellow eyes shone insolently, taking her in, while from behind her,
from the same spot the whistle had come, a boy's voice soft with
wonder said: "Hey. Are you the librarian?"

"I am the *summer* librarian," Maria said with deadly calm, ignoring the speaker and continuing to address the redhead in front
of her, "and it just happens that there *are* people who read in the
summer. We will all be spared a great deal of unpleasantness if
you just move, without further comment."

"Well, now, ya don't say . . ." mincingly began the redhead as
she turned to leave, but a husky blond boy now in her line of vision, undoubtedly the whistler (and leader, she belatedly realized), quietly said, "Shove that, Rourke," and the mimicry
stopped. In a tense, simmering silence, Maria started back to the
porch, rage making her catch her heels in the rain-softened earth,
making her clumsily lurch. Once back inside she stood watching
at the window—after a dawdling conference, they finally followed
the whistler's lead, straggling across the patchy lawn, majestically
ignoring the gate and pushing out through the high privet hedge
where they left a wounded gap—and she began to tremble with a
fury the situation hardly warranted, a fury left over from another
time.

"You were just wonderful, Miss Foss," Carol Danziger damply
breathed behind her, "just marvelous. Those disgusting boys.

Even the teachers are afraid of them. Of course," she added swiftly, daintily, "I've only been *going* to the public school since Miss Maitland's closed last year, and Mummy and Daddy are sending me away to boarding school next year. But I still had to be with them all this past winter. And you know the girls are every bit as disgusting as the boys . . . but then, you wouldn't know." She blushed heavily. "I mean I happen to know you went to Miss Maitland's because I saw you in one of the hockey team pictures hanging in the lunchroom. I remembered because you were by far the prettiest on the team."

Prettiest, thought Maria as she turned from the window and ironically smiled at the girl: the one slender form among eleven beefy ones, all lined up against an ivied gymnasium wall, right hands stolidly clutching hockey sticks, left hands vainly trying to hold down navy serge pinnies whose flapping pleats revealed lumpy, chilblained knees. "Thank you," she said dryly, inclining her head, then could not resist: "Actually I do know about boys and girls like that, and disgusting is an ugly word."

"But how could you possibly know about them?"

"It's quite simple. I went to the high school for my senior year."

"You did?" Gaggling, the girl jabbed her glasses back on the bridge of her unfortunate nose. "But wasn't that silly? I mean, leaving Maitland's in such a *crucial* year. I mean, with Miss Maitland so thick with all the deans at the good colleges?"

"I'm sure it was silly, but it wasn't a question of choice."

"Oh. Dear. I'm terribly sorry, Miss Foss."

"There's no need to be. I really liked the public school very much." As the poor girl, in an anguish of thrashing and swallowing, reached for her book, Maria was filled with remorse—why was she being so cruel?—and in a softer voice said, "I'm going out back for a cigarette, will you rap on the window if anyone comes in?" and hastily went out the back door.

The air was now so thick, so filled with moisture, it was difficult to light a match. Succeeding, she fiercely drew in on her cigarette and with troubled eyes stared out at the library's sad ruin of a backyard: on the left, at the end of an unused driveway, a rotting shingled garage was piled with cartons of moldering junk, its doors coming off the hinges; straight ahead and to the right trees, spaced wider than those out front, had let down enough sunlight to nourish a high wild expanse of grass. Neglect. Decay. Waste. Mostly waste. How vicious and pompous, how ironically like her mother she had just been, and all because the poor girl had unwittingly brought just that back: the waste, the needless waste.

But as overbearing as she had been, she hadn't lied. She *had* liked the public school, the jangle of bells and the shouting and laughter in the halls, the warm density of the overcrowded classrooms, all of it such a relief after the deathly hush of the frame house, and after years of Maitland's chill, sparsely filled rooms. She had also truly liked her wild and noisy schoolmates and had secretly longed to belong, to be taken in, and would have had there been time. For there she had been, a strikingly undistinguished student, suddenly bereft—of a devoted father, of the necessary funds, of the boost of Miss Maitland's invaluable connections—a student who either won a scholarship to college or did not go at all. Since her father had always stressed the importance of college, particularly the right college (though she now did not understand why), she had managed to go; by discovering a dormant "brilliance" of sorts in History, and by living a merciless, constricted life, she had succeeded in winning scholarships for three years at the college her father had most admired. For three winters she had supplemented a meager allowance from her mother by waiting tables, typing manuscripts, doing cataloguing in the library, shortening hems and altering dresses for classmates, and for two summers she had gone off with strange families to be a combination Mother's Helper and tutor in History for their petulant children. She had never complained or considered herself any sort of martyr, but at the same time she never permitted herself to dwell on the dangerous thought: None of this would have been necessary had her mother sold the house.

Maria's father, a Philadelphian, had inherited the pretty white Colonial house from an uncle just shortly after the end of the First World War. After much deliberation, he had accepted a long-standing offer from a New York banking firm, and had come up from Philadelphia with his bride and settled in Marberry Pond Park. Since they already knew many people in the Park, they instantly became a part of its quiet, secluded social life, and lived there happily, and uneventfully, but for the arrival of Maria at a time when they had long reconciled themselves to being childless. Maria's mother passionately loved the Park, her house, her garden, her friends. Maria's father liked the Park well enough, but he was an extremely practical, unsentimental man who, sadly enough, had never prospered, and when the town had begun its sudden violent expansion, he had seen opportunity, and wished to act. He wanted to sell and move to the city nearby: the land had quadrupled its value, he wished to spare himself the exhausting daily commute to the Wall Street banking house where he worked. But his wife was almost hysterical in her opposition. She detested the city. She hated apartment life. Life would be unendurable without her garden, her house, her friends, and the subject of friends brought up the most important thing of all: If they sold they would be the first in the Park to do so, which would amount to a betrayal of the other Park residents, their dear friends, since *he* knew the sort of people ready to jump at the chance to invade their private Park. He did not know, for he was the least snobbish of men, and the fate of "their private Park" did not remotely interest him, but the maintenance of precious peace did. He finally gave it up and soon afterwards succumbed to that strange, terrible exhaustion which it turned out had not been caused by the grinding daily commute at all. He was never told the name of what he had (multiple myeloma), nor did he ever learn that the dread disease which literally ate the marrow out of his poor bones also devoured the hard-won savings of many years. "It would kill him right now if he knew," warned Mrs. Foss. Maria, anguished, deeply loving her father, hardly needed any instructions to be silent. But taking root then, and after her father's death putting out tendrils that were never permitted to break through the surface of her conscious mind, was the ugly suspicion that her mother's real motive for silence had not been compassion, the wish to protect her husband, but fear, the deep well-grounded fear that had the dying man learned the true state of their financial affairs, he would have ordered the house sold from under him. And this spring, when the letter from her mother arrived at college, the suspicion burst out in full bloom at last—proven.

The first sentence in the letter, ending with three exclamation points, stated that the house had been sold. The following staccato sentences explained how it had come about: their house, it seemed, along with four others, had been the last ones left, and the contractor for the middle-income development that was to replace Marberry Pond Park, frantic to get on with things, had in desperation offered unheard-of sums to all of them. Quickly scanning paragraphs documenting betrayal—who had sold out first, who next and next—Maria came to the last and most important page. The house had to be vacated by mid-August, the latest: since there was now not only enough money for Maria to have a "carefree" senior year at college, but also to release her from the hateful summer tutoring, she would expect Maria home. Although, of course, she would need Maria's help in dismantling the house, and moving into the apartment she had leased in one of those new buildings on the station plateau, the rest of Maria's time would be her own—she would have her first real summer of freedom in years. Seeing that she had no choice, she had to go home, and knowing all too well what those hours of "freedom" would be like, Maria quickly made a mental note to write Miss Leonard about working at the library, then sat back to contemplate the enormity of what all this meant. It was not the proof that the house and what it stood for always *had* meant more to her mother than her husband or child, but the dark turn her mother's mind had taken, now that the house was doomed, that chilled Maria through and through. Instead of leaving, clearing out, starting a new life somewhere else, her mother had fanatically encamped on the battlefield, as it were, on the scene of her bitter defeat, and with her few friends rallied round her, clearly intended to make some symbolic sort of Last Stand, pathetic, senseless, yet filled with all the fury of obsessive hate.

Shivering, lighting a fresh cigarette, Maria now heard a ripping swishing sound, and looking to her right she saw a tall blond-haired boy, hands in pockets, striding through the tall tangled grass, making for the porch. The whistler, she remembered, as undaunted by her forbidding glare, he came right up the steps and put out a hand: "Hi. I was just going inside to look for you."

Though she pointedly ignored his extended hand, he was not put off. He let it fall, and continued, smiling: "My name's Harry Strickland and I came back to apologize for Rourke. He's a real wise-guy and doesn't know anything. I mean, you shouldn't mind him."

"I didn't," she said precisely. "And it certainly wasn't necessary to come back and apologize."

This time he reddened and began to blink, and she was instantly sorry, for the handsome face under the inevitable slick haircomb was disarmingly innocent, the blue eyes as clear and candid as a child's. "Well, I didn't really come back for that," he began again, taking courage from the sudden softening he perceived in her face. "The truth is I came back to find out what someone like you's doing here, in a dump like this. This town, I mean."

Because she had to forcibly hold back a smile, she said, almost sternly: "As I told your friend, I'm the summer librarian."

"Well, you talk awful funny. You sure don't *come* from this town and that's what I mean."

"I've lived here all my life."

"Yeah? Then how come I've never seen you before? In the village or anything. You been away?"

"That's right—at college." She flicked her cigarette down into the spongy black loam, and put her cigarettes into the pocket of her cotton shirt-dress.

"College? Phew!" Pursing his lips, he studied her with wide soft eyes; then bent his long neck and watched one of his sneakered feet kick at the rotting top step as though it belonged to someone else. "That must make you about eighteen."

"Twenty," she said with dry finality, and turned and opened the door in the same instant that Carol Danziger began rapping on the window with her garnet ring.

When the firehouse siren went off at noon, she prodded Carol Danziger from her wicker entrenchment, locked the library, and walked into the village for her lunch. Like thousands of growing small towns all over the country, it had completely changed its face in ten years. As low-priced developments mushroomed on its outskirts, and Garden Apartments (restricted to two stories by zoning laws) sprang up in its heart, the merchants had either rallied to the challenge by bravely remodeling and expanding, or had been vanquished by bolder, more inventive new competitors. Maria's route to the drugstore was a purposefully devious one, which took in an extra block of glittering new storefronts, a detour that skirted the Woman's Exchange where her mother's graying sandy head was always visible in the gloom behind the plate glass.

Her first week at the library, to pacify her mother about having arranged for the job in the first place, she had dutifully gone to the Woman's Exchange for lunch every day. The moment she came in her mother, Mrs. Knowles, and Mrs. Hollis stopped whatever they were doing (nothing), and began bustling about like girls, dragging four Hitchcock chairs with peeling gilt stencils (from Mrs. Peterson's dismantled house, and up for sale) into a small alcove formed by a ceiling-to-floor bookcase in the rear of the shop. There, placing them about a beautiful cherry Lazy Susan table (from Mrs. Knowles's dismantled house, and not up for sale), they took out thermoses filled with hot coffee, wrinkled brown paper bags of homemade sandwiches, and sat down to their lunch. When the last sandwich crust was gone, one of them went out front to the case of "home-baked goods" (Mrs. Luther, the cabinetmaker's wife) and brought back a plateful of something crumbling—*Linzer torte, lebkuchen*—or of strudel so damp or brownies so hard they could no longer be decently offered for sale. Maria did not see what they ever *did* sell, since most of the wares were contributed by themselves or by friends who were hardly likely (or able) to repurchase their own handiwork, and since she had witnessed the reception given to strangers, having helplessly watched the whole thing through spaces in the room-divider bookcase that formed the little alcove. The bell over the door would tinkle, there was an aluminum clatter as the young housewife from one of the developments, wearing slacks or shorts, tried to maneuver the baby-in-stroller through the door; whoever had risen from the cherry table and gone out—her mother or Mrs. Knowles or Mrs. Hollis—would come to a stop in the center of the front room and remain there, arms crossed, watching but not attempting to assist, airily asking "Yes?" when the complicated entrance-operations were completed; there was the inevitable shy murmur, ending ". . . just like to look around," and whoever had gone out would say "Ah *yes*" like someone successfully grasping a sentence in a difficult foreign language, and would remain there, arms still stolidly crossed, while the stranger explored. The poor self-conscious young woman would then begin to timidly finger and inspect the tin trays decorated with *découpages* of flowers and fruit and the wastepaper baskets glued with hunting scenes and Audubon prints (the work of old Mrs. Davis), the string gloves, potholders, crochet trivets, tea cozies, baby bibs embroidered with bumblebees (all from deaf Mrs. Wade), the little satin pillows filled with sachet, netted bags holding dried potpourri, pomander balls (Mrs. Hammond's specialties)—and finally, since nothing was tagged, would shyly ask some prices. The outrageous sums were always given with a negligible smile, a smile which changed as the stammered explanations began ("didn't dream . . . only a tiny present") into a grimace so chilling, accompanied by a murmur of ". . . but of *course*, my dear," so patronizing, that Maria, hidden behind the bookcase, had often trembled with rage. She knew she could not change the three bitter women, but she also knew she did not have to sit and passively witness their senseless games of spite. She managed to stick it out through the first week, but then thought up the lie which would release her for the rest of the summer: on certain days, she told her mother—and she never knew which days they might be—she could not close the library promptly at noontime, for there were people there doing special research with a deadline, or other people who had phoned and asked to come during the lunch hour; since she did not want to hold up their lunches at the Exchange, it was best to count her out from then on; she would grab a sandwich in the village when she could. Though her mother had violently objected—did she realize that would mean needlessly spending at least six dollars a week?—Maria had been happily eating her lunches at a big new air-conditioned drugstore ever since, a wonderful lively place full of clatter and chatter and jukebox din.

Big drops were staining the pastel slates as she hurried back up the library walk after her lunch. She had only been safely inside a few minutes when the rain came down at last, and the whole building began reverberating with cozy pittering sounds. She had finished the "overdue" postcards and dropped them in a mailbox on her way to lunch, so she now went into the musty back stacks and turned on a dim overhead light, browsing in the narrow book-lined aisles which smelled of leather and binder's glue, until at last she found what seemed a light frivolous novel and carried it back inside. To her relief, the rain kept away all comers, even Carol Danziger, and for two hours she traveled about Mayfair, Paris, Rome, worlds away. The library was singingly quiet, the rain closed in the mind. When it finally stopped at four, it lifted the heavy curtain of silence, of rapt peace; tires began wetly cracking out on the boulevard, a horn blew irritably, someone ran thumpingly up the street frantically calling a dog or cat or child named "Kim." Yawning, stretching, she rose and went to the glass-paned door where she stood staring out with amazement at the violent drenched green of the grass, until the front door rattled open behind her and a now-familiar voice said: "Thought I'd see if you drowned."

Without even turning, she put her hand on the knob of the door in front of her and angrily yanked it open. "You leaving just because I came in?" he asked forlornly, and when he got no answer, relentlessly padded across the room and followed her out the door. On the tiny ledge of back porch two colonial settees faced each other, kept dry by the capacious overhang of the roof. When he came out she was sitting resolutely in the dead-center of one of them, but instead of taking the empty bench, he ignored her forbidding glare and jammed himself into a corner of hers. Fury, exasperation—and despite herself, fear—made her fingers so stiff and clumsy she could not light her cigarette. After quietly watching two of her futile attempts, he leaned forward, calmly striking a match from a book he had held hidden and ready in his hand all the time. When a gust of warm damp wind blew it out, he frowned and quickly struck another, cupping big protective hands about the plumy flame. Defeated, Maria bent to light her cigarette, trying to think of something to say that would be so nasty, so cutting, he would go away and never come back, but as she withdrew, puffing on the cigarette, she accidentally glanced into the eyes above the flame. Her face going hot, she hastily retreated to the far corner of the settee: *Never* had any boy, any man, looked at her with such violent worship, such complete and vulnerable surrender, and the sight of these things in his eyes made her almost sick with shame and fear—fear, not of him, but of something struck deep, deep within herself.

"Just tell me one thing," he said in a perfectly ordinary voice that had nothing to do with his swooning eyes, briskly lighting his own cigarette. "It's what we were discussing before. Why aren't you off somewhere on vacation? Why did you come back here?"

"I came back here to help close up the house."

"The house?" he asked in a tone Maria would have recognized as rapture for just this much confidence, had she not been so muddled and distressed by the strange turn of events. "House where?"

"Marberry Pond Road," she snapped tensely and stood up.

"Oh. Where all those fine old houses are coming down for the lousy little ones?"

"They're nothing but white elephants."

"What?"

"Nothing. *Nothing*," she said, finally coming to her senses and realizing she had talked too much. She took a last deep draw on her cigarette.

"Well, why did you have to come? Couldn't your mother and father manage to close the house themselves?"

"My father's dead."

Blinking, mortified by what Maria had deliberately made him feel was a stupid blunder, he fiercely muttered something that sounded like, "You and your big mouth Strickland," and without another glance at her, stood up and went plunging off the porch. As he disappeared around the driveway corner, Maria wondered for the second time that day what was the matter with her—why did she lash out at everyone, particularly at anyone who admired her?—and bewildered, unhappy, stared through tears at a spaniel snuffling among piles of leaves the rain had brought down.

"I got us some pork chops," said Mrs. Foss, putting the brown paper bag between them on the front seat. Saying nothing, Maria started up the car, wanting to say a great deal about the broiler that would have to be lit on such a hot night, the greasy pan *she* would have to scour, not to mention the more appetizing choices they could be having for the same amount of money—frozen crabmeat, African lobstertails, shrimp or chicken salad neatly put up in plastic containers—if her mother and her friends were not crazily involved in a boycott of the new supermarkets, having sworn eternal fealty to Mr. Humbert and his like.

The sun had come back out at four-thirty, bringing a swarm of life to the village. Now, added to the beetling lines of traffic, were the cars coming from the station where the five-seven had just disgorged a load of commuters. At the first chance, Maria took a turnoff to the right, a maneuver which got them out of the honking jam of cars, but which put them on a longer round-about route to their house. "I hear that's coming down in September," said her mother, at last breaking the silence as they passed an ugly turreted building with boarded-up windows, sitting back on several acres of scorched lawn—the remains of Miss Maitland's Country Day.

"Coming down for what?"

"A Recreation Center. Whatever that means." There was a snort.

Maria sighed heavily, but not, as her mother thought, for the soon-to-be-demolished school. She sighed because for the second time that day she was reminded of the waste, of all the money that had been scraped together just so she could walk that building's drafty corridors, sit cheek-by-jowl in its underheated classrooms with girls like herself, daughters of parents not rich enough to manage a good boarding school, yet too proud to consign them to the public high school, parents who fervently hoped that Miss Maitland's one asset—influential connections—would work the saving charm.

The weed-tangled meadow that had once been a neatly taped-off hockey field fell behind, the car sped along roads where the houses became spaced farther and farther apart. Then finally they were on the dirt beginnings of Marberry Pond Road which wound for three mazy miles along the bay's wooded shore. Once a fence with a locked gate had separated Marberry Pond Park from the rest of the world, a gate to which only residents of the Park had possessed keys. Now pointed fence-slats lay fallen, rotting, while the gate itself had been removed from its hinges and carted off, leaving its two fluted supporting pillars standing sentinel on either side of the road, the head of the one on the right nailed with a gaudy green-and-yellow sign shaped like an arrow: MARBERRY ESTATES—$26,500!!! As the old gray car rolled through this doorless portal, sweet earthy smells blew in through the rolled-down windows, sun glanced off Mrs. Hollis' water-beaded trees and shrubs, filling the windshield with glinty brilliance. Then they passed a muddy gouged-out stretch bristling with the toothpick frames of three new houses, the place where the Dixons' lovely old house had once stood surrounded by stately elms, and Maria steeled herself against some remark or gesture from her mother. But tonight her mother was ominously still. And tonight Maria felt a strange and terrible prickling of the skin, for it occurred to her that each evening, as they rolled through that bare and gaping gateway, it was as though they had just passed from the real world of the living into a twilit one like Limbo, all shades of things long dead.

The sun stayed out from that day on. Lawns turned a bleached yellow, leaves hung flaccid on the high old trees. The village was deserted after ten o'clock every morning and all activity at the library stopped. Even Carol Danziger defected, coming by two days after the rain to select three books and to triumphantly announce that Mummy and Daddy were taking her away for two maybe three weeks in the mountains—good-by, good-by, good-*by!*

There was just one daily visitor to the library.

Bent over a book, Maria would first hear him out beyond the high hedge, loudly declaiming to some real or imaginary friend (his way of heralding his impending arrival), and not long after the screen door would twang open, floorboards would creak under sneakered feet. When she finally looked up from her book, he would be standing there all red in the face, wearing a foolish sheepish grin: "Morning. Thought I'd just browse around." Coughing nervously, he would then abruptly turn his back and the game began: for a while he restlessly prowled about the front room, peering at the covers and tables of contents in any new magazines put out in the reading rack, or pulling down children's readers at random, snorting and chuckling at things he found in them; when he tired of this or sensed that she had come to the end of her patience, he padded back into the stacks, and after a long time would emerge carrying something thick and improbable (once, seeing it was Ruskin, she had almost choked) and settle himself in one of the cushioned window seats; there, with much scholarly wetting of thumb and forefinger, he turned pages at a considered pace, his expression irreproachably preoccupied—a deft imitation of the one she wore when she read.

The first few times he came to the library and all this happened, she barely managed to keep from exploding into the green silence of that leaf-shaded room, to keep from asking what on earth was the matter with him, acting like such an idiotic child— had he nothing better to do with his time? Why wasn't he off with his friends, boys and girls his own age, instead of plaguing her? Why wasn't he outside somewhere on such a beautiful hot day, down at the beach like everyone else? As exasperated as she was, she never did explode and ask any of these things, for she knew all the answers. There was nothing the matter with him because he *was* a child, and to his mind there was nothing better to do than hang around the inspiration of his first really serious crush. As for his going to the beach, she had only to look at those carefully mended, washed-thin suntans to see that his family could hardly afford one of the expensive beach clubs commandeering every foot of a shore that had once been free. And after the initial irritation, she began to relax, began to stop being angry and resentful—he was a funny yet somehow pathetic boy—and she even began to enjoy his visits. Not only was the elaborate pantomime he went through rather amusing, it was also strangely touching and even flattering: he was not like the rest of the boorish teenagers who hung about the village, but was a sweet and gentle and well-mannered boy, quite bright, really very bright, and given the proper advantages could do well for himself, a boy whose simple and direct devotion seemed to refresh and restore her, give her a sorely needed lift of the heart. What harm could there be in that?

Too late she saw the harm, saw how much she had come to depend on his visits, when four days went by and he did not come to the library. Despising herself, she nevertheless spent the fourth day listening for the shouts beyond the hedge, waiting, worrying. Was he sick? Had he suddenly gone away? Had he . . . had he found a replacement for herself, someone his own age, someone sensibly accessible to all that adoration?

On the fifth day, a Wednesday, she went to the drugstore later than she ever had, after shamelessly dawdling at the library, waiting. The noontime rush was long over, the place was almost empty, the whirring whoosh of the air-conditioning was the only sound. Without looking around she made straight for a back booth, gave the waitress her order, then sat pushing her leather cigarette case back and forth over the speckled plastic tabletop with her thumbs, wretchedly wondering what had happened to make her sink so low that she fed on the worship of a schoolboy. Had she lost all sense of proportion? When the waitress set down her hamburger and french fries she gave a guilty start. Troubled, dazed, she looked up and immediately saw him beyond the waitress' starched hips, sitting swung around on a stool at the counter, gravely watching her.

As their eyes met he gave one owlish blink, then swung down long legs and nonchalantly sauntered to the booth. "Hello, Maria," he said, towering over the table, sneakered feet planted imperiously wide apart.

It was the first time he had ever dared use her name. "Hello," she said coldly, pointedly not using his.

"Well, isn't this nice," he said with what she guessed to be carefully rehearsed urbanity, lowering himself into the blue leather seat opposite.

She blinked at the trim collegiate haircut replacing the slick blond water-wave and, despite herself, smiled.

"It's cooler this way," he said quickly, blushing as he saw she had guessed the real motive for the visit to the barber.

"I see." To keep from smiling again, she began to eat her hamburger, but found it difficult to chew and swallow under that fixed, rapt gaze. When he finally realized he was making her uncomfortable, he looked away over the low wall of the booth, and keeping his eyes on a tower of Summer Cologne on sale, a tray of Drastically Reduced bathing caps, he began to talk about the beach club where he had spent the last four days as the guest of some well-to-do classmate named Marvin. Maria barely listened to his descriptions of the cabanas with built-in bars and television sets, of the ladies who wore pearls with their bathing suits, but kept covertly glancing at him, with a strange sinking feeling noting the dazzling color changes the sun had wrought in his skin and hair. She also heard the new note of self-assurance in his voice, and from this and his new manner, she realized that he had come to some sort of decision about her—probably that the library relegated him to an insufferably juvenile position, and that he must try to meet her in other places where they would be on a more equal footing. She knew this guess to be correct when he suddenly broke off, got up and went to put a quarter in one of the little chrome machines sitting at each place along the counter, tune-selectors connected to the huge jukebox on the store's back wall. As all the glassy pyramids of bottles and jars began vibrating with the booming bass of some romantic song, he came and sat down with an air of unmistakable satisfaction: *Now*—they could almost be out on a date together.

Her course clear, she pushed away the plate of untouched french fries. "Exactly how old are you, Harry?"

"Seventeen." He solemnly stared at her, then picked up a paper napkin and began folding it into an airplane. As the eloquent silence from Maria's side of the booth prolonged itself, he glanced up, then down again, sheepishly smiling. "Okay. Sixteen. But seventeen in December . . . and that's the honest to God truth!" He launched the napkin-plane across the booth. It gently nudged her shoulder then fell into her lap. "Four years' difference. Almost three. That isn't much, Maria. That isn't much at all." He spread begging hands flat on the tabletop, and the cold tips of his fingers grazed hers as they nervously toyed with the sugar bowl.

"That's where you're wrong," she said in a choked voice and, trembling, stood up and threw down money for her lunch. "It's all the difference in the world. All the difference there could ever be. And don't you forget it." Then she fled.

A week went by and he did not come to the library. It was their last week in the house on Marberry Pond Road. Since her mother was at the Exchange and she at the library in the daytime, they spent the nights finishing up. Loading the car with cartons of breakable things her mother would not trust with the movers, they shuttled back and forth between the hushed and fragrant cricket-ticking back roads, and the cement station plateau where lighted evening trains clattered emptily in and out, blowing commuter newspapers and chewing-gum wrappers across platforms still hot from the sun.

One stifling night when even this leisurely carting and dumping seemed impossible, they decided to treat themselves to a few hours of relief in one of the new air-conditioned movie houses, and they set off for the village without phoning to see what was playing. They separated in the lobby as they always did, her mother proceeding down a gently inclined aisle to the unpolluted air of the orchestra, Maria climbing a flight of thickly carpeted steps to the smoky balcony. As she settled herself in an empty row, she shivered at icy blasts of air pouring down from a vent above her, and put on the cardigan she had snatched up as they were leaving the house. Then she lit a cigarette and stared hopefully at the screen where multicolored giants moved suavely, their bodiless voices confusingly booming at her from all directions. For

a long time she stared and listened, unable to summon any interest, and finally, bored, began glancing about the balcony. Her restless gaze came to a stop on a row two down from hers, where riot-
ous light splashing off the screen variably made silhouettes or
bas-reliefs of four long-necked boys and four girls. In a sudden
shift to brighter light the head of the boy on the end of the row
flashed goldenly, a head, she instantly noted with a sinking feeling, which was not big-eared like the others, and which held nestled, in the hollow between jawbone and clavicle, the tousled dark
head of a girl. Going numb with dread and other emotions she
could not bear to acknowledge, Maria watched the gold head
bend, ministering to the curly one, until, maneuvering to place
a more ambitious kiss, the boy turned his head—and revealed a
hook-nosed profile with a receding chin.

Rising, Maria stumbled down the steps to the lobby, where she
took a seat on a bench next to the soft-drink machine. She stayed
there until crashing chords of music announced the end of the
film, and her mother, as always, rushed out first to avoid the
crush. As she came up to Maria, rising from the bench, she gave a
smug little smile: "I see you couldn't even sit it out. Have you
ever in your life seen such trash?"

Though the moving men were scheduled to come on Monday,
they decided to try and finish up the house on Saturday. Late Friday afternoon as Maria was leaving the library, she hung a little
wooden sign on the front door—LIBRARY CLOSED TODAY—and told
herself it was perfectly all right, Saturdays were always quiet, and
one day would hardly matter. But the next morning when she
opened her eyes in her stripped bedroom, she saw that the uncur-
tained windows looked out on a mistfilled garden like blind white
eyes, and as she listened to the drops of water softly plopping off
the eaves and branches, she knew at once that it was a perfect "library day," it ought to be open, she ought to be there. Groaning,
she shut her eyes, trying to postpone the necessity of making a decision, but as she lay there the busy sounds of cupboard doors

slamming and quick footsteps on uncarpeted floors made the decision for her: she had to help her mother. She got up at once,
threw on a cotton bathrobe, and, as her first move of the day,
took the still-warm sheets and pillow and light blanket off the bed
where she had slept, and stacked them in a grocery carton in the
hall.

At eleven-thirty she methodically went through all the upstairs
rooms to make sure none of the small things had been missed,
pausing last in the doorway of her father's old room. Light like
dark water poured in through the windows over the uneven peg-
ging of the floorboards, the rolled-up mattress on the springs of
the bed. A beautiful walnut four-poster, the bed bore blue tags on
two of its posts, for it had been sold to a New York dealer for the
true and flawless antique it was. As she looked at the bed, and the
similarly tagged maple chest-on-chest, Maria thought of how
much this would have pleased him, how in fact the sight of that
whole dismantled house would have filled him with joy. "Daddy,"
she said softly to nothing, no one, and fled down the hall, down
the stairs.

She went into the living room, filled with crates of books from
the shelves on either side of the fireplace, and where the couches,
tables, and armchairs were pushed away from the walls in readiness for the movers and stood huddled in the middle of the room
like a herd of mute lost beasts. The house was strangely still, still,
there was a peculiar smell of sulfur and slate in the air—the
dampness in the fireplace, she decided, looking at the charred
bricks in the cleaned-out grate. "Mother?" she called uneasily.

"Cooahhh, coo, coo-o-o," answered a mourning dove from the
magnolia by the cellar door.

"Mother?" cried Maria on a rising note of fright. "Where are
you? Mother? Are you all right?"

She was not. Maria finally found her in the kitchen, sitting in
the middle of the floor next to a deep cardboard carton she had
been wadding with paper and packing with cooking utensils. She
sat holding a cast-iron skillet and a sheet of newspaper in her mea-

ger lap, her thin legs pushed straight out in front of her. Though her face, streaming with tears, was strangely calm, the throat beneath the sharp chin was violently working, either in an effort to hold back sobs or to bring out words, which it apparently could not do. Though she was terrified, Maria calmly went up to her mother and, acting as though this were a place she often sat, quietly raised her up and supported her to the benched inglenook where they took most of their meals. Passive as a child, her mother let herself be led and fussed over, and when Maria was finally inspired to ask, "Should I call Myra? Would you like to see Myra?" her mother nodded almost simple-mindedly.

Five minutes after Maria phoned, Myra Hollis came clomping in, wearing a hooded plastic raincoat that made her look like a cellophane-wrapped package, brogue tongues flapping over muddy rubbers, plump cheeks scarlet from her agitated walk down the road. "Well now, Liz," she said heartily. "Having a bit of a crying jag, are you? It's high time—I'd been wondering when you would. Goodness knows, it's only natural after—what—forty years? Have you packed your kettle? Good." She proudly patted her huge shabby tapestry purse. "I stuck in some tea bags and a little nip of brandy as I went out the door. Now all we need is some sugar and cups. Ah lovely, Maria, *that's* the good girl. Now we're all set."

They accepted Maria's story without question: Now that it was raining so hard, she had better go and see if any books had been left in the little wooden box on the library porch. And as long as she was in the village, suggested Myra, she might as well pick up some sandwiches for their lunch—since they had defrosted and cleaned out the icebox after breakfast, it was silly to bring in any other kind of food.

"No need to hurry," said Myra Hollis, winking at Maria going out the door, as if to say the longer she gave them the more likely it was she would find everything restored to normal by the time she got back.

Once off the muddy back roads Maria drove wildly, blindly,

trembling with the horror she had so bravely suppressed for the last half hour, the rain streaming and muddling over the windshield like the tears she could not seem to shed. Ignoring the peeling sign that prohibited parking in the library's driveway at all times, Maria turned in the car and parked it halfway up. She crossed the patchy wet grass, looked in the book-deposit box which was empty, then let herself in with her key, leaving the LIBRARY CLOSED TODAY sign hanging on the door. Though the front room was dark with storm light, she did not turn on the desk lamp. Sitting down, she put her throbbing head into clammy hands. Rain slipped down through the maple and beech leaves, slapping the windows, hitting the roof like hail, making such a rushing racket she did not hear the tapping on the door. When she finally did, she knew without lifting her face from its shelter of icy hands just who it was, and she did not move. The tapping on the glass panes continued. Realizing that the desk was plainly visible from the door and that it was impossible to pretend she was not there, she at last rose and went to the door, throwing it open with a violence that rattled the panes. "Can't you read? Don't you see that sign?" she cried through the screen door, glaring at him as he stood pale and blinking on the frayed WELCOME mat.

"Sure. But you're here," he said implacably, and opening the screen door marched in past her.

"I'm the librarian."

"I know," he said softly, without any irony, and stopped in the center of the room, crossing his arms.

"Please, Harry," she whispered, feeling the tears rushing up on her at last. "Please," she begged. "Please go home. I have work I must do."

"I won't bother you if I just sit and read."

"But you *will.*"

His face broke up into quivering brilliant planes. "Maria. That's the nicest thing you ever said to me."

"You have *got* to leave. D'you understand?"

"Listen Maria—I can't stand it anymore. I have to know. Is there someone you love?"

"Oh God," she said weakly, taking her hand from the door and passing it over her face. "Don't start being awful, Harry. You're not that way. Don't start now. Just go home."

"Tell me if there's someone else," he whispered, tortured, coming slowly back to the door.

Helpless, she watched him slam the door shut with one shove of his broad palm.

"I'll bet there isn't," he said, forcing a smile, coming so close she could feel his warm breath on her face as he took her elbows into his hands. "I'll bet you don't really even know how to kiss. Maria. I'll bet."

"How horrible you are! How disgusting!" she cried, passionately throwing out her hands to push him away, out of the library, out of her life. But the hands stopped, splayed on the chest, feeling the scudding racking beats of the heart under the ridges of rib, until he took them away and squeezed them, powerless, in his own.

Silenced, they stared, wide-eyed, dazed. Drowning, she thought. Drowning, drowned. As the hands released hers and went under her hair, she shut her eyes, and the hands pressed the nape of her neck until her burning face rested against his burning throat. Tears scalded her lowered lids. Shame, fear, desire and shame— each as she had never known. She jerked back her head to finally speak but "Don't . . ." was all she ever said, for he found her mouth, and then there was only glassy green underwater light, the fleet image of a child curled reading on the window seat, and the sound of a squirrel jumping from a tree, running teeteringly, crazily, across the slippery roof above their heads.

Under the Trees

Who wishes to understand the poet
Must go to the poet's land.

GOETHE

He came to them in January of the year after the war, at the start of a new year and a second term, arriving in a season of freak blizzards, power failures, and a new strain of grippe named Virus X. He came straight from a large Midwestern university where, it was said, he had first been a student, then graduate student, bringing with him a strange aura of Quonset huts, huge underheated dorms, thick-calved girls in sloppy jeans and bearded boys in army tans. He came in maroon or violet or canary yellow sleeveless sweaters, a hairy gray tweed suit and saddleshoes, carrying several large, string-tied manila folders abulge (they decided) with poems the little reviews had turned down. He came to teach them the second half of Eleventh-Grade English and to help prepare them for their College Boards, a last-minute replacement for gaunt Miss Cripps, who had come down with pleurisy over Christmas and gone to Saint Petersburg for the balance of the severe winter. Without being told, they knew they were lucky to get him, particularly on such short notice, for that peculiar supply of aging men and women who had served as teachers during the war suddenly seemed to have given out, and all the young men who, in normal times, would have replaced them were either at college, starting from scratch on the GI Bill, or picking up where they had left off. On his second day he made a point of telling them where he had been during the war. After taking the attendance, he got up and came around his desk and, lounging back against it, blinked at them with sleepy, greenbrown eyes. "I have asthma and congenital flat feet," he said. "Several months after the war broke out, I left college, and went to work in a defense plant. For almost two years I made wing-flap actuators for bombers. After a month and a half in the hospital with staphylococcal pneumonia—which, I may add, almost did me in—I went back to college. I tell you these things because of the gold stars on the Roll of Honor in the station park, and because I know many of you have older brothers who fought in the war. Since I am here to teach you English, I felt it wise to remove at the outset anything that might block your . . . amh . . . receptivity, anything like suspicion or hostility. Thank you." With that, while they exchanged looks of sheer astonishment, he went back around his desk and sat down and, with something like a sigh, opened Emerson's *Essays*.

Though, according to their calculations, he could not have been more than ten years their senior, he looked almost middle-aged: medium tall, with sloping shoulders and a shapeless body, he had a round, bland, blunt-featured face and wispy reddish brown hair that had already receded a good three inches from where it had started out. Hardly what one would call physically appealing, he also had the unfortunate habit of spitting when he talked; often, as he read or lectured, specks of spittle would either fly through the air like unpleasant sunmotes, or settle, shiny, in the corners of his big, chapped mouth. Yet, despite his physical drawbacks, he was not at all self-conscious. On the contrary, he seemed to be completely insulated by self-esteem and self-confidence, and was not at all affected by the fact that the other masters clearly disliked him. They observed that this was so from the start, for none of the older men ever greeted him in the halls, and at the end of the first month, when the curtains on the masters' smoking room door were taken down to be washed, they all saw him, day after day, standing and smoking at the window overlooking the football field, his back turned on the gray-haired men sitting, wreathed in smoke, in wicker chairs. While they could understand how the older masters, most of them at the school fifteen or twenty years, might resent his intrusion as a stranger, or even fear his youth, they decided it was probably just that these older men found him too peculiar—too arrogant, too moody. All of which he was. And the swings of his moods were violent. On his good days he would bound springily down the varnished halls on his pink rubbersoles, buoyant with elation, his face taut with some inner excitement, and his dry and boring lectures would suddenly bloom with purple words like "splendid" and "glorious" and "sumptuous" and "grand." On his black days his face was pale and sullen, and he seemed to have such difficulty speaking that he made them do all the recitation in class. Ugly, almost sinister on such days, he would often stand at the top of the gray-painted iron stairwell while shepherding them to assembly, his lips ceaselessly working—cursing, some said, roundly cursing *them*, reciting poems, his own, others claimed, while there were those who said he was just talking to himself, just as every crackpot did.

For, despite themselves, they found him overwhelmingly peculiar. A character. And mysterious. Mysterious because no one seemed to know anything about him. Who was he? What was he? Where had he come from and where was he going? He had come to them out of the Middle West, but he was clearly not a native Midwesterner; his accent, if it could be said to be anything regional, was Eastern, but he had peculiar ways of pronouncing certain words ("hawd" for "hard" and "biwds" for "birds") and at certain times would suddenly roundly roll his *r*'s, as if trying to be funny and to parody something, but never making clear what he was parodying. And then, though there was a rumor that he was there to teach them that one term just to kill time while waiting for the start of a job at Columbia (or CCNY or NYU), no one could confirm it. And his being a poet only confused things more. They learned he was a poet his first day, when Mr. Stillman, the headmaster, had personally introduced him; suddenly giving one of his nasty pink-and-porcelain smiles, the headmaster had said, ". . . and I would like to add that our Mr. Morgan writes poems. In fact, I have had my ear to the ground, and it seems that Mr. Morgan is . . . ah . . . one of our more promising Young Poets." They had greeted this news with a baffled, near-hostile silence—he certainly didn't *look* like a poet—and their bewilderment had only increased when, in February, one of the magazines in the library reading rack was said to contain a poem he had written; those that took the trouble to investigate—and there were only a few of them—turned to the page bearing a poem titled "The Seven Seasons" by someone named James Morgan (was *his* name James?), and found a "poem" which had no rhymes at all, was filled with words like "blood" and "fire" and "lions" and "centurions," and was utterly incomprehensible.

Because there was so little known about him and because they found this strangely annoying, provoking, they grasped at any clue. Just a simple thing like his reading a letter assumed importance. It was positively an event the day they were on their way down to the first-floor history room and passed him on the stairwell coming up, one guiding hand on the rail, his feet fumbling for the risers, his rapt face bent to the letter in his hand. But though they were all able to see that the writing was so tiny and fine he had to hold the tissuey pages close to his nose, that was all they *could* see—no giveaway postmark or signature had been visible. And it had only added to the mystery in the end, for he did not seem like someone who would have letter-writing friends. He seemed like someone completely alone in the world. Then, shortly thereafter, one of them rode all the way to the city with him on the same train. It had been assumed he did not board or live in the country like the other masters, for every afternoon at two-twenty he could be seen loping down the curving driveway, heading for the station two blocks from the school. One afternoon Polly Seaver, who had an appointment with an orthodontist in the city, was excused from algebra and gym so that she could make the two-thirty-nine train. He had come bursting out of the candy store next to the platform just as the train began to move, Polly reported, and with a daring leap had boarded the front end of the car where she sat. For several moments he just stood there, dangerously swaying as the train lurched along, first turning to make sure of the SMOKING sign, then facing back to scan the empty seats; after looking straight at her and then (Polly swore) deliberately through her, he slumped into a seat near the door. Lighting the first of six cigarettes, he took up a newspaper, neatly folded it back into quarter-sections like some meticulous, commuting-businessman, and began to read; twenty minutes before the train dipped into the tunnel under the river, he put aside the newspaper, took what was unmistakably a racing form from his overcoat pocket and, spreading it open on one of his bulging folios, sat intently studying it and marking it with a pencil all the rest of the way into the city. When the train reached Pennsylvania Station, he bolted for the phone booths on the upper level, where Polly, tenaciously scurrying after him, saw him feed quarters into a phone, then talk rapidly, agitatedly. Though she had longed to linger and perhaps even follow him, Polly, due on Central Park West in precisely twenty minutes, had sadly left him shouting into the phone and fumbling in his pockets for more quarters, and had dutifully gone and boarded the Eighth Avenue Express.

But after he had been there a month, there was at least one thing about him that held no mystery, one thing they knew for certain: he was a terrible, abysmally dull teacher, worse, if possible, than poor old Miss Cripps, who at least had been earnest. Plainly detesting the material he had to work with (American literature), he infected them all, so that listless, bored-in-advance, they were often barely able to get through their nightly assignments. This in itself would have been bad enough, but on certain days, when his disgust seemed to have reached an insurmountable peak, he would cut short the day's classwork and read aloud to them. Charming and entertaining as this could have been, they knew they were not there to be charmed or entertained; the work curtailed was invariably the Vocabulary Building Exercises (collate, ancipital, glabrous, indue) which were to help them excel on their College Boards, and the authors he read aloud—G. K. Chesterton, Shaw, Proust, Rilke, Flaubert—were the creators of things they would not be asked to answer for several years. Yet, disturbed as many of them were, some fierce adolescent code of honor kept them silent . . . with two or three exceptions. They were able to tell at once when someone, overanxious about the Boards, had complained at home and as a result Mr. Stillman had had a "talk" with him, for days would go by without his looking any of them straight in the eye, a week or two without his reading anything but required material. But eventually he always did resume the reading, and this was the pattern until the mid-March day he read them Baudelaire. Class began that day with an unexpected fifteen-minute quiz on Edgar Allan Poe. When the papers were collected, and lay in a neatly folded stack on his desk, he murmured something about "a man who magnificently translated Poe into French," and, adding something almost inaudible about "affinities" and "influences," he took up a shabby paper volume. After announcing the title of the volume of poems was *The Flowers of Evil*, he read six poems—four in English, two in astonishingly fluent French—the language making no difference as to intelligibility. Putting down the book, he clasped his hands and turned big, dazed-looking eyes on the sleet-streaked windows. " 'Flowers of Evil,' 'Flowers of Evil,' " he said softly. "Now . . . ah . . . Miss Gordon. Could you, by any chance, see what Baudelaire might have had in mind in using that word? *Evil*, that is?" Staring out at ice-coated boughs, he did not see Miss Gordon's white, panic-stricken face. Musing, gentle, he added, "Or perhaps it would help if we approached it another way, the long way round. For instance, what, Miss Gordon, would you say is the *evil* of our own particular time? . . . Violence? Sadism?

Indifference? . . . Could you possibly think of one word which might . . ." The bells in the hall drowned him out. Saved, Miss Gordon gratefully shut her brimming eyes, and that night reported her trial at home. From that day the reading aloud ceased, apparently never to be resumed. The weeks went by, their vocabularies burgeoned (frugivorous, recondite, buccal, shive), they learned no end of useful things: Mr. Hawthorne had been born in Salem, Massachusetts, Mr. Longfellow, in Portland, Maine, and "evil" was a word that could safely be applied to a simple thing like a Great White Whale.

Then, one late April morning, it was spring at last. After weeks of freezing rain the sun came out, the air was soft as silk. In their classroom, though the four long windows were shut, shades rolled tightly at the top, the panes were filled with the lucent blue of the sky and the chartreuse of willows exploding into bloom; mysteriously, the smells of washed-down chalk and bookbinder's glue were gone, replaced by the fresh, loamy scent of the green-threaded earth outside, which penetrated glass.

Yet, despite the weather, it seemed that it was going to be one of his bad days. Ominously pale and subdued, he took the attendance, never once looking up. When he had finished, he put aside the little spiral notebook, picked a fleck of tobacco from his lower lip, and turned toward the windows with a brooding sigh. Exchanging looks of resignation, they waited. "We'll go outside," he finally said. "We'll hold today's class out under the trees. The ground is damp, but the air is warm, and we can sit on the steps." He had more to say, but for a moment paused, suspended out in the blue like a man in a balloon, oblivious to the stir he had created: Classes were never to be held out of doors; this was a school rule dating back to a June day in 1932, a day when freak lightning had stuck an old oak on the school lawn and killed a boy taking shelter under its boughs. Despite the unusual circumstances—it had been after school hours, the storm had come up out of nowhere, the boy, a notorious dawdler, had been dismissed long before the storm—the rule had come into existence, all the same, and had been strictly observed ever since. Now they stared at him with a mixture of consternation and exasperation: Why didn't he know this? Hadn't he been told? Or, while being told in some briefing conference with Mr. Stillman, had he been, as now, off somewhere else? Well, whatever, he did not know, and they, looking out at the sky and listening to the open pock of a bat on the playing field, *they* were not going to tell him.

At last he turned from the windows, addressed them directly: "I guess the girls ought to take sweaters. The boys will be fine in jackets. That's all you'll need. Leave your books and notebooks here. Just for God's sake be quiet in the halls!"

And for once they were. Shuffling, not even whispering, they followed his bouncy lead down the echoing well of the stairs, through the quiet first-floor corridor—past the history room, past the two dangerous doors of frosted glass—out the swinging front doors.

The modest red-brick building had a strangely pretentious entrance—a high, white-columned Georgian portico, from which twelve marble steps descended to a macadam drive. Across this curving drive, another flight of just five steps led to sweeping level lawns. It was here, at the top of these second steps, that they came to a jostling stop, dazed with light and joy. On either side two huge, old weeping willows rose high in soaring arcs, then spilled down branches; blinking up, they seemed to be standing under a yellowgreen waterfall. Between the slender, pointy leaves a strong midmorning sun beat down, warming the crowns of their heads, baking the stone of the steps. "Sit down, sit *down*," he urged with a munificent gesture, and so they did. Shyly, still unable to believe their luck, they gave the lower window nearest the front doors a last fearful look, then seated themselves on the steps, the girls choosing those nearest the bottom, modestly shielding their white-socked legs with their skirts, the boys ranging themselves higher, just below him on the topmost step, their spines straight, their hands respectfully on their knees. Settled, they all looked up at him with confidence: nothing—not even something peculiar he might do or say—could spoil this occasion.

For a moment he seemed unnerved by their unusually attentive, upturned faces. Then, running a hand over his thinning redbrown hair, he said: "I thought that we would forget Mr. Whitman today. Though there are those who might think that a poem like 'These I Singing in Spring' would be appropriate on such a day, I feel something more is required. And so, I shall read you Mr. Joyce. Some of you may have heard of him, some not. I do not see the point of going into Mr. Joyce just now, it would only confuse you if I tried to explain him. All I'm going to do is read you something he has written, something to match, in a way, this perfectly glor-r-rious day." Though, as usual, they found his rolling *r*'s unfunny, even annoying, they waited patiently. "I don't think any of you will understand a word of what I'm going to read," he continued, his tone neither patronizing nor ironic, "but that isn't worth a damn. Just *listen* to it. That's all. Just listen to the sound of it. To hell with the meaning—just listen and don't even try to understand." So saying, he took up the large, blue book he had brought with him and opened it on his gray tweed knees. Frowning, he rapidly flipped pages, turning to consider places he had marked with torn scraps of paper and then rejecting them. He finally gave a decisive little grunt and turned back to what was clearly the first page of the book, and wetting his lips he began: "'riverrun, past Eve and Adam's from swerve of shore to bend of bay, brings us by a commodius vicus of recirculation back to Howth Castle and Environs. Sir Tristram, violer d'amores, fr'over the short sea, had passencore rearrived from North Armorica on this side of the scraggy isthmus . . .'"

A rainbow of spittle flew through the air. The voice, pitching and spluttering, labored on. At last, with something like a collective shudder, they began to stir. For the first few moments they had just sat there, paralyzed by embarrassment, staring at his straining red face, listening to the ludicrous voice: somehow he had managed to do it; he had spoiled everything. Now, unable to sit passively motionless any longer, they began to move; slowly, careful not to risk the contagion of the exchanged glance (knowing the explosion into gasping laughter would demolish him), they, one by one, turned away from the distressing sight of him and faced front, gazing out almost beseechingly at the scenery.

Dead ahead, brilliant new grass stretched to an asphalt road. Across this boulevard stood a neat row of mock-Tudor houses built in the flush of the late Twenties—little monstrosities of stuccoed gables, "weathered" oaken beams, stained and mullioned glass. As the voice at their backs struggled on, they all eagerly watched a large, gray garbage truck pull to a stop at the first of the houses. The moment it stopped, its huge garbage-devouring treadmill turned on with a grinding whine, and two men in graygreen suits hopped down and ran off, quickly returning, staggering, under cans, which they upended and dumped into the back of the truck with much grand-opera shouting and gesturing and thumping. On one of the tiny squares of lawn that fronted each house, a small, smooth-haired terrier stood beneath a creamy magnolia tree; as the garbage men scurried by to fetch a fresh supply of cans, the terrier jumped up and down on stiff legs like a china dog, yapping hysterically, the noise bringing down a shower of sickly sweet petals on his head. Frightened by the dog, a small boy of four or five, who had been proudly pedaling a tricycle up the sidewalk, tried to brake the bike but fell off, tipping it over on top of him. At his screams a coffered, oaken door in one of the houses flew open, a woman in a blue hairnet and matching blue bathrobe came bursting out: "What happened, Michael? What-happened? *Whappened?* You break anything?" she shrieked, and, scooping up the kicking child, slammed back into her Mermaid Tavern of a house.

"'. . . Macool, Macool, orra whyi deed ye diie? of a trying thir-stay mournin?'" serenely continued the voice behind them as the din across the street subsided, but a different voice, a voice so different it brought their eyes, like fluttering birds, veering back to roost. The voice was different and *he* was different, sitting bathed in dappled light, no longer straining, thoroughly enjoying himself. But it was the voice that did it, that took them and led them—a voice so naturally, perfectly Irish they all boggled, even the dimmest among them finally seeing what had long been overlooked: in the green of the eye, the red of the hair, the turn of the nose was confirmation of the voice, faint clues to an identity, if only national, at last. Mister Morgan. Mister Mor-r-gan. Their Volatile Celt. Their Irish Bard. Trite and pat and foolishly glib, but at their age that was what hit the mark. Always wanting to like him, they had only needed something concrete which they could understand. And now, as they sat and listened to him reading, deft, witty, winning, wearing a bemused little smile, they also began to smile, baffled, but strangely moved. For as he had predicted, they really didn't understand a word of what he read, but as he'd also said, that didn't seem to matter at all. What mattered was the somehow pleasing rightness of the sounds that poured from his lips, what mattered was the shining beauty of the day and being fifteen in a spring without war.

At the flash of sun on moving glass—the swinging front doors—only a few of them raised their eyes. But their silent horror immediately communicated itself to the rest of them, and they all looked up at the man on the top of the school steps, his matte navy blue suit quite black in the sunlight, his albino-pale hair and steel-rimmed glasses giving off platinum glints. Though he stood motionless, squinting impassively down at them, this immobility had the effect of someone holding a commanding finger to his lips. Then he finally started down the steps, making no attempt to muffle the gritty scrape of leather on marble, but the reading man either did not hear him or, hearing, gave no sign. Crossing the driveway, the headmaster came to a stop two feet behind the gray tweed back, where, after gathering them up in a slow and chilling smile, he clasped his hands behind his back and shut his eyes, as if the better to listen. "'This is the wixy old Willingdone picket up the half of the three-foiled hat . . .'" read the unsuspecting man, still half-smiling, and as his light, shrewd voice tripped on, the pale head behind him began to nod: Yes. Ah yes. Ah yes *indeed*.

Then suddenly, blessedly, bells began to ring. Through windows pushed wide to the balmy morning came the explosive scrape of chairs, the babble of released voices. But the reading man did not stop. Putting up a hand to detain them a moment longer, determined to finish properly, he raised his voice and read, " 'Tip (Bullseye! Game!) How Copenhagen ended. This way the musey-room. Mind your boots goan out.' "

With a resounding clap he brought the two ends of the open book together and at last looked up, his face like a swimmer's coming up from the deep. "Well, that's it for today. Not the Good Gray Poet, to be sure . . . but better for you. At least *I* think." Then, apparently not wondering why they just *sat* there, looking stupider, if possible, than they ever had, he jumped to his feet and turned, ready to go bounding off on his pink rubber-soles, when he saw the man behind him.

"Oh hullo, Mr. Stillman," he mumbled—as though the head-master were always to be found, midmornings, rooted in the middle of the driveway—and was about to bolt past him, when a look from the older man made him stay where he was.

Having accomplished this much, the headmaster now turned his pale, glaring eyes on them, sitting, doltish, on the steps. "Where is your next class?" he demanded.

"With Monsieur Farnol, sir," timidly ventured one of the girls.

"Then what are you waiting for?" he exploded. "You're going to be late as it is!"

A second set of bells rang, instantly confirming his prophecy. Trembling, they rose and hastily stumbled across the drive, up the steps. When the last three of them seemed to dawdle, the head-master lost control of himself: "You. You *three*. If you know what's good for you, you'll get a move on!" he bellowed, and they did get a move on, almost knocking each other over in their haste. But once inside the swinging doors, hidden from any outer view by dimness and glass mirroring sky, they exchanged long, mute looks, and turned back to peer down through the tops of the doors. One moment, one long, last glance, and they worried no more: while the older man angrily gestured and raged, he stood very still, his reddish head bowed—patient, deferent, wisely accepting—a poet under the sheltering trees.

The Pride of the Morning

"She isn't coming," Fiona announced from the top step, then came bounding down the other three; opening the door, she squeezed into the coupe, joining Bessie on the back seat.

Fiona's father absorbed this, hands on the wheel, a questioning profile turned toward the white house. It was just past mid-May, but the Vierecks already had put up all their screens. Most windows were pushed high, the front door stood open, and from the dim hall behind the screen came a mirror's mute flash and the rich beesy smell of freshly waxed floors. "Not coming, eh?" said Mr. Viereck at last.

"No," said Fiona, precise, and settled back close to Bessie, waiting for him to start the car. He turned the key in the ignition, the motor turned and coughed. But then, instead of releasing the hand brake, he gave a stagy remembering shake of the head; reaching over to snap open the glove compartment, he began to rummage through the junk inside.

Why, he's just stalling, realized Bessie, startled, as he groped past a flashlight, whisk broom, heap of rags. He's hoping she might still come running out and say she's changed her mind, she'll come. But she won't, because they've been having a fight, which is just what's been happening all this time. Bessie thought this over. It was now twenty minutes to ten. She had come on the dot of nine, as asked, to find Fiona waiting outside.

"Mother may not come," Fiona had said by way of greeting, waving to Bessie's father in the Ford. Bessie's father, who had met Fiona just once, neither returned her wave nor smiled. Then, as though she had explained something, which she hadn't, Fiona led the way into the house, going through the living room, where they usually sat, to the glass-enclosed porch at the side of the house. As a room it always disconcerted Bessie, for unlike all the sun parlors and solariums she knew, it had no wicker chairs, straw rugs, or rubbery jungle of potted plants. Here the floor was thickly carpeted in green, the chairs and couches had walnut frames, and the only thing blooming was the roses on the slightly faded chintz.

For ten minutes she and Fiona went over, once again, the list of things they wanted most to see at the fair. As they wrangled about the order of their choices, the Vierecks' voices, unwrangling, low, and the restless tread of someone's feet drifted down from the room overhead.

"Is she sick?" Bessie finally ventured, impatient to start and growing annoyed; she'd had to wake her father from his Saturday sleep to get there on the dot of nine.

"Oh, no," said Fiona, very cool, getting up. "She's just been asked to lunch at the club. Come on, let's go and wait outside."

The glass-paned door opened onto the garden, a large old-fashioned garden that Bessie loved, with straight turfy paths between the beds, a birdbath, a rose arbor at its far end, and in the center, at the crossing of the paths, a silver ball on a classic stone column which mirrored the world in miniature. On its right side was a netted steel fence over ten feet high, which Bessie had always assumed was there to protect the house and garden from any wild balls winging in from the greens. The Vierecks' house stood uncomfortably close to the fourteenth hole of a private course whose clubhouse topped a distant hill. Neither girl's parents belonged to this club. Fiona's had once, but no longer did, just as Fiona had once gone to a private school three towns away, but no longer did. Though with Bessie's parents it would also have been the money, this had never come up; they had not been and were not ever likely to be asked to join the club.

For ten minutes they wandered about the garden, trying not to muddy their shoes. It was the first sunny day after two weeks of rain. The earth was spongy, the air soft and moist; the flowers seemed to lean up toward the sun. Beyond the fence tiny golfers trailed up and down the rolling greens, thick as carpets, stuck with flags. Maple seedlings floated down from the big tree, looking like pale-green shiny moths. From an upstairs window came the ringing of the phone. Fiona stopped in her tracks, looked up, then wandered away from Bessie, going to an apple tree just in bloom. Perplexed, Bessie watched her break off some fat buds, shred them, fiercely grind them into the sod with the heel of her shoe. Then at last there was the crunch of tires on gravel, a honk from the front of the house. They went around and found Mr. Viereck alone in the little gray coupe. As they came to the car he rolled down his window. "Fiona, will you please run upstairs and see if your mother is off the phone."

Now, clutching a road map, Mr. Viereck slammed the glove compartment shut and, releasing the brakes, let the car roll down the gently graded drive. Both girls looked at the road map he was shaking open with his right hand, then both looked quickly away from this unsuccessful delaying tactic: Fiona's father had lived on Long Island all his life. As the car jolted over the muddy ruts of the lane which led to an asphalt boulevard, Fiona rolled down her window and leaned out, sniffing, taking the air like the family spaniel out for a drive. Mr. Viereck began to whistle gaily, but Bessie, like Fiona, was not deceived—he was clearly shaken by her not coming, by their long and secret fight. What she could not accept was their fighting at all, and with such artful softness to boot; when her own parents fought, which was always, doors slammed, choking voices strained and rose. What could be so important about lunch at the club? she pondered, knowing very well

Mrs. Viereck went there too often to make this any sort of special event. Or *who* could be so important? Then, inexplicably, she began to sneeze.

"'*Sundheit*," said Mr. Viereck up front.

Bessie groped wetly for a handkerchief.

"What's that?" asked Fiona, peering into Bessie's opened purse, seeing very well that it was a crisp new ten-dollar bill.

"Some money," said Bessie casually, but blushing.

"Some money." Fiona laughed, and explained to her father: "It's a ten-dollar bill."

Mr. Viereck caught Bessie's eye in the rearview mirror and winked. "You planning to treat today?"

"Mother thought I ought to have it," she mumbled, for the moment hating both of them, particularly Mr. Viereck, for hitting unerringly on the truth. "You should offer to treat for something," her mother had said, her brow earnestly furrowed. "It's only right after they've been so nice to you all the time." Bessie, knowing very well that it was not right at all, had taken the money rather than hurt her mother's feelings.

"Your mother's quite right," said Mr. Viereck, turning off the asphalt boulevard and entering a freshly paved highway that branched away from the town. "It's a good thing to have. It would come in awfully handy if you were to get lost."

Bessie smiled grudgingly. Fiona said, "Imagine getting lost in a place like that."

Mr. Viereck stuck a cigarette between his lips, then punched the dashboard lighter in. "I gather the trylon and perisphere are first. Then where do we go from there?"

Fiona, perking up, rattled off their list but, to Bessie's surprise, concluded with something they hadn't discussed.

"The parachute jump!" Her father laughed. "What on earth is that?" He patiently listened while Fiona explained, then said, "Oh, I think we can pass that up."

"But why?" Fiona demanded, frowning.

"It just doesn't sound very special to me. Cheap thrills. All

that. There are hundreds of better things to see." To show that
the subject was closed, but completely, he turned on the car's little radio. A barrage of static, then the coupe was afloat with melting trombones, loud and sweet. Benny Goodman? wondered Bessie, who had just been given a bedside radio; she listened happily,
waiting for him to change the station, but to her surprise he left it
on. Fiona sniffed disdainfully at the music and sulkily slid down
on the seat. "Oh, don't let *them* fight now," Bessie prayed. Seeing
her lovely day slip away, filled with forebodings, she stared out the
window on her side, scanning the muddy marshland, too soon, for
a reassuring glimpse of sunstruck white towers rising, like the
spires of some New Atlantis, from Flushing Bay.

He kept several paces ahead of them, hands bunched in
pockets, shoulders sloped, never moving his head to look at the
wonders freshly unfolding on every side. The air was a singing
blue, alive with fountains, flags, birds, musical horns. On the
ground, flowers bloomed in brilliant mats, their unfurling petaled
heads packed so close they could not stir in the faint warm wind
that fanned the beds. People walked the newly paved streets wearing tremulous smiles, blinking in sun; wearing the dizziest smile
of all, Bessie walked like someone in a dream.

Suddenly he stopped and waited for them. "You hungry, girls?"
he asked when they caught up. Shocked, Bessie could only stare at
his face, gone a waxen yellow-white, glistening on the brow and
upper lip.

"Not really. Not yet," answered Fiona, thoughtlessly speaking
for Bessie, who had had breakfast at seven and who suddenly realized she was starved. To Bessie's further annoyance, Fiona now
reached out and, picking up Bessie's arm as though it were some
sort of object, pushed back her sleeve to peer at the Mickey Mouse
watch she wore on her wrist. "It's only twenty past eleven. Could
we wait a little while?"

"Anything you want. It's your day," he said with false hearti-
ness, to Fiona alone, and began to look searchingly about. They

had come into a large dazzling square, formed by four white buildings soaring high, aflutter with blue, red, and yellow flags. In its center was a large round fountain, where arcing stone fishes jumped through golden hoops and sent fizzing jets of water, which crisscrossed in rings, from their open mouths. Nestled against one of the large buildings across the square, through polychrome mist, was a small squat structure of glass and brick which Mr. Viereck spied with relief. "I tell you what," he said. "You two go and sit on the edge of the fountain there and wait for me. I'll only be a minute, so don't you dare move or talk to anyone—you hear?"

He glared at Fiona as he spoke, as though trying to force her to drop her eyes, narrowed, piercing, from his own pale face. "Yes, Daddy," she answered sweetly. "Of course." And while he watched she marched, docile, to the basin's rim.

Bessie followed, and in a strange tense silence the two girls sat down. Fiona began to hum to herself, keeping time with her feet, letting her rubber heels bounce with an annoying resilient thump off the stone. In an anguish of indecision, Bessie finally felt she must speak, acknowledge what she had steadily tried to ignore for over an hour. "Fiona, are you mad at me? Is there something I've said or done?"

"Don't be silly," said Fiona lightly, devastating Bessie, who had needed the complete acquittal of, "Mad? Why should I be mad?"

Bessie stared at the couples ambling by, wistfully noting the open pleasure on every face. Determined, she tried another tack, and with grim brightness said, "It's really like another world. Don't you think it looks something like that place in *Lost Horizon*—I forget its name."

"I wouldn't know," said Fiona, heartless. "I didn't see it. Mother wouldn't let me go."

Bessie, whose mother had all too willingly let her go alone to a Saturday matinee, sat frozen, mute, finally letting herself see what she had sensed Fiona was doing all along. But how *hurt* she must be to sink to this, Bessie thought, trying to be fair. The miracle of her friendship with Fiona had been that this had never happened before. Up until now she had been spared all corrections that might have been made, the endless differences that might have been pointed out. She couldn't blame me for their fight, thought Bessie. Does she think *she* stayed home because of me? She wouldn't. She likes me, thought Bessie, immediately hating herself for the lie. The truth, which was negative, was simply that Mrs. Viereck did not dislike her actively. She tolerated Bessie as the one new friend Fiona had made at the public school, as she tolerated many other irksome things that Fiona brought home—a mania for reciting "knock, knocks," a craze for collecting playing cards, an insistence on owning a "beer jacket" where she could crayon witty maxims like "Vas You Dere, Charlie?" In her case, Bessie had clearly seen that Mrs. Viereck was surprised—she could have been worse.

Though she fell in love with the Vierecks, Bessie never expected them to love her back; she was at an age where the unrequited crush is a law unto itself. The months she had spent as Fiona's friend, a person privileged to glimpse her home, her parents and their way of life, had kept Bessie happy, but she had always known it would end. She had just not expected it until next fall, when by some mysterious means Fiona would be sent away to boarding school. Seeing the end loom threateningly close, Bessie thought: She's angry with me because for the first time I can see it's not what I thought—and what she needed me to think. It's not at all perfect; there is trouble, real trouble, and probably always was.

Spray, lifted by gentle winds from the basin, mirrored sunlight, made rainbow mists. Bessie faintly shivered and stood up, announcing, "I'm getting wet."

"What do you care?" asked Fiona flatly, staring off.

"I care. My new suit will get spoiled."

"Oh," said Fiona politely, and looked away from Bessie's suit. It was pale Junket-pink with a dotted swiss blouse whose piping and furry dots were pink too; on her thirteenth birthday Bessie had at last been given permission to help her mother pick out her clothes. Without envy or rancor Bessie stared at Fiona's blue cotton dress and Shetland cardigan; she had long ago seen that neither she nor her mother could ever arrive at the rightness of what Mrs. Viereck chose. But she could not let Fiona do this. She sat back down and, turning half around, peeling off a cotton glove (another mistake), trailed two fingers in the basin. The water was as cold as her heart. "Do you suppose your father's all right?" she asked idly, watching her fingers' miniature wake.

"What do you mean? He only had to go to the john."

"He's taking so long," said Bessie, hating what she was doing, yet unable to stop. "And I did think he looked rather funny when he went in."

"Funny how?"

"Oh, pale. And sickish."

"Oh, that," drawled Fiona, then gave an arch laugh. "Haven't you ever seen anyone with a hangover before? No, I don't suppose you have," she went on, much too rapidly. "They were at a dance at the club. When I woke up at two to get a glass of water, they still weren't home. It's a wonder he got up at all."

Bessie, not listening really—she knew the signs of a hangover well, and Mr. Viereck had none of them—sat fidgeting, then finally rose. "I'm going in there too. You want to come?"

"No. I don't have to. Besides, one of us has to wait. If Daddy found us both gone, he'd have a heart attack."

Five minutes later Bessie came out through the swinging door, blinking at the blinding sun, pulling her gloves back on over hands that reeked of liquid soap.

"There you are!" cried Mr. Viereck, pouncing on her breathlessly. "You thoughtless girls—didn't you know you might give me a terrible scare?"

Behind him Bessie saw the fountain, fizzing spray; on the rim where she had left Fiona, two fat women sat massaging their feet.

"I'm really surprised at Fiona," he went on, looking past her, still watching the opening and shutting door. "She's really so considerate—" He trailed off, taking Bessie in. Wheeling about, he stared at the fountain, then turned on Bessie furiously. "Where did you leave her?"

"Sitting on the fountain rim. She wouldn't go along with me just because she didn't want you to be upset." Remembering precisely what Fiona had said, she wondered if he had trouble with his heart.

For a moment they both stared, rather dully, at the fountain basin, ruffled by wind, where the bright blue water was not more than four feet deep.

"Are you sure she didn't follow you?"

"Well, no. I'm not quite positive. She may have decided she had to after all," said Bessie, and confusedly blushed. "She could have been in the other room while I was washing my hands."

"Would you please go back and have a look," he said through his teeth.

For five minutes Bessie stood in the center of the room, deafened by rushing water, gabbling women, slamming doors, turning like a top to scan the basins, mirrors, scales, towel machines. Afraid of the man outside, she went back out reluctantly, but found, to her relief, he had already decided she would come back alone. "Though it isn't like her, she's probably gone into one of these buildings to have a peep. This place has really bowled her over; she can't seem to bear to miss a thing. No sense in trying to guess which one she's in—we'll just sit down here and wait for her." With this he went to the fountain and sat down on the rim exactly where Fiona had been; the two women had put on their shoes and tottered away. Bessie threw a longing look at a dry blue-and-orange bench, but followed him. As she sat down he lit a cigarette and from her careful three feet away she could feel his dislike and blame fuming at her like the smoke he exhaled through his nose. The unfairness of his blaming her for leaving Fiona—self-possessed, cool Fiona—all alone, filled her mouth with a bitter taste like tinfoil. He smoked in nervous jerky puffs, the way his mind, Bessie thought, would be jouncing from one explanation to another of where Fiona might really have gone.

"Did you two talk to anyone?" he asked at last, reaching around in back to douse the cigarette in the water of the pool.

"No, we didn't, Mr. Viereck."

"Did you notice anyone hanging about?"

"No, Mr. Viereck. No one at all. Fiona and I both know about that."

"Fiona knows about what?"

"Strangers that try to talk to little girls."

With a look of utter repugnance he took her in, all eighty-five beginning-to-change pounds of her. "You're thirteen. Fiona's only twelve and a half. Fiona knows nothing about the things you claim to know about."

Seeing how he already hated her, Bessie saw no point in contradicting him. Clearly he did not know that other Fiona, the one who could tell without a blush or giggle or smirk about the man on the bus, the man in the shoestore, the old Russian dancing master who had taught her ballet. He's nothing but a bully, she thought, maddeningly close to tears, beginning to hate him reciprocally. She was now so hungry she had faint cramps, and was not at all ashamed to have an appetite under the circumstances. Wherever she was, Fiona was quite all right—she was certain of it.

"I don't see any sense in going to the police," he was muttering, reasoning with himself. "It's only been about twenty minutes. No sense in making a fuss. She'll be along any second now. And when she does, I'll give her a thrashing she'll never forget."

No you won't, thought Bessie wearily, and watched him light another cigarette. Where was the face, the fine, composed face she had once thought so remarkable for anyone's father to own? The cheeks suddenly looked too full, pallid and puffy, the broad mouth never stopped working as he licked his lips or chewed on the cigarette, the smooth brown hair was raked into tufts by his hand. How weak he is, she thought, astonished. *He* is weak, and *she*—she is cold and proud and cruel, as Fiona is going to be.

With sudden strange longing she thought of her own mother, dowdy with tears and rage as she cried out to her husband, "I *called* there. You weren't there. Think of something better this time!" But what the Vierecks do is worse, Bessie thought, ashamed of her own shame in the past, her intricate schemes for keeping Fiona from her house.

Feeling almost giddy, she got up and stood in front of him. Unwillingly he looked at her. "I think I know where Fiona might have gone."

He said nothing, waited with narrowed eyes.

"I think she might be at the parachute jump. It isn't far. You could see it in the sky as we came into the square."

Though he deeply flushed, she saw that he knew this was precisely where Fiona could be, and would never forgive Bessie for being the one to think of it. "She wouldn't do that," he said, but knowing better than Bessie that she would, rose and for a moment squinted helplessly about. She watched him consider what would happen if their paths crossed, if Fiona came back to find them gone, and finally offered, "I could wait here while you went."

"You will come along with *me*."

Fiona stood with her back to them, fingers curled through the loops of wire fence that separated idle spectators from those who wished to jump. She was a little to the right of the ticket turnstile, her head thrown back as she looked up, up at the moving wires, taking a new load of adventurers to the top. A few already regretted their daring; tentative shrieks and moans floated down from the blue. Mr. Viereck's voice called above them; Fiona started, slowly turned.

Unblinking, blank-faced, she took them in, barely glancing at Bessie, watching the man coming at her, fast. From over the shoulder that came down to her level, held her pinioned, immobilized, in a hug of relief, she stared at Bessie with cold and vacant eyes. *Hit* her, Bessie silently urged, seeing Fiona desired it with all her heart. Hit her *hard*—it's your only chance. But he finally stood up and brushed at his eyes with the back of his hand and, breathing hard, said, "Do you know what a fright you gave us? Do you have any idea of what you've done?"

"I'm sorry," said Fiona, simply, offering nothing else.

"Sorry?" he repeated, his voice now cracking. "I ought to give you the whipping of your life!"

Patiently standing, Fiona nodded.

"Why did you do it?" he went on, damning himself forever.

As Fiona shrugged, her beige Shetland cardigan boxily jerked up and down. Bessie saw that she had removed her arms from the sleeves and now wore it as her mother always wore hers, jauntily thrown about the shoulders, one fastened top button holding it in place. "I don't know," Fiona said irritably. "I just felt I had to. You said we couldn't. It's not at all cheap. It's loads of fun."

"Just felt you had to." Mr. Viereck's laugh was as bad as Bessie feared. "Just wait until your mother hears that explanation of—" He stared at the two estranged girls. "But she won't. She'd never forgive you if she heard about this, Fiona." You mean she'd never forgive *you*, thought Bessie, listening because she was there but feeling as remote as the jumpers silently dangling overhead. "No. There's no sense in making a fuss. We simply won't tell her about it, that's all. It never happened, the whole foolish thing—you *hear*?" He glared at Bessie, his last words drowned in the screams of the jumpers, dropping like stones until the silken blooming of their chutes.

Without Mistletoe

For three years the routine had been the same. She would arrive home from college for Christmas vacation, having worked up momentum (it could hardly be called excitement) for weeks, returning to that mock-Tudor house, the Elizabethan fantasy of some Thirties builder, and see what could be done to create some illusion of holiday spirit. The need to capture some of the look and feeling of the holiday had been instilled early, compounded partly out of early school days when they had all sung "Deck the Halls" and decorated the Lower School with a tree, boughs and festoons of greens, swags of multicolored paper loops—but mostly from having a German nurse who had received parcels from Germany packed with gingery cookies shaped like gnomes and Kris Kringles and *Tannenbaums* all wrapped in pastel tinfoil, and cards with merry rosy-cheeked peasants and snowbound forests and laughing angels stamped in bas-relief and hand-painted in brilliant colors, but never (at least so it seemed) any nativity scenes: it wasn't until years later she discovered that her parents had arbitrarily drawn the line there, and had asked her nurse not to stick the richly gilded cards with the manger, the refulgent Mary and infant Jesus, the adoring Kings and shepherds in the frame of her bedroom mirror along with the others . . . actually more inconsistent than arbitrary, since during her childhood they had always permitted a tree. There had been no tree, however, since the year she turned thirteen and her brother seventeen. Now her brother was married and living in California. He would not be home for Christmas. He had not been home for Christmas or any other occasion in three years. Long before that, when he'd been in college, then the Navy Air Corps, then working for an aeronautics firm in Chicago, he had come back to this house as seldom as possible. As she did now. Taking a leaf from his book she returned from college only for the big holidays, buckling on invisible armor when she did, trying as best she could to protect herself from the emptiness and poverty and chill of that house, even though the thermostat was set at 70° and most of the rooms were thickly insulated with deep-pile carpets and silk and satin double-drapes, and cluttered with furniture covered in damasks and brocades. But most of all she hated the stucco walls, which had inspired endless fantasies (as she'd lain lazily in bed over the years) of some master paperhanger coming and magically smoothing over the rough walls and covering them with delicately printed papers, transforming the cornyellow stucco box of her room into a green-and-white striped bower; wallpaper had become symbolic of the life and house she wished she had—a rambling white-clapboard house with sashed windows filled with wavery old glass panes, and a giant maple outside her bedroom window where phoebes and finches fluttered and sang.

But there was *this*, the real house with its stucco walls outside as well as in and leaded casement windows, that she had to return to, and only two places in it where she could place decorations for some Christmas spirit: the long walnut mantel above the fireplace, a cold cavern with a waxed slate floor, where fake iron logs sat on black wrought-iron andirons and a hidden red light bulb glowed when a switch was pressed; and the front hallway, with a dropleaf English table, an oblong Federal mirror, two harp-backed chairs, and a glass-and-brass English chandelier, where she truly *did* deck the hall—and it was the boughs and greens needed for this that had set up the routine.

The routine: once home, the first thing she did as soon as she could gracefully get out of the house without provoking bitter accusations ("You just got home, and you're running right back *out!*"), was take a bus to the florist at the farthest end of the village. She didn't drive and so couldn't use the green Buick in the garage. At the florist, she would browse outside the shop where the windows were steamy with the loam-smelling warmth of the greenhouse, and stroll down the windswept sidewalk, feeling a childish yearning as she passed the dense line of trees leaning against a makeshift board fence, going to the spot where ropes of greens lay in coils next to stacks of loose boughs (pine, spruce, fir), and baskets brimming with pine cones and sprigs of holly; the mistletoe was kept in a refrigerated glass case inside the shop, along with bouquets of freesia and sweetheart roses and stiff sprays of ugly salmon-colored gladiolas. Taking her time, eking out the pleasure as long as she could, she would finally get one of the high-school boys hired as extra part-time help for the holidays, and would say, pointing, "I'll take thirty feet of that, cut into six five-foot pieces, please" (this invariably produced a look of dull confusion, necessitated a quick explanation of long division), "four of those and six of those" (mixed boughs), "and a dozen of those" (ungilded, unpainted pine cones), "five of those" (sprigs of holly), "and I guess I'll pick out a bunch of mistletoe inside." "Charge and send?" the boy would ask. "No, I'll pay cash. And would you please see that it's all delivered as soon as possible," she would answer, tipping him with a dollar bill held in readiness in her coat pocket—a proven guarantee of quick delivery. She would then follow him into the mossy-ferny fragrant shop, picking her way between the pots of Jerusalem cherry and red-ribboned poinsettias to the refrigerated glass case, where she would choose a bunch of mistletoe with the plumpest white berries, then edge carefully through the clutter of fake white or blue trees, miniature orange trees, stacks of ornate gilded wreaths, to the cash register. As she counted out bills from her beloved old calfskin wallet (mellowed to a brilliantly supple chestnut patina by countless ap-

plications of saddle soap), she would try to hold back the bitterness and anger: the money in the wallet was what she'd been able
to put by out of the monthly allowance her father sent her, plus
what she had made waiting tables in The Pub and working part-
time in the Co-op bookstore in the weeks before coming home.
Her parents refused to pay for the decorations. They tolerated
them once she had arranged them, but they didn't really want
them, said she was "too old for that sort of thing," it was a waste
of money, and so would not pay. She had learned to ignore them.
And though there had been a time when she'd been hurt, she no
longer gave a damn.

When she'd finished at the florist, she would walk home. It was
a long and freezing hike, but she took the edge off the distance
and biting cold by dropping into many steam-heated places along
the way. First would be a detour down a side street to the many-
gabled old private house (part model for her wallpaper house)
deep within a grove of towering trees, that had been converted to
a library, a place of inglenooks and windowseats and bready-
smelling mazes of bookracks; the haven she had escaped to for
endless hours during her childhood, sitting curled, reading, dreaming, building herself a life, a world, with Miss Parsons hovering,
offering books, encouragement, affection, visions, hope—Miss Parsons, now white-haired and white-lipped and blotchy-cheeked and
shaky from her years of secret drinking, but still beloved and loving, the mottled purple of her cheeks fusing into a solid pink flush
of joy at the unexpected visit from her old pupil and protégée.
Next stop might be the record store, where she was permitted to
charge things; a session in one of the listening booths, the
purchase of one or two albums, perhaps the latest King Cole Trio
release and Traubel and Melchior singing *Tristan and Isolde*, the
latter bought solely for the *Liebestod* (which couldn't be bought
as a single record, and which she just heard for the first time in
her Music Survey course)—all that churning, yearning, tumultu-
ous music embodying feelings deep within her, feelings partly
given expression in her love for Bailey, but not yet fully tapped.

After that it might be the drugstore, for a bottle of Arpège cologne and a new lipstick, but never any of the sumptuous new dress shops along the way: in an attempt to curb what he called her "wild spending," her father had put her on a clothes allowance, an allotment so small she had tried having a dressmaker in Arlington make her two dresses—a disastrous experiment she did not repeat.

Dawdling, glancing at her watch (had the greens been delivered?), she worked her way down the bustling village streets, never bumping into anyone she knew. Most of the people she knew would be in the Benson village, seven miles away, where she and Margy Reichlin, her oldest friend, would go when Margy got in from Smith. Passing the old Maplehurst theater, where she'd first sat roped into the zoo-like children's section, chewing Good 'n' Plenties and staring, transfixed, at Sonja Henie's white skates skimming across ice like black glass (yes, *that* was the way)—then later graduated to the balcony, where she'd watched some idol like Van Johnson chastely embrace Phyllis Thaxter or Doris Day, while her body bloomed, took fire under expert, gentle hands and lips (yes, *that* was the way). Past Mac's diner, where she and her high-school boyfriends, then Bailey, had ravenously wolfed down hamburgers and chili at one, two, three in the morning. Past the Woman's Exchange, a place where she had her first brush with the genteel brand of anti-Semitism it was known for—a shop scented by bowls of potpourri, the dried flowers and herbs grown in the gardens of the women who ran the place; spare, austere ladies in tweeds and shetlands and pearls, who presided over tables and shelves of handmade potholders (shaped like Humpty Dumpty and Cheshire cats), wastebaskets and trays glued and shellacked with Audubon and Currier and Ives prints, pans of homebaked brownies and shortbread; ladies who suddenly busied themselves in the back of the shop, or stood stonily, arms crossed, not offering assistance, when someone outside their "social circle" (almost the whole town) walked in. Past the Chinese restaurant they had not entered since the day her aunt had told her mother she had seen cats' heads in the garbage cans out back. Past the new two-story "garden apartment" building, then the row of sagging old houses, to the entrance to her street. And back to the mock-Tudor house where she prayed the greens had been delivered while she was out.

At the sound of her key in the heavy front door, her mother would call out, "Sarah?" Accusing, sharp. She always slipped out of the house while her mother was busy or was on the phone. Bracing herself, she would go into the living room where her mother, reading the papers, would be sitting in her favorite wing chair. (Later, not too many years later, when television came, her favorite would become one of the ugly, elephantine chairs in the sun parlor, where she'd sit glassily staring at the flickering screen for hours on end.) "Hi, Mom," she would say, untwining her long Black Watch plaid scarf, unbuttoning her camel's-hair coat.

"Where were you?" A fierce accusing glare over the rims of her glasses.

"At Ludlow's, picking out some greens."

"Isn't it time you outgrew that?" Then back to Walter Winchell or Ed Sullivan. Always the *Mirror* or the *News*. Her mother was an educated, intelligent woman, but she had not read the *Times* for years. Gossip columns, lurid murders, and horoscopes had become her pipeline to the world.

This year, the fourth, the script did not vary. ". . . time you outgrew that?" concluded her mother, then adding, as Sarah turned away: "Your boyfriend called. Ernestine took the message." And returned to the *News* centerfold photograph of a smashed-up car.

She hung up her coat and went out to the kitchen. The greens hadn't been delivered yet. Ernestine said that her "boyfriend," Bailey, wanted her to call him only if she got back before three; it was two-fifteen.

She went up to her parents' bedroom and dialed the pink phone on the lavender velvet bench.

"Can't talk long, sweetheart. That bastard Sawyer's been beefing about my 'hanging on the phone.' He's out until three."

"Oh, God, Bay. I'm *so* glad you called."

"Things rough?"

"Rough."

"What time can I bail you out?"

"After eight-thirty."

"I still don't see why you can't eat dinner with me."

"You know why, darling. If I have dinner here most of the time, they won't mind our going out every night so much."

Silence on the line.

She knew that hurt him, but there was little she could do. Her parents had never approved of him, and it wasn't just because he was a Catholic. He wasn't good enough for her, they said. He hadn't gone on to college, but had gone straight from high school to a job in a CPA's office, where there was little likelihood he would get very far. He did not have, as her father put it, "class." Love wasn't a word they understood. Bailey was her first real, true love. And though marriage was something else again—she had a lot she intended to do, become, the future was something she did not want to tie up—love him she did, and wanted to be with him every night, laughing and drinking in their favorite local bar, later making love, confirming the life-force within her that she knew would take her far beyond that mock-Tudor house.

"Okay. Eight-thirty, then," Bailey finally said. "Hang in there. I love you," and hung up.

Feeling no better, in fact feeling worse, she went downstairs and found two long white florist's boxes on the kitchen counter near the back door. Ernestine stood at the sink, peeling potatoes to go with the leg of lamb that lay, heavily seasoned with garlic, in the roasting pan on top of the stove.

"Are there any old newspapers around, Ernestine?"

"No, Sarah, your mother throws out all the papers soon as she finishes them. Says they draw the roaches . . . won't even let me keep them in my room."

Ah yes. Charming. Poor Ernestine. (Poor Caroline. Poor Selma. Poor Jessie. Poor Anita. Her memory faltered at all the names.) She cut the thick green cord tied around the boxes, and spread some of the tissuey green paper from inside them on the counter top, a token gesture of self-preservation, in case her mother came in and, finding her breaking the boughs to fit the mantel, began to shout about getting needles on the floor.

"M-m-m-m, that smells good," said Ernestine, breathing in deeply. "Where you going to put all that?" It was Ernestine's first —and undoubtedly last—Christmas in that house.

"Some on the living room mantelpiece. Some in the hall."

"Your mother know that?"

"My mother knows that."

They both laughed.

Sarah settled down to work. There was also an unwritten script for this part of the routine. Using her extremely fine eye (she was a talented but not quite first-rate painter), she would break the long boughs into smaller pieces and carry them, two or three at a time, into the living room, placing them on the mantel, building, constructing, interweaving with expertise. During the first few trips from the kitchen, her mother would glance up from her paper and offer comments, which ranged from "Don't you get tired?" to "You're getting needles all over the place." Sarah would keep on working, trying not to respond. And the mantel, when finished, was always a small work of art: a mingling of boughs— pine, spruce, fir—intricately meshed and interwoven, peaking in the center to the fullest mass, with sprigs of holly and natural pine cones tucked in between the sprays of needles, all looking as if they had grown that way.

"That's very nice," her mother would always concede at this point. Never, "You were right, it's worth the trouble, it really does brighten up the room." Or, "What did you lay out? I'll pay you back, Sarah dear." Just, "That's very nice," and back to Sidney Skolsky or John Chapman, or the daily Horoscope, which would offer her mother, an Aries, some cheery little message to brighten her day: "*Today finds you at the peak of a personal cycle, good influences going in your favor; make your wishes and feelings known.*"

After the mantel, she would tackle the hall, first turning on all the lights, then getting a stepladder, rolls of Scotch tape, scissors, a ball of string: tacks or nails, it had been stated the first year, could never be used. The lamp hanging on a brass chain from the middle of the hall ceiling was the centrum of her decoration—a brass-and-glass English lantern with many ribs and spokes, where she first secured the ends of the greenery ropes with string, then fanned them out, maypole-style, into a loopy canopy of swags, fastening the far ends to the tops of doorways and ceiling moldings. The crowning touch was a fat bunch of mistletoe, which she would tie to a round brass ring on the bottom of the lamp with a flaring moss-green velvet bow. It was hard work; all that scampering up and down the ladder was tiring, but when she was finished, the hall smelled like a forest and looked like a piney circus tent.

This year, as she stood on the top ladder-step, tying the end of a swag to a rib of the lamp, the telephone rang in the little alcove off the hall. Ernestine quickly picked it up and told Sarah it was for her.

Letting the rope drop, Sarah backed down the ladder: Bailey again?

But no, it was Margy, home two days early from Smith. Sudden joy made Sarah's face hot, made her laugh aloud. They chattered excitedly, then Margy said: "I'm not seeing Toby until tomorrow night. But maybe we can double—you going to see Bay tomorrow night?"

"Every night, sweetheart."

As they laughed together in the same surge of happiness, Sarah knocked on the wood frame of the alcove door. All that fall and winter she had thought about this, marveled that there could be a time in one's life when one *knew* just how precious and rare that time was. They had never discussed it (they were both superstitious), but she and Margy knew just how lucky they were to be young, in love with young men who loved them, sharing a deep and true friendship—and for that moment in time carefree and free, free to enjoy a world just done with a war and geared for pleasure.

"Can you come over?" asked Margy. "I can't come there. Mommy has the car." Of course Margy drove, had her license. Margy was the personification of practicality and effectiveness. She drove, she sewed, she cooked, she baked. She did all these things expertly, with dispatch, because she loved the doing of them, and the fact that they helped her mother and eased the running of the house only added to her enjoyment. It wasn't remotely the Plain Jane's defense, the learning to be a Little Homemaker to make up for deficiencies. Though Margy was, in fact, plain, she had always been a great favorite with the boys. *And* girls. And adults as well. Lovable. A lovable person. Joyous, with great zest for living and a fine, subtle sense of humor and an open freckled face that registered every emotion she felt. Margy. Sarah loved her, and she had been her closest friend for eleven years.

"I can't come there because I'm still doing the greens," Sarah lied, the real reason being that if she went out again, she knew her mother would make a scene. "Take a taxi over here, I'll finish up as fast as I can, and make a pitcherful of martinis we can carry up to my room."

Margy sighed at this irresistible bait. They both loved to drink. Margy's family had finally given her permission to drink at eighteen. Her own family, or rather, her father, the final arbiter in such matters, was broad-minded about alcohol (undoubtedly because he took so much of it himself), and had not only given her permission to drink when she was sixteen, but had also performed the initiating rites. "I know you're going to be drinking now *any*way, so you might as well learn how to handle and hold the stuff at home," he had said as he mixed her first highball, which she hadn't been able to get down. She had hated the taste of the Scotch, but along with the highball had come the stern dictum:

"Only drink Scotch. Never rum or bourbon or rye or gin. They'll make you sick. Scotch. And always dilute it with water or soda—*plain* soda, not soft drinks." Despite her aversion, she took his advice. Slowly, she learned to like Scotch and hold it. Well. Later, she came to love martinis, but didn't hold them as well. They became a special treat, and now, just mentioning them to Margy made her mouth soft and moist with anticipation. Delicious: the cold dryness, taken in little sips while she and Margy sat up in her room, laughing, gossiping.

"It isn't just the car. I can't come there," Margy plaintively explained, "because Larry's got a fever with some strep thing, and Mommy doesn't want him left alone." Larry was Margy's twelve-year-old brother; the Reichlins had never been able to afford a maid.

"Hell," said Sarah, achingly disappointed.

"*Yes*, hell. But I know I can get out tomorrow. Let's have lunch down at Zimmer's and then go up to the Benson village and poke around. Okay?"

"Okay," said Sarah, feeling the hum of happiness start up again. "I can't wait."

"I can't either. I've so much to tell you, I'm popping at the seams."

"Me too."

They both laughed. Then, before they got sentimental—something they always tried to avoid—they quickly said good-by and hung up. Sarah remained in the alcove, smiling to herself.

"Who was that?" called her mother from the living room.

"Margy Reichlin."

Silence. Then: "*I* never hear you laugh like that. You never laugh around here unless you're talking on the phone with your boyfriend or one of your friends."

She said nothing. There was nothing to say. She felt the joy ebb, leak away, but her eyes, which just a few years before would have filled with tears, stayed dry.

As she picked up the end of the greenery rope and reclimbed

the ladder, the anger came in a rush. She didn't want to be angry. She knew her poor mother couldn't bear to listen to or witness happiness—particularly in her own child. She knew, she understood—oh she understood her mother all too well, and what's more, deeply pitied her, but dammit, *dammit*, she didn't want the joy she'd been feeling to be destroyed.

"How *is* Margy?" her mother suddenly asked, as Sarah quickly tried to finish the swags. Margy or no Margy, she was going to have those martinis—and fast.

"Just fine, Mother."

"Why didn't she come over?" Suspicious, almost sly. Her mother had always suspected—and quite rightly, since it had been true when she was a child—that she was ashamed to bring her friends home. Ashamed of her mother's fatness and strangeness, ashamed of their having a maid when none of her other friends did, but ashamed most of all of the thick atmosphere of anger, unhappiness, and despair that filled the mock-Tudor house like the greasy black smoke that had surged through the rooms the time, years ago, the oil burner had backfired.

"Because her mother's out, and her brother's got a fever and her mother doesn't want him left alone."

Silence. A rustle of newspapers. More silence. Her fingers shook as she tied the last swag to a spoke of the lamp. As she backed down the ladder and snapped it shut, she decided to leave the mistletoe in the icebox and hang it later on. "You want a martini, Mommy?" A token gesture she felt she could afford; even when her mother *was* drinking, she only took bourbon and hated gin.

"Yes, thank you. I think I would."

Now she'd done it. Would she have to sit and drink with her now? Of course. Of course. "Very dry, Mommy?"

"Yes. But with an onion, not an olive, please."

"We have any?"

"Any what?"

"Cocktail onions."

"Don't be silly, Sarah. We have everything in this house."

Ah yes, thought Silly Sarah, going woodenly into the dining room. Forgive me—I forgot. Of course we have everything in this house. *Naturally* we have cocktail onions *and* olives. We have cabinets overflowing with jars of onions *and* olives, sweet gherkins, sour gherkins, jellies, jams, sauces, spices, and pyramids of cans and tins packed with meat and fish and soup and vegetables. We have closets and drawers just crammed with clothes and linens and china and crystal and silver and jewels—all in splendid condition, all of the Very Best Quality. Everything. You just name it. We have it. Everything everything in this house.

She opened a drawer in the dining room sideboard and took the liquor cabinet key from under a stack of ornate damask tablecloths that hadn't been used for years. The swinging door to the kitchen was open, and Ernestine might see this brilliant hiding place for the key—but what did it matter? If Ernestine wanted to drink, like most of the maids who'd worked for them had (after even the briefest tenure in that house), she would do as they had, and keep her own bottle hidden in her room.

She stirred the martinis in a glass pitcher on the little portable bar—tink-a-tink—eight to one. Leaving the mix to sit on ice, she went into the kitchen for the onions. Ernestine stood, arms folded, staring blankly out the window above the sink, not seeing their neighbor's bleak backyard, not aware of Sarah's presence in the kitchen.

Rushing back, Sarah poured out the drinks, then carried them on a tray into the living room, where her mother sat fixedly staring off into space, her eyes exactly like Ernestine's.

But the moment Sarah moved into her line of vision, the eyes changed—clearing, focusing on the tray. "You could have put in more than one onion," she said, reaching for a glass.

Sarah took the other, and put the tray aside.

"Are you going to stay here and drink with me, or are you going upstairs to lock yourself in your room until dinner time?"

Not dignifying that with an answer, Sarah carried her glass

across the room and sank down on the maroon-and-cream striped satin couch. *Whoosh*, went the puffy cushions.

Frowning, hardly placated by her staying, her mother raised her glass with a shaking hand: "Happy days." The official family toast. No one in that family—with the exception of her grand-mother who said *L'chayim* when she drank her beloved *kümmel* —ever said anything else. Not a chipper "Bottoms up" or "Here's looking at you" or *Skoal*. Just a flat, sober-toned "Happy days" with glass held high.

"Happy days," said Sarah without a trace of irony, and raised her glass.

They drank, her mother taking a greedy gulp, Sarah, a delicate sip.

Across the room her mother sat stiffly upright in lamplight, the recent loss of weight accentuating the largeness of bones, the sal-low face sagging and furrowed; she sat, eyes glassy, unfocused . . . until Sarah leaned forward to set her glass on the burnished sur-face of the coffee table.

"*Here*, Sarah. Take a coaster!" came the harsh command. Opening the drawer in the lamp table next to her chair, her mother took out two ugly pearly rounds cut from Jamaican conch, souvenirs from one of her father's long-ago cruises. Cruises he'd taken alone. Or supposedly alone.

She set her glass in an ashtray and went to take the coaster.

"Want a cigarette?" her mother asked brightly. "I have a pack of your brand right here in the drawer."

She couldn't tell which pained and touched her more—her mother's taking the trouble to buy her cigarettes, or the way she was trying to make an occasion out of this, yes, dear God, unusual event . . . their sitting together and having "cocktails." "That was sweet of you, Mommy—I would like one," she said, and bent her head as she tore open the pack, so her mother wouldn't see the tears welling up: she couldn't help it, it had happened at last.

"I'll take one too," said her mother, setting her glass on a coaster, extending a beautiful hand. Delicate, long-fingered, aristocratic, kept supple and fresh-skinned with rich creams, the flawless ovals of nails always brightly tinted—her mother's hands had always rightfully been her pride and joy. And looking at those hands, one caught a glimpse of the woman who'd gone awry, the woman (Sarah had heard from aunts) who had once been pretty and lighthearted and proud, full of eagerness for life. The woman who for years had been buried, lost, under layers of gross fat, and now, with the fat gone, had emerged thinner and lighter—but was still lost. Lost.

The beautiful hand took a cigarette and stuck it between unbeautiful blotchily-painted lips, inserting it at a comic upshooting angle meant for jauntiness. As Sarah lit the tip, her mother childishly sucked in, then withdrew the cigarette, pursing her lips, sending out a jetty little plume of smoke.

Sarah abruptly turned and crossed the room, resolutely lighting herself a cigarette and picking up her glass.

"Isn't this nice?" said her mother.

"Yes. Very nice." Sipping, she kept her eyes averted from the sight of her mother, mistily smiling, pinky coyly curled, lips pursily sucking, then forming a round which blew out tiny puffs of smoke signals: I'm drinking a martini, smoking a cigarette—I'm a sophisticated woman of the world! And sharing it all with my daughter. How *nice*.

Out in the kitchen Ernestine banged a pot. Her mother sighed. And sensing what was gathering in the silence, Sarah thought: Please don't say it. Mother. Don't. Leave it unsaid.

But of course her mother could not. "Isn't this nice, my daughter. To sit together, like other mothers and daughters, having cocktails?"

"Yes. It *is* nice."

"It's lovely to know I have a daughter sometimes. Too bad it only happens once in a while."

Stop now, Mother. For God's sake, *stop*.

She was saved by the sound of a key scrabbling in the front door-lock—her father, home early for a change. At the slam of the door, her mother did stop. Stopped smiling, stopped talking about how lovely it was to have a daughter sometimes.

"Fred?"

"Yes."

"You're home early."

"Yes."

Her mother couldn't see him as he came out of the tiny entranceway, into the hall, but Sarah could: moving slowly, heavy-handedly clowning, he took off his hat, peered into the living room at her, then looked up at the green canopy, forcing a foolish grin, shaking his head.

"Hi, Daddy." With an acid edge.

"Hi, Sarah." Cruelly mimicking, exaggerating the edge. "What happened to the mistletoe? No mistletoe this year?"

Fortunately her mother heard none of this, being off on a tack of her own. "Come join us, Fred. We're having cocktails. It's very nice."

He's already *had* a cocktail. More than one, thought Sarah as he now came into the living room. "Cocktails, huh?" he said, looking from Sarah to her mother—stocky, medium-tall but seeming shorter than he was, pink-faced, the nasty caricature of a silly grin gone. He ran a smoothing hand over the beautifully barbered silver hair his hat had slightly mussed, glanced back at her mother with a narrowing of amber eyes. ". . . should you? I mean, Dr. Wolpert said . . ."

"Dr. Wolpert said I could take a drink now and then." The sallow face had turned a mottled pink, the voice had lost all its lightness, was sludgy, thick.

"Okay—but not a martini. Why didn't you take bourbon like you always do?"

Leave her alone, thought Sarah. Leave her *alone*.

"Because Sarah was making herself a martini and offered me one. That's why."

Turning toward Sarah, her father bowed from the waist. "Ah yes. Our Vassar sophisticate."

Her eyes enormous, her mother gave Sarah a beseeching look; the splotchy flush was gone, the face was drained and haggard and waxy-pale.

"Get yourself a drink and join us, Daddy," said Sarah in a strange, new, imperious voice.

The silvery eyebrows lifted, the yellow eyes gave her a piercing look. "Okay, I will," he finally said. "But first I'm going to listen to the closing prices upstairs." Another intense look at Sarah. "You going to grace us with your presence at dinner, or are you dining out?"

"I'll be home for dinner."

"Well, well. Wonders never cease."

As he went up the stairs with a thumping careful tread, Sarah and her mother avoided each other's eyes.

"Don't mind him," her mother said suddenly. "He's been drinking."

"I know."

Even as they spoke, a radio voice drifted down the stairwell—faint, but unmistakable—the swift, garbly, tobacco-auctioneer voice of the announcer who gave the racing results.

Her mother suddenly laughed. Ironically. Her heart lifting, Sarah smiled back: she hadn't heard anything remotely resembling irony from her mother in years.

"Are you going out with Bailey?"

"Yes."

"I'm glad." And as Sarah stared at her with astonishment: "He's a nice boy, Sarah darling. He just doesn't have a future, that's all."

"That's not all that matters."

"So you think. You think love matters . . . when all you know is puppy love."

Sarah stood up. "There are some dregs in the pitcher. You want to share them with me?"

"I still have some left in my glass. Sarah. Don't be angry about what I said."

"I'm not angry, Mommy."

"Come back with your dregs. When your father comes down, we'll all drink together. Be like other families for a change."

She nodded and went out, thinking: Come back with your dregs—a perfect title for a snappy little ditty. She added more gin to the watery mix in the pitcher. Straight gin. No vermouth.

When she came out of the dining room, carrying the brimming glass, he was stepping off the stairway, starting across the hall. He stared at the glass in her hand, and was about to say something cuttingly vindictive—she could tell—but changed his mind, laughed, and settled for, "Chip off the old block!"

Grateful for even that much restraint, she went and kissed him on the cheek. He reeked of Scotch. Slipping back into the role of clown, he took a little sidestep, bowed from the waist. "Well, *thank* you," he said, straightening up and squinting at the ceiling lamp. Then grinned lopsidedly and shook his head. "Well, what do you know. My daughter kissed me. Without mistletoe. Wonders never cease." And went into the dining room for his Scotch.

An Injection

It was a hot June night and all the green patches of lawn were being tenderly watered by hose or sprinkler, while families sat on their screened porches rattling the evening papers. Her father stopped first at the stationery store to buy the late edition with the closing Market prices, then drove her straight on to the doctor's for her seven-fifteen appointment.

"Though you think so, it *isn't* the money. After all, we decided on the whole thing a long time ago. The money's been waiting. We keep our promises. If you took the time to think you would realize it's the world situation—my god, just take a look at those headlines!" He put the evening paper, folded headlines-up, on her lap, then turned into the doctor's driveway and snapped on the brakes. The house was a small brick box with an open-work porch on the right side, and a brass knocker shaped like a stirrup gleaming on the office entrance door.

"What do you want me to do?"

"Cancel."

She turned and gave him an incredulous stare.

"I'll bet they've had hundreds of cancellations. Nobody in his right mind would want to get caught over there with things the way they are!"

When she just sat, hands in lap, he began to glare.

She tried to keep her voice calm. "But everything is *set*. I've even gone and bought a passport case!"

"That makes it imperative, eh!" He gave a short hard laugh.

"Nothing is going to happen."

He gave a little sniff to show what he thought might happen to the world situation, and looked out the car window to a lot across the street. A new house, just in the framework stage, was going up. "This is a fine growing town. A fine place to live—you couldn't *find* a nicer spot. It seems to me that with all the advantages around you, you wouldn't want to go trotting off to places where people are starving, on the verge of a *revolution*. Here we have a club, a beach . . . and all the nicest young men. If you give up the trip, I'll add to the money and buy you a little car."

She looked unhappily down at her hands folded over the headlines. "A car is not a trip."

"What logic! A car is not a trip! You're as stubborn as your mother!" He took the keys out of the starter and gave them a little flip. "And what about doctors over *there*? Have you ever thought of that? What happens if you find yourself in some godforsaken little Italian town and you get an attack of appendicitis?"

"I had my appendix out that summer at camp. When I was thirteen. Don't you remember how they flew me down to Portland?"

He didn't answer but got out of the car to go in with her. He would worry if I stayed home all summer, she thought, he would worry his head off no matter where I was, and if I stayed here it would be driving too fast or swimming out too far. Just because he was made that way was not reason enough to give up the trip.

The trip had been promised ever since her sixteenth birthday, when the War had just ended and a trip to Europe as a college graduation present seemed a very special thing. They had started putting the money away for it then, and each year her anticipation had grown almost in direct proportion to the funds. She had always wanted to travel and the farthest she'd ever gone was to Rochester, to visit a cousin. She was traveling with four other girls from her college, on a detailed itinerary carefully worked out even to the time spent on platforms between trains. It couldn't be more safe. London was first, where her father had arranged for her to stay with some old friends while the others would stay at a hotel. She didn't want to miss any of it, not even a London hotel, and giving in on that score had seemed an enormous concession. Now he wanted her to give it *all* up and stay around home— tacitly, to find a husband.

As they sat far apart on the leather couch of the waiting room, she idly turned the pages of an old *Esquire*, pretending to survey the cartoons from an abstracted distance, but really listening to the sound of silver scraping on china, audible through the glass-paned door that connected the office with the main part of the house. Ever since childhood the doctor had seen her through the spate of expected diseases: measles and mumps, scarlet fever and impetigo, and later a light siege of pneumonia. When she had gone away to college, a staff of starched women had taken over the treatment of her minor aches and ailments, so she had not really seen him for four years. She had only caught glimpses of him around the club, where he was part of a circle her father belonged to—a group of men who played golf and cards together. The injections had brought her back.

The doctor came in now, still chewing a last mouthful of his dessert, rubbing big dry hands across each other in a gesture almost imitative of washing. Tall, assertive, he had wiry gray hair, a thickskinned lined tan face. He wore soft loose tweeds with a definite air, and from the easy gait and the hearty thrust-out of his hand, one could see that he considered himself more of a sportsman than a doctor.

He greeted her father in a deep gravelly voice, pulling him to his tired feet with a powerful grasping handshake, towering over him, smiling. "Just thinking about you. How was the Market today? News have much effect?"

Her father gave a short glum grunt. "What do you think? I was just saying that I think it's *crazy* for her to be going abroad at such a time."

"Now's as good as any other time. Things are not going to get any better."

She smiled her prettiest smile at the doctor, seeing that he was on her side, and he added: "Why not let her have her fling? You can't tell when she'll have the chance again. By next year she'll be married. Just look at her: she'll be married all right! This way she'll get it all in. Six months over there will last her a lifetime."

She beamed now and looked gratified, as though at any moment she might kiss him.

"She's only going for *three* months. Believe me . . . that's enough as it is."

The doctor laughed at his troubled face and clapped him affectionately on the shoulder. "Come, come, come now," he said in the sickroom manner that charmed patients into thinking themselves immediately better. "She's old enough to take a trip like that—remember, she's a *woman* now."

She gave her father a look that said: You see, someone understands. Gratefully she followed the doctor into his darkened office, where the shades were pulled against the summer dusk in the street. The heavy soundproof door clicked shut behind them, insuring complete privacy for a patient in consultation, and the doctor very carefully hooked a lock over the doorknob. Then they passed through the consultation office with its tidily appointed desk on into the immaculate white-tiled dispensary, where a black leather examining table and glass-fronted cabinets full of flashing cutlery—probes, knives, scissors, tweezers, syringes—confronted the anxious patient.

He told her to take off her blouse so he might inject the upper arm more easily, and she did as she was told, unbuttoning her faded boy's shirt and putting it over the back of her chair. She tried to calm her nerves, but shuddered and prickled all over with gooseflesh as she sat down and watched him select a long glass tube, a needle, and a little bottle from an ice compartment where all the serums and perishable medicines were kept. She had never ever completely recovered from the traumatic experience of her childhood vaccination, when it had been necessary to hold her down with two strong nurses.

"This is the last one," he protested. "Don't look so frightened!" He fastidiously washed his hands with pink disinfectant soap, making merry splashing noises in the corner sink. "You were such a good brave little scout the first two times . . . this is only the same thing. Just think of it as the last step, and that after this you'll be free to leave. You'll be traveling, seeing the world—and how many of us get a chance for that nowadays?"

She looked very pretty sitting there with her dark hair just brushing her shoulders, frowning at him. "Don't you start talking like that too." With the fascination of aversion she watched him break open the tiny bottle and fill the tube with the serum, careful to guard every dangerous drop.

"It's natural for a father to worry. He's thinking about all those young Frenchmen," he teased, nonetheless coming at her with the needle poised menacingly in the air, an alcohol swab in the other hand.

"What young Frenchmen?"

"The ardent young men of France. Don't tell me you haven't thought about them!"

"I'm afraid I haven't."

He laughed playfully, then suddenly peered at her over the top of the glasses which he had waited until the last moment to put on. "Fine sunburn. Where'd you get it?"

"On the beach." She knew that all this patter was his way of trying to divert her from the coming injection. She tensed herself for the terrible moment as he rubbed her bare arm with alcohol-soaked cotton, which was cool yet burning on her newly tanned skin. Then there was the needle plunge, the tingle of the solution as it entered her vein. Next to her ear (she had hidden her head as he sat down on the wire chair next to her), she could hear labored asthmatic breathing and smell the briny tobacco scent his body seemed soaked with.

"That's quite a sunburn."

"I always get this way the first time out."

"Put on a coat of Noxema before you go to sleep or you'll be up all night."

She nodded, unable to speak, grateful for the small-talk which took her mind off the unpleasantness at hand. She thought of the times when she'd been a child, and he had come to their house with the symbolic little black satchel, remembering these same big calming hands, and the talking and teasing he set up as diversions while he poured out a dosage, or prepared a swab for a sore throat. She had always let herself relax under this resonant voice that rambled on so soothingly . . .

"I suppose you're going to Paris and Rome?"

She nodded again.

"Paris and Rome," he sighed. "You'll be so taken up with a good time, with all the sights and all the young men, that you won't remember any of this. You won't give the old men at home a single thought . . ."

She laughed and he chose this moment of levity to draw out the needle with a tense jerk, painting the wound with iodine and taping it over with a Band-Aid. Her relief that it was all over gave her back her confidence, and she complained in near-coquetry: "Oh *that* sort of talk! 'Youth.' Whenever people want to sound important or pompous, they talk that way about 'Youth.' I've never thought you such an old man. When I was a girl I had quite a crush on you."

"You *did?*" Despite the exaggerated incredulity, she knew he had known.

"Yes I did."

Amused, she looked up innocently into staring flat blue eyes and then blinked, suddenly aware of her bare shoulders and sunburned body, hardly a child's now.

The doctor rose abruptly and turned his back as he dropped the equipment into a sterilizing bath. "So now," he said with his back still turned and his voice all different: "Now you're saying that you've grown up and lost all interest in your crush."

"But I didn't mean it to be insulting," she protested, confused and upset at the turn things were taking. She hastily pulled on her cotton shirt and buttoned and tucked it into her skirt.

Persistent, he came across the room and stood heavily by his little functional white desk. He absently fingered the slip of certification that he had signed for her passport, breathing quickly. Then he looked at her with an odd, unpleasant expression. "Well, I suppose that's what happens when you grow up and see things in a new way," he said significantly, and before she knew how to answer with delicacy and extricate herself from a situation she had entered in the extremity of innocence, her arms were locked to her sides and he was pushing, pressing her back against the wall by the chromium sunlamp.

"Please let go," she begged in a whisper. "It's ridiculous. Doctor Johnson . . . please be fair!" She squeezed her head to the left in the direction of the reception room. "Dad would honestly kill you if he thought . . ."

But the trembling doctor was intent on his purpose, and echoing her "Fair?" closed down on her with unsteady lips in a long kiss. "*There!*" he said when he chose to let her go. "That's all there is to that. 'Youth'? Guess I can still keep pace."

"Oh-h-h," she moaned in a rage of embarrassment, certain that the whole world had gone mad. "You've got lipstick all over you!" And as he furtively rubbed at his mouth with a paper tissue wad, she rushed from the dispensary to the heavy bolted door in the outer office, and throwing the lock, stepped into the now-crowded waiting room. It was the consultation hour. Several of the patients looked up curiously over the tops of their magazines at her explosive entrance.

Then the doctor was right behind her, suavely greeting the new arrivals, shaking her father's hand. "She's a grand little patient," he said smooth-as-silk to her father. "Stop fretting about her. She'll have the time of her life."

Her father's smile was stiff, as though saying: "Oh, it's easy enough for you to talk like that, since she isn't your daughter."

"I suppose you're right," her father said aloud, and reminded the doctor that Sunday they had a date to play golf.

There

The Rescue

They were bringing the bicycles up on deck—the Youth Hostelers' blue-tagged ones coming first—swinging them out of the opened forward hatchway on giant cranes, dangling them high in the misty air, then uneasily lowering them to one side of the deck where they were checked on a mimeographed list and put under tarpaulin: though the rain hadn't started, they had, as Dutchmen, an abiding respect for bicycles. The last day of the voyage, it was the first bad day they'd had. For nine days the potbellied Dutch vessel had slid so slowly, across a sea so calm, it had often seemed not to be moving at all, at times had seemed some huge pleasure barge moored to some invisible bank. For those nine days a sun, merciless for June, had beaten down through the webs of stays and rusted masts, melting the tar that caulked the deck boards, blistering paint that covered rust, burning the young bared bodies stretched on every inch of space. Young, because it was a Student Ship, a Dutch cargo vessel converted to a troopship during the war, now carrying one of the first postwar loads of American students abroad.

Today, despite the rawness and dampness, the decks were as crowded as on a sunny day, the only difference being the thick sweaters and warm wool slacks pulled over sunburned arms and legs. They were all there, on deck, because it was the one place that assured a full view: on this, the last day, no one wanted to miss a thing. They were also on deck because there really was no other place to be. The so-called "Rec Room" was a standard joke, a tiny room just big enough for a Ping-Pong table and upright piano, both of which were claimed by the same fanatics day after day, both producing a racket that only the players could endure. Then there was the dining room, quite large, low-beamed, filled with wooden trestle-tables they'd been informed they could use for their chess and checker and card games, but this too had become more or less of a joke: if it was not being used for their meals (which they took in three long sittings), it was being swabbed down by the Dutch kitchen boys, which left mere minutes in a place that reeked of undercooked noodles, greasy wurst and rancid mops. The only other places were the holds where they slept (boys, forward, girls, aft), but no one, unless seasick or sick, ever lingered in them once awake and dressed; vast, dim, creaking, ribbed concavely like the innards of Jonah's whale, hung with bunks in tiers of four, their air held some baleful staleness that was oppressive and drove one out—perhaps some lingering essence of the young soldiers, buckled into full equipage, who had lain sleepless, waiting, in those bunks five years before.

Today, even had the sun been out, few would have lain stretched out on the deck: there was simply too much to do, to be wrung out of this the last day. The damp air buzzed with a restless excitement, students scurried feverishly back and forth, making sure of addresses ("You can *always* reach me c/o American Express!"), rechecking routes ("We get to Paris the twenty-first . . . when does your damned group arrive?"), consolidating, firmly, any gains ("Oh, yes, I promise, every day. You'd better promise too!"). These latter, the lovers—at least those whose romances had withstood the nine-day strain—were out in full force, busier than everyone else; defying the fog, they took last snapshots, they sat solemnly in corners murmuring vows, they stood arm-in-arm at the rails plotting ways to meet despite the different routes of their groups. The only pause in all this came shortly after breakfast, when the loudspeakers hung all over the ship, gave the violent popping and snapping that prefaced announcements of any kind: "Good morning," said the faintly accented voice they'd come to know well, then discreetly coughed; they had just entered, it continued, its English a trifle more fastidious than usual, a zone cleared of mines the previous year, a "path of safety" two miles wide. With this it stopped. That was it. That was all. "*Dank U. Dank U*," it said, signing off as always in its native tongue, and in a cracking burst of static was gone. For a moment the decks were silent. "So what?" the stillness asked. "So what does that mean?" Then the same old voices began their game. "Dankoo!" they hooted, "Dankoo!" they falsetto-shrieked, "Dankoo, dank-o-o!" they roared until the laughter of their same old audience drowned them out. With this, the cards and checkers and chessmen were picked up, the ardent conversations resumed, pencils scribbled in address books, camera shutters clicked and clicked.

On the starboard side, paused by a coil of rope, Mitchell Shroeder listened and watched and swore to himself: The ship would have to sink before anything got a rise out of them. To him the announcement had meant something portentous—just what it was he didn't know, but while the voice spoke his skin had crawled, some part of his mind had answered Yes. Straight ahead of him now, blocking his way to the afterdeck, was a group sprawled about a bearded boy in bluejeans playing a guitar. The boy was singing a song about someone called "The Lily of the West." Mitchell dreaded having to pick his way across them, dreaded having to call attention to himself. He'd been feeling this way for fifteen minutes, ever since he'd come on deck. Despite all the racket in the hold—the shouting and cursing that started each day—he had slept right through breakfast, and when, drugged with sleep, he'd come up and found this overcast day, he'd been utterly thrown off, he did not know where to put himself. For nine days the sun, refracted blindingly off the salt-bleached decks, had strangely covered his solitude, he'd moved, unnoticed, ignored about the crowded ship. Today, he felt the deadwhite glare of the fog focus him, single him out; unnerved, self-conscious, he'd begun a turn about the boat, certain that people were staring at him.

As it happened, he was quite right, not merely paranoid. When he set off again now, gingerly stepping over legs, wearing dark glasses, book under arm (today, Camus' *La Peste*, in French), his flannels too creased, his sneakers too white, his British raincoat far too clean—he did, in fact, draw curious stares here and there. Once past this group, he headed straight back—he had a wild hope he might be alone on the poop-deck—but found the stairs leading to it blocked by still another group. He recognized them as an "Economic Study Group" going to Denmark, assembled for a last-morning lecture by their Group Leader, a bald professor from the Middle West togged out in a bright yellow slicker and beret. Sullen, glassy-eyed with boredom, they barely moved to let Mitchell pass. He almost stepped on a pair of hands tightly locked and concealed beneath a raincoat flap, he joggled a looseleaf note-book where obscene doodles were being drawn, he almost kicked an expensive camera; glares followed him up the stairs.

Muttering to himself, he walked past the crew's quarters, and when he turned the corner, could not believe his luck: he had got-ten his wish, he had the place all to himself. When he crossed to the rail he at once found out why—wind flapped his raincoat, spray hit his face—but he was too grateful to be alone to care, and was resolved to stay. The fog was turning a mustardy yellow, he noticed, as though the sun were trying to come through. Perhaps it would be clear when they docked, after all. Perhaps he would get this wish too: He had a cherished little vision of Rotterdam (where they would land next morning at six)—all turning wind-mill arms and neat De Hoochian houses glinting a Welcome to Europe in sun. He stuck his paperback book in his raincoat pocket and, pulling the collar high about his neck, hunched over the rail and stared down at the wake, which furled away from the huge propellers and flattened itself into a long mottled lane on the pitchy sea. It made such a positive path it immediately made him think of that other one, the "path of safety" two miles wide that presumably they were traveling in now. He went back over the brief announcement, fascinated, his skin prickling again, and as he stared down at the water below his mind took a dive beneath the churning wake, and there he saw them, loomy black shapes, rene-gade mines cut loose and escaped from the sweepers, soaring up and up through the singing greeny deeps like truant balloons from a vendor's hand. Slowly, like someone mesmerized, he let this morbid vision complete itself—hearing the explosion, the screams, and seeing the animal clawings for the lifeboats which were far too few.

Giving his head a shake as though to clear it, he straightened up, appalled at himself: even *he* could see this was getting pretty crazy, was carrying things too far, could see how really unbalanced he had gotten during the last nine days. The worst part was remembering how way back in New York in March, he had con-gratulated himself. A Student Ship? he had thought at the time, What a *deal:* it not only was the cheapest way to get abroad, but since he was practically still a student himself, it sounded highly promising. He saw his mistake the moment he laid eyes on his fellow passengers, convening in the lobby of his hotel in Quebec. Dismayed, he watched them, pinned with plastic identification badges like conventioneers, racing about, as explosively excited as students at a rally before the big game. With just one look he saw everything, saw that though the difference between him and them was at most six or seven years, they were years that made all the difference in the world. In grade school when the war began (he'd been finishing high school), in boarding school when it was done (he'd been in an Army hospital recovering from malaria)—for them the war had simply never been. Honest enough to know he couldn't resent (or even envy) them on a personal score—he hadn't seen action, he had gotten to college on the G.I. bill—he despised them on first sight for poor battered Europe's sake, he told himself. He, Mitchell Shroeder, twenty-six, was going to Europe on hard-earned savings (he'd worked on a newspaper as a researcher for two years) to "see" it in the classic sense; that is, quiet, unobtrusive, in a state of indecision (he knew now he did not want to be a journalist), he was going to make the old-style pilgrimage to places his studies and unending reading had made deeply meaningful to him. He was going not only hoping to receive some sort of guidance, but also, simply, just to stoke up while he could, well aware that if he didn't go now, while still relatively free, he might never get there at all. But they? he asked himself right off in Quebec—they with their stupid shining faces, lettered sweaters, drip-dry clothes, their too-expensive cameras and matched luggage—what on earth were *they* going to Europe for?

He'd had his answer once aboard the boat, where, his attitude blatantly clear to all, he was left alone (just as he wished), and he moved about the boat as good as invisible. Though this sometimes became uncomfortable—a couple stretched out mere inches away would carry on their seduction as though he did not exist—and though he certainly hadn't *intended* this role of eavesdropper-cum-voyeur, he nevertheless, by being insubstantial, had managed to find out everything. He learned that those rawhide suitcases held, aside from more sneakers and drip-dry clothes, secret caches of nylons, soap, whiskey, and cigarettes to be declared as gifts (to whom?), but really to be sold on the Black Markets of a Europe that hadn't seen such things for years; he learned that their wallets (some even wore money-belts) bulged with parental "allowances," dollars they knew just where to take in each city to get the best rate of exchange; from their frequent reverent mention he'd learned that the Ritz and the Dome (which they thought still there) and Harry's Bar were shrines, of a sort, to be visited, and several times had seen the actual volumes of Hemingway and Fitzgerald carried like Bibles under their arms; he learned of the drinking parties carried on in remote corners of the upper deck on certain nights, learned too that the lifeboats were busy all night long, and that certain members of the crew could be persuaded for certain sums to rent out their cubicles. He learned, in short, what the Group Leaders did not see or, seeing, wished to ignore: the ship was a seething little orgy afloat. He did not think this out of any kind of prudishness—there was nothing at all the matter with him—he liked sex and liquor as well as anyone else, in fact, far better than some on that boat. It was just that there was something so forced and self-conscious, so almost *compulsive*, in fact, in the way they went about it all, which was repellent to him, and which to him was just more sign of what they seemed to be trying to *be* . . . a sort of self-styled Lost Generation Number Two. To them, Europe, still shattered by war, was some glorious long-promised playground they'd read and heard about, and where they now meant to have the same sort of lark the others had had thirty years before. And it was for Europe's sake he despised them most, he repeatedly told himself, assuming what amounted to an almost national guilt and shame for them. Too busy wondering what they, who had suffered, could possibly *think* when they found themselves overrun by these spoiled stupid brats, he never wondered the basic thing: Who would see or care enough to see any difference between his visit and theirs? And what *was* the difference, really, between them, for either devoutly touring the Louvre or rapturously sipping a first pernod, weren't they simply Americans all, the same old restless thoughtless Innocents come Abroad again?

The fog seemed to be lifting as well as thinning, Mitchell, sobered, noticed now: there was about a quarter of a mile between its smoky hem and the sea. He straightened up and lit a cigarette, and looking out at the water suddenly saw, with a skip of the heart, something he'd been too preoccupied to see until now: two or three huge nervous-looking gulls had materialized out of the mist, and were dipping and wheeling over the wake newly littered with breakfast debris. He stood there, suddenly trembling with excitement, and though they were still almost twenty-four hours out of land, it seemed to him he could feel the giant muffled activity of the continent nearby. But as he stood there, roused, elated, another kind of tremor made him throw the cigarette overboard: that old saw about seasickness striking an empty stomach seemed to be quite true. He watched the cigarette disappear in the waterfall of the wake, then moved back, licking his lips. It was only ten-thirty; the first sitting for lunch, his, was not for another hour. He had learned by now that one could, for the magical dollar, buy almost anything on board that boat, and decided to go down to the kitchen and see if he could get something simple—some bread, a roll—to quickly fill him up.

Growing queasier by the minute, he turned and walked carefully past the crew's quarters, and when he went down the iron stairs, little flecks of orange paint from the handrail came off on his clammy palms. He had reached the main deck, and was painfully trying to pick his way back across the Economic Study Group, thinking perhaps he just ought to go lie down in his bunk, when the cry came—thin, gull-like, not to be believed. It came from up high, from some place near the navigation bridge. Mitchell froze, his sneakered feet straddling a pair of khaki legs. The banjo, the singing, the slap of cards, the droning voice beneath him stopped. A terrible muffled silence covered the ship, and then in the damp air it came again, loud and hoarse and clear this time: *"Man overboard!"*

All at once the senseless running began. Rising, wide-eyed, mesmerized, scattering cards and books and fountain pens, the students started blindly off, none of them knowing where they were heading, but all empowered by the same panic impulse to go *some*where, just anywhere else. Mitchell too began to move, walking, not running, in a daze heading for the port rail without having any idea why. In his confusion he noticed that the Dutch crew, always invisibly employed at tasks below decks, were suddenly everywhere, striding, grim-faced, among the churning boys and girls, and noticed, too, with a strangely sinking heart, that many of the girls were mutely weeping, the tears streaming from their huge, glazed eyes. He was almost at the rail when there

was a violent clanking, a tremendous vibration beneath his
sneakered feet, and with a heaving iron groan the boat came to a
halt. This was followed by silence in which there was only the
eerie docile slap of the sea against the sheer sides of the boat.

Then a sudden scuffling and shoving for places at the rail began,
and, pressed forward, Mitchell found himself staring down into
the kneading gray sea, realizing with a dull sort of amazement
that his queasiness had gone. The sound of hard breathing,
shuffling feet filled the silence. Then a loud laconic Southern
voice rang out: "How did it happen?" it asked with lazy curiosity.
From far down the line another voice answered, Midwestern this
time, but just as matter-of-fact: "Coupla guys were horsing
around in the lifeboats, taking pictures and things. This one
climbed to the edge for a trick shot and slipped. He must've
jumped clear when he felt himself going . . . he hit the water far
from the ship."

There was a deathly hush along the rail; everyone thought of
the giant grinding screws. Then "Where *is* he?" someone burst
out, at last giving voice to the question no one else had the courage to ask. As far as the eye could see there was just the mucky
surging of claycolored water, the faint sifting lift of the fog.

Another voice, tense with self-importance, yet strangely shy, announced: "He jumped on a bet. For a thousand bucks. I happen
to know that that's a fact."

"Who the hell *said* that?" demanded the Midwestern voice,
then roundly swore, this burst of profanity immediately drowned
out by sympathetic shouts and curses breaking out all along the
rail. In the midst of it Mitchell stood very cold, very still, having
finally realized what he had just barely missed: had he stayed on
the poop-deck one minute longer, he would have actually *seen* the
boy—would have seen him surface, his streaming terrible gasping
head suddenly coming up on that flat mottled lane like some
dread materialization of his shipwreck fantasy.

"Anyone know who it is?" someone just behind Mitchell called
out.

"A boy named Youngman. Part of that study group going to Rome." This again was the Midwesterner, clearly the only witness, or at least the only one who would speak.

Again there was silence. A girl on Mitchell's left began to sob, quietly, dryly, trying to stifle it with a wadded handkerchief. A big useless white life-preserver, thrown wildly into the sea when the first thin cry had come, drifted slowly by on the water below.

"Why isn't anything *happening?*" someone cried hysterically, and at once, as if in answer, the huge motors beneath their feet began to grind again. Slowly, massively clumsy, the potbellied ship began to turn, pushing away tons of water as it moved, leaving a flat wide marbleized sheet that spun on the surface, then suddenly stopped. It was clear they had done a complete turnabout, for now, up ahead, two more life preservers bobbed on water that moments before had been the wake. "No sign of him," someone gratuitously offered. "Thank god the fog's *lifting*," put in someone else. Then a fierce metallic squeaking amidships made them all turn their heads. The huge crane, which had been bringing the bicycles out of the forward hold, was now swinging a lifeboat full of men up high in the air. Breathless, not daring to move or speak like spectators at a circus aerial act, they watched the boat, jammed with stocky sweatered Dutchmen, oars stuck out as useless as pins, swing out over the water, then go down, down. When it smacked the surface a feeble cheer went up along the rail, in the lifeboat several fleshy pink faces angrily turned upward. The cheering ceased. One of the crewmen released the boat from the hook, then shouted gutturally; the oars began to dip and lift rhythmically.

"*There he is!*" someone screamed. "See him? Over there . . . way out to the left!"

Mitchell finally snatched off his dark glasses and frantically scanned the rocky watertop.

It could have been anything—a barrel, a log, a porpoise, even a gull. Ridiculously small and shapeless, a meaningless black blob pitching on the sea, until suddenly an arm shot up, there was no mistaking it: an arm. "Thank god," murmured voices all around Mitchell, who stood, eyes blurred, his whole body gone icy cold and numb as though it were trying to reproduce the sensations of the boy in the sea. But his mind reeled at the thought of it, could not encompass how it must feel to bob on the surface above one of the craters of the earth, fathomless leagues dropping away under one.

As the rescue boat labored on the swells, the silence along the rail was like a prayer. To Mitchell it seemed to take minutes for the boat to move a foot or two. The strapping Dutchmen, clearly picked for their job, seemed as puny as college crewmen in their battle with the strangely sucking sea. Yet, slowly, inexorably, it drew nearer, nearer the black shape still miraculously afloat. Then at last a long and flaccid black shape was being hauled from the water—it did not move at all—into the small safe dry world of gunwales, oars, and sweating men. As they saw it put in the bottom of the boat, a hoarse cracked cheering broke out, unrestrained at last.

It was still going on when the loudspeakers at their backs began to pop, but went unheard. As the popping grew louder—the volume was turned up—the cheering at last died down. "*Attention!*" a voice shouted. "Attention. Attention. This is an emergency! Everyone will please move to the center of the ship. We repeat—this is an emergency. The boat is listing dangerously. We request immediate cooperation. At once . . . *Dank U. Dank U.*" In an earsplitting crackle of static it was gone. "Dankoo . . . Dankoo," feebly echoed the usual voices, but no one laughed. And no one moved. Assuming responsibility, several Group Leaders moved back, shouting, then swearing, but no one listened, no one moved: the boat could heel over and sink them all—no one was going to miss the sight of the lifeboat coming alongside. The loudspeakers gave a tentative buzzing hum, but then, as if up on the bridge they suddenly acknowledged defeat, popped twice and went dead.

Ironically, coming back, the lifeboat moved quite rapidly, or so it seemed. When it swam into their ken below, the crush at the rail became dangerous; Mitchell could hardly breathe. But oblivious to elbows, knees, unbearable pressure against his back, Mitchell, feeling here was some lesson to learn, stared down at the boy wrapped and propped up in the boat amid the fiercely silent men. So that, thought Mitchell, was what it looked like to have almost gone under with the rinds of cheese and cocoa-stained paper cups, and to finally been pulled out by a redfaced Dutchman, grim as death, because he had heard the crew's rumor that you were to get a thousand dollars for this. The boy's red hair was plastered in strands to his forehead, his skin was shadowed with green like a corpse, his eyes were almost swollen shut; the whole face, in fact, was strangely bloated and tumid with something more than the brine of the sea—a sort of bursting fright and hysteria. When some hollow cheers broke out along the rail, they looked up for the first time. As he raised those red and terrible eyes, and slowly took them in, a shamed hush fell over the crowd; something enormous turned over in Mitchell's chest, and then lay still. But then the face below, a boy's face after all, slowly reclaimed itself—life and youth returned. He gave a wan grin, their playmate returned to the fold, and the cheering, hoarse and wildly jubilant, began in earnest now.

Quickly, efficiently, the boat was lifted from the sea by the cranes and set down, neatly, to one side of the yawning forward hatch. The crowd at the rail shifted, began to surge forward now; taller than many of those around him, Mitchell stayed where he was, still able to see. He saw the boys in starched white jackets with a stretcher, but more important, he saw their Captain, a strangely enigmatic man whom they rarely ever saw. He was a tall, portly Dutchman with a black beard and sharp black eyes. He stood importantly off to one side, hunched into black oilskins, his mouth clamped cruelly on a pipe, surveying the shaking boy with a narrow-eyed analytic calm; when finally, buried in blankets on the stretcher, the boy was spirited away up the winding stairs that led to the officers' quarters and bridge, the Captain followed, his ruddy face grim: If it *had* been done on a bet he would get to the bottom of it!

Strangely dissatisfied, unhappy, the crowd began to disperse, milling all over the decks, released once again to normal speech. Murmured speculations were endless: ". . . there were porpoises yesterday, and sharks are always around too when you see porpoises . . ." ". . . mincemeat by the propellers . . ." ". . . if the fog had been closing in instead . . ." ". . . not even for a *million* bucks!"

Pushing through the restless crowd, Mitchell sat heavily down on a bench beneath the stairs. He felt so peculiar he could not stand up—suddenly weak and strangely helpless with rage. Once again he felt queasy, but not quite in the same way he had before; this was not seasickness, this was something else. When the grinding and clanking of the motors started up, and the boat prepared to right itself, he shut his eyes. Where was Youngman now? Were they asking him questions? Was that squinty-eyed Captain cross-examining him? With all the vibration, he still felt the bench shake under the impact of someone sitting down, and reluctantly opened his eyes. Wearily he took in the girl who had sat down— one of the homely ones, one of the few unlucky ones who had remained alone for nine days. He particularly remembered this one, for her darting hungry looks had fastened on him once or twice. Slumping back, he shut his eyes, hoping she would go away.

"He looked half-*dead*, didn't he?" she said brightly, as he might have known she would. Reluctantly, he opened his eyes. "What an awful thing to *go* through," she went on, encouraged by the sight of his dark eyes. "Imagine. Just imagine. Do *you* think he did it on a bet?"

"Who started that rumor?" said Mitchell, his voice trembling with anger. "My god. Who's sick enough to start a rumor like that!"

The girl stared at him, astonished to have provoked so much emotion—of any kind. Then, going coy, she shurgged with elaborate nonchalance: "Probably the crew. They hate us enough . . . think we're all rich and stupid brats. Haven't you noticed? I'm sure you have—I've seen you *watching* everything. I suppose that's because you're a writer. Someone said you were a writer, and I suppose you're going to Europe to write the Great American Novel or something like that. I'm going to Arles with that art group. We'll only be there two weeks. Art is my major, you see."

Left speechless by this barrage, Mitchell stared at her pale and ugly face. When she began to blink at the silence, he finally said: "I'm not a writer."

"Well, what are you then?" Her voice was rasping and aggressive now; she was of course wounded—her type always was. "Why are you going to Europe?" she demanded as if it was her right to know.

Now Mitchell shrugged elaborately and, sitting up, pulled out cigarettes: "Because it's there."

Baffled, blinking once again, she accepted a cigarette; watching her daintily begin to puff on it, Mitchell saw that she now hated him. Since she hated everyone else, she sat on, smoking, not really having any other place to go. In what looked like a companionable silence, they sat there smoking, side by side. The boat was sailing straight for Europe once again, and as it slipped smoothly now through the sea, Mitchell thought that the water looked different—it seemed to him to be turning from its muddied gray to true bluish green. To their left, around the corner and stairway, the cranes began to lift the bicycles from the open hatch again. From somewhere in the still-thinning fog came a muted horn of a passing ship; piano chords, tinny, faint, drifted down from the "Rec" room, along with the hollow plastic pock of the Ping-Pong balls. Though most of the crowd had scattered, a few stood in resolute clumps here and there, rehashing, reliving with relish the drama of the boy, *their* boy, in the sea. A few feet away from the bench where Mitchell sat with his poor tense companion, two lovers began to take some pictures again. The girl was trying artfully to pose herself on a coil of rope, while her boyfriend shouted like a Hollywood cameraman: "No, don't smile—it looks too phony. That's it, sweetie . . . yes, that's it. Perfect, perfect . . . Ah Christ, you moved, you *moved!*"

"You don't have to sit here," the girl at Mitchell's side burst out. "I mean you can get up and walk away."

Before Mitchell could open his mouth to wearily smooth her down, the loudspeaker right above their heads began to pop. "Attention," said the dry precise voice, "Attention, please. This afternoon at four o'clock there will be a meeting of all passengers on the forward deck. Landing procedure for Rotterdam will be discussed. Students are reminded to have ready customs declarations and quarantine slips." In the pause that followed someone hissingly whispered in Dutch. Then: "On orders from the Captain all students will refrain from leaving the A deck or going beyond the poop-deck stairs. Any students disobeying these orders will be placed in confinement until we land. The first sitting for luncheon is now to be served. Please to be prompt. *Dank U, Dank U.*" With a strange smooth electrical click the speaker went off.

"Dankoo!" hooted a group of boys passing the bench, shoving and heading for their lunch of cheese and noodles and bread. "Dankoo," said the lover, his hands furtively slipping and groping as he helped his pretty friend down off the coil of rope. Mitchell stood up and looked at the girl still peakedly smoking, her head turned away, and said: "That's your sitting too. I know. I *watched* you." With a henlike movement of the neck, the girl turned and blinked at his kindly, teasing smile. "Come on," said Mitchell, "don't sit here and brood. You've got to keep up your strength for Arles. You'll feel much better after you've had some lunch. Come along now—believe me, you'll see."

Tea at Le Gord

Where woods and wall began, she got off the bicycle and wheeled it the rest of the way up the hill, glancing uneasily at the wall. Higher than a man, it was topped by jagged triangles of glass—a clear statement that the De Rogiets had no use for intruders. The gate at the hill's crest was made of barred iron and a printed plaque just above the handle proclaimed: *"Le Gord. Chien Méchant."*

Madelaine hesitated, looking wistfully back at the cathedral which sat like a tiny spired crown in the distance. It was much farther out than she'd imagined, and now the sign warned of this fierce dog. She wondered why Mrs. Talbott hadn't mentioned the dog, although she knew she was being childish to worry about it. She pulled the little gold bellchain on the gate.

Entering, she stood still and blinked at the sudden change of light. The ringing of the bell had carried far, for at the end of the densely wooded path she heard the ominous baying of three or four dogs, not of just one as the sign had indicated. She feared dogs, even the pawky little poodles her mother affected, so she waited and stared anxiously at the foliage about her. When she decided they were penned in or tied up, she proceeded along the cinder path until she emerged into brilliant sunlight.

It was a steeply-built house, trimmed with intricate cuttings and shutters of wood, more a Hansel-and-Gretel cottage or a post-card Swiss chalet than the "little château" Mrs. Talbott had described. The lawn was dry, rankly weeded, running to the wooded park inside the gate.

A redheaded girl stood on the wide porch that ran around the first floor of the house, holding back a struggling dog. She called: "*Attention!*" warningly, and Madelaine's flesh prickled as she glimpsed a snarling mouth, straining haunches, as she turned and saw two more big dogs clawing fiercely at the wire of a steel-net-ted enclosure by the house. She could not tell what kind of dogs they were, but they seemed some species of Great Dane, with pale brindled coats and dark muzzles. Probably they were not always penned in. If she were to obtain a pension here, how could she come and go with ease, when she would even be afraid to come in alone from the gate?

The girl chained the dog to the newel post and came down the steps, her homely face breaking wide with a smile. "Mademoiselle Barker?"

"Yes," answered Madelaine, still eyeing the dog. "Is Madame De Rogiet at home, please?"

"She has been in town since the morning, Mademoiselle, but she expected your visit and will be home soon. She rode in with Monsieur on the 'jeep' to pass the morning at her mother-in-law's house, but she must come back for tea, for that is when she feeds the dogs." The girl blinked shyly at Madelaine, her pale-lashed green eyes darting enviously over her clothes.

For tea. Madelaine looked at her watch. She was tired and hot and thirsty from her ride. She was about to ask if she might go in-side and wait in the shade for Madame De Rogiet when two little boys of five and six years suddenly appeared in the flamboyant arch of the front door, where they clung to the doorknob and gog-gled at Madelaine with round, weak pale-blue eyes. The delicacy of their limbs made them seem miniature children, and their faces were blanched in shadowed pallor, marks of malnutrition. With-out taking their eyes from her face, they moved leggily out onto the sunny porch, avoiding the chained dog and jostling each other for moral support until they had gotten down the steps and reached the security of the maid's skirts, where each grabbed a handful of calico. "Marie? Marie-Paul?" they bleated in unison into the flowered material, *"Marie-Paul, qui est cette demoiselle?"* They had half-singing, half-crying voices and in their open mouths the little pointed teeth were bluish.

The girl put a hand on top of each dark head. *"C'est une demoiselle américaine. Alors . . . silence!"*

"Perhaps I ought to go away and come back later," said Madelaine. The children, like the dogs, were something else Mrs. Talbott hadn't mentioned.

"Oh no, Mademoiselle," said Marie-Paul, "Madame distinctly told me to ask that you wait. Perhaps you wish some water? It is a long ride from Chartres on such a day."

Madelaine said she would very much like some water, so the girl, giving the dog ample berth, led her back along the porch to the kitchen, the two little boys stumbling along at Marie-Paul's side, peering back owl-eyed at Madelaine.

The kitchen looked like a Vermeer interior gone to seed. A resinous smell hung in the air, the black and white checkered floor was covered with footmarks. Flies buzzed and settled everywhere, drowning on the gummy surface of cream bowls lined up for boiling, slipping down inside the necks of green bottles holding milk. Marie-Paul opened the rheumy icebox and poured Madelaine some water. As she drank it the two children watched her with blinking round eyes, and when she put down the glass and smiled at them they became convulsed in a paroxysm of shy delight, doubling over to giggle shrilly.

"What are their names?" she asked.

"Philippe and Charles. They are *très gentils*. But very nervous: they tremble so when they drink their soup, they spill it all over themselves. I think perhaps it is because their mother is not with them often." Marie-Paul looked with troubled eyes at the two boys, then turned a deep and lucid gaze on Madelaine, making her feel that though they were total strangers there was between them a bond of communication that could be depended on. Madelaine felt that a hand had been mutely outstretched, and she shivered at the empty dankness of this house where the past lay like frayed tapestry on the wall . . .

Outside the dogs began to trumpet joyously. The two little boys pressed into a corner, startled into silence.

"That will be Madame De Rogiet," said Marie-Paul, quickly taking Madelaine's arm and leading her out of the kitchen through a dark hallway to the front door. "Madame would be angry to think I had invited a guest to the kitchen."

Madame De Rogiet was kneeling on the top step of the porch, making crooning, loving noises to the chained dog. As soon as Madelaine appeared, the dog stood up under her caresses and began to growl. Giving the dog a mock admonishing tap, the woman smiled, and with an arching forward of the neck, a dip of the head, she moved down the porch holding forth a long thin hand. Her face was narrow, hollowed under cheekbones and eyes, the nose reaching out from between deepset brown eyes. Her only beauty was a perfect transparent wax-colored skin and winging dark oval eyebrows. She gripped Madelaine's hand with slender tensile fingers. "I hope you have not been waiting long . . . Mademoiselle . . . Mademoiselle Bar-kair."

Madelaine assured her she had not.

"I am sorry that I did not give you a ride out, but there were visitors at my *belle-mère's* house. It is so seldom one sees old friends these days, I did not want to set a limit on the time." She shrugged and smiled without any trace of warmth, tweaking pale wisps of brown hair into a Paisley scarf knotted like a turban about her head, looking carefully at Madelaine. "I can see that you are tired from your long ride. We will go inside where it is cooler and we can talk."

"How wonderful to have a car," said Madelaine, following the slight figure into the dim cool house.

"Car? No. It is a 'jeep,'" laughed the woman as though she had made a successful joke. Madelaine smiled politely. She was acutely ill at ease, sensing measuring glances at her person, her clothes, sensing more veiled laughter. She was wearing an outfit her mother had selected for her at Best's: a striped chambray dress (her mother said stripes were thinning), a cardigan about her shoulders. She looked completely American, from the gold barrette holding back one side of her well-brushed blond hair to the tips of her seasoned moccasins. Did she look funny? Was she in some way funny like the "jeep"? Judging from the smile on the woman's face, it would seem so.

"How long have you been in Chartres, Mademoiselle?"

"A little over two weeks."

"And you were pensioned with another family then?"

"The Villets. They live down in the *Vieille Ville* back of the cathedral."

"Villets? . . . Villets, Villets? They are the butchers?"

"No, there are *two* Villets, Madame. This one is the Contractor. Monsieur is very tall, gray-haired . . . almost white. Wears heavy glasses?"

"I am afraid I do not know the Villets," said Madame De Rogiet coldly. "So. You stayed with the Villets two weeks, and now you are searching a new pension?"

"It isn't because I didn't like them," Madelaine explained hastily, feeling that somehow she was betraying the other kind family, "but it was awfully crowded. The house is very small and they're quite a big family. Even though I was paying them, I felt that I was in the way."

"You paid the Villets?"

"Of course," said Madelaine faintly.

"*Combien?*" asked the woman, lapsing into the discretion of French.

"Five hundred francs a day."

Madame De Rogiet leaned back, her face assuming a somnolent, pearly look. "And did your Madam Talcott tell you how much we wish for a pension at *Le Gord?*"

"No, Madame, Mrs. *Talbott* didn't," said Madelaine, annoyed that the woman couldn't remember the name of her study-group leader. "She said that she thought it was important for us to meet. She assumed we would discuss prices later."

The woman smiled. "We are asking eight hundred francs a day, Mademoiselle."

Madelaine sat up straight. "Oh! But Mrs. Talbott gave me no idea there would be any change in the price of the pensions." Confused and embarrassed, she decided to tell the truth at once. "You see, Madame, each individual in our group was told to bring a certain amount of money to France. It was all worked out very carefully in advance, and there was to be just so much allotted for pensions each week. Of course our parents provided for a little spending money, but that was to be saved for the gifts we might buy in Paris at the end of the summer."

Madame De Rogiet laughed. "Ah, I can see your mother appreciates Parisian chic!"

"Mother has wonderful taste," said Madelaine. "She's an editor on one of the biggest fashion magazines in the States."

The woman appeared not to have heard. She said almost indolently: "But surely, Mademoiselle, with the rate-of-exchange being what it is, being completely to the advantage of Americans . . ." She sighed, shrugged, and rose to straighten a little mahogany pipestand on the desk. "My husband and I have always liked Americans. We wish to travel there someday . . . my husband has a distant cousin in Boston, a cousin on his maternal side. We have seen so many Americans in Chartres this summer, and we watch them all with interest. We have been watching your group for weeks now. You see, my husband's mother lives in the *Rue de la Cygne*, right by the cathedral. Each morning I go there and see you all in front of the cathedral with your pads and pencils. You seem such a handsome, energetic group. We thought it would be charming to have one of you live with us . . ."

Madelaine could see the others in the group as the woman had, peeping out from behind lace curtains at the *Rue de la Cygne:*

the pretty girls (who might well have been picked for their looks rather than an interest in Gothic Art) tanned and slender in their Bermuda shorts and shirts, smiling as they emerged from the dark cathedral into the noon sun. Yes, it would be *charming* to have one of those other girls as a guest at *Le Gord*. Wretchedly she remembered one of the first mornings at the cathedral when an old guide in the black robes of the church had taken them up to the triforium gallery, proud and eager to show such treasures to *les américains*, who must surely have a great love and understanding of such things if they had come such a long, long way to see them. The girls and boys in the group had whispered, nudged, and laughed above the droning voice of the poor old *corbeau*, making it impossible for Madelaine, who was one of the last in line, to hear what he was saying about the stained-glass transept windows.

The silence was broken by the sudden gusty bang of a door upstairs, followed by running tiny bare feet, then fretful crying, long drawn-out sobs, hiccoughs, whines. Madelaine, her heart beating, stared hard at the Frenchwoman but saw nothing on the smooth pale face to indicate she had heard her sons. Then Marie-Paul came chinking down the stairs bearing a tray with two half-finished bowls of milk sliding back and forth, boiling skims still sticking to the sides of the bowls. Relieved to see her, Madelaine smiled warmly, but the green eyes were blank, the freckled face closed.

Disheartened, Madelaine surveyed the room as though hoping to find a conversational subject in the *faïence* plates on the wall, in the leather-bound volumes of De Musset and Lamartine in the bookcase. One wall was completely covered with photographs of large, fierce, beautiful dogs like the ones outside. Nailed to most of the frames were blue cockades, *Grand Prix* gold-stenciled on their fat satin hearts.

Then Madelaine looked up at the ceiling, a ruin of peeling cracks and oily stains.

"Ah, you must not look at that!" protested Madame De Rogiet.

Until now she had been proudly watching Madelaine's reaction to her possessions. "That happened during the war when the Germans were in this house. They used it as their headquarters so that all the officers came here to have their parties, to make it a club. They took all our beautiful rugs, heirlooms that had been in our family for centuries. To say nothing of our wines. My husband was inconsolable."

"But . . . judging from what the Villets told me, you were *lucky*, Madame! Lucky they didn't burn the house. Weren't you afraid?" Seven years, she thought, seven long years since all that has been over, done, and almost forgotten by some, and still they have not tried to repair the ceiling.

"I was not afraid because I was not here," Madame De Rogiet explained with almost insulting patience. "We were at my mother's house, near Dreux. We were safe. My husband came back to Chartres one day to see how the house was faring and managed to talk with the officer in charge. This German was truly an educated man and he loved dogs, too. My husband showed him the trophies we had received for breeding our *caniches*, and the officer, at the end of the afternoon, promised my husband that the house would be protected. He was a *bonhomme*. They were not all beasts, you know. And though he could do little to prevent the parties where they drank up all the wines in our cellar and ruined our ceiling," she pointed to the oily stain, "he kept his word of honor—a true officer and a gentleman."

Madelaine heard the word "gentleman" and shuddered. In the quiet she fancied she could hear heavy boots thumping up and down the thin wooden stairs, voices calling out gutturally in the echoing rooms, metallic equipage scraping against pink plaster walls. How silent the house must have fallen after their surrender, damp, soiled, deserted, full of uncertain sounds . . .

"We will have tea," said Madame De Rogiet, rising. "And then I will show you the grounds. You will see something of what it was when it belonged to my husband's father." She smiled vacantly, talking more to herself than to Madelaine. "In those days it was only used as a summer home, and in the fall, as a hunting lodge for the *chasse,* when everyone would come out in carriages from Paris. I will show you where the old stables and kennels for the hounds once stood. It will be a pleasure to show you these things, because I am certain you have little chance to see such things *chez Villet.*"

After tea they began a tour of the house. On the second floor, Madelaine heard the light, chanting voice of one of the little boys, talking to himself behind a heavy door. Madame De Rogiet hurried her to the third floor, where they entered a wide sloping-ceilinged room with a shuttered window. In the dim light, Madelaine could see that the wallpaper was in tatters.

"This is the room available for a pension," said the woman as she flung the leaves of the shutters wide, letting in late afternoon sunlight. "It was my husband's room when he was a boy. The pattern of the paper, as you can see, is the noble *fleur de lis.*" She pointed to an intact section of the wallpaper. Madelaine half-expected her to begin a recitation of her husband's lineage, beginning perhaps with the Duc de Berry and working up to the present.

"See the view," said Madame De Rogiet, gesturing imperiously.

Madelaine looked. Over the tops of dipping trees, the distant cathedral spires were blue and gold in the late light. "We once had a house in the country," she said, the words slipping out before she knew why she'd uttered them.

"You have a large house in America?"

"Oh no. Not now. But when I was very small and my father was alive, we had a big house in Pennsylvania." She took a deep breath. "Mother and I have an apartment now."

"And your mother? . . . She works on a magazine?"

"That's right," said Madelaine, quietly yet almost belligerently.

"And you, Mademoiselle, are studying to be an artist?"

"No. I'm an Art major in college. I'm studying painting and its

history, but don't do any painting. I don't know yet what I will
do."

Madame De Rogiet smiled, and in that moment Madelaine
knew she almost hated her. The lilting unequal cadence of the
woman's phrasing was an affectation, and the mannered vocabulary of shrugs, moues, dips of the head, articulations of long
pointed fingers, seemed graceless to her, without point of refer-
ence in her own experience. It was a Gothic sort of elegance, once
precious, but now unbeautiful, like the highwaisted tubular
women who advanced in procession, abdomen first, trains over
arm, across the miniatures of Van Eyck.

Madame De Rogiet looked at her watch. "Time to feed my
beauties!"

Madelaine had little choice but to follow her downstairs and
wait as Madame De Rogiet went into the kitchen and returned
with two huge pails of a yellowish stew. She hung back as the
woman unchained the dog on the porch, but it ignored her as it
caught the scent of the food in the pail. With the dog eagerly
panting at her side, the woman went to the high-wired enclosure,
unlocked the door and entered, calling out lovingly to the fawn-
ing, ravenous dogs inside. "Micelle, Gruette, Mélusine," she
crooned, laying light fingers on their veined necks, calling them
well-mannered beauties, highborn ladies, waiting so patiently for
their food. But as the gluey mash was poured into their bowls,
manners disappeared, and the snapping jaws, heaving ribcages,
and tensely rooted haunches brought out a rash of prickles along
Madelaine's spine. Perhaps she could leave now while they were
so busy.

But after interminable singing: "How hungry they are! How
starved my little babies are today!" Madame De Rogiet picked up
the empty pails and rehooked the door as she came out. "When
we return from our tour of the gardens we will let them out for
some exercise. Then you shall see how sweet and gentle they are!"
She smiled. "You must not be so frightened, Mademoiselle, for

they would not harm a child. One must be educated out of fears such as yours." She swung the empty pails at her side, bending her slender body forward. "You shall see how sleek and glossy their coats are. From eating only the best, you understand—raw meat and eggs—their coats shine like polished brass."

"Perhaps some other time . . ." began Madelaine, but the woman was already up on the porch, putting the emptied pails back in the kitchen.

They began their tour by crossing the lawn and entering the park inside the wall. Silently they walked in piney shadows until a sharp turn where they entered a long spanning arch of trees, a natural Gothic arch.

"This is exactly as it was when Monsieur le Comte of three generations past owned it. Only the arch has grown higher. Our rose arbors, our gardens in the English manner, our tennis lawns are gone, and there is no longer the will nor the money to restore them. But this is as it was."

And gesturing dramatically, she led Madelaine in proud, stately procession to the center of the mossy arcade, where the light filtered down through foliage as through the triforium gallery in Chartres Cathedral, making crisscross patterns on the grass. In the center, another spanning arch of trees crossed at a right angle, a squaring transept. They paused. Madelaine stared, strangely moved.

"Now for the gardens," Madame De Rogiet said, hurrying Madelaine along until they reached a clearing where sparse cornstalks, cabbages, and carrots grew in confusion. Then on to an old mill where dust seeped quietly from a beamed ceiling, then to the spot where the rose arbor had been, growing in fine disorder over latticed wood, like the gardens of Madame Pompadour in Boucher.

When finally they returned to the house, Marie-Paul was just disappearing in the door, Philippe and Charles each attached to an apron string. Madelaine knew she must tell Madame De Rogiet her decision.

"Madame . . . it's very late and I'm afraid I've already taken too much of your time . . ."

"But not at all, Mademoiselle! It is a pleasure to see someone appreciate fine things." Searching Madelaine's troubled face, she seemed to read her thoughts: "If as you explained earlier, you feel that you cannot afford a pension with us, I understand. On the other hand, I am sorry *we* cannot be more accommodating."

"Oh, I wouldn't dream of asking that, Madame! But you see, as I said, I did promise to do some shopping for mother in Paris . . . some perfume . . . some gloves . . ."

"I quite understand. Then, I did not mention this, but I see you are an intelligent girl and will not take offense: I did not reckon with the children. I saw that they were unusually upset this afternoon and could only conclude that it was the presence of a stranger under their roof, a stranger speaking an alien tongue, which upset them. They are such *delicate* children, susceptible to any influence—even my beautiful darlings upset them." She pointed to the dogs in the wire enclosure. "I think it would be best for everyone concerned if we considered the pension a closed matter."

"Yes," said Madelaine, hating the woman, for the children had *liked* her.

"I will walk you to the gate, Mademoiselle. But first you must meet my ladies. We have been impolite to them, you have not given them a chance."

Madelaine saw no way of refusing. She let herself be led to the enclosure, where Madame De Rogiet opened the door. Only two of the dogs came out, working velvety black muzzles against Madelaine's bare legs, snuffling inquisitively. She remembered an incident in her childhood, when she had run, run across a wide lawn from a collie charging after her. Her father, who had been there to catch the dog before it caught her, had first soothed her, then patiently explained that she must never show a dog that she feared him, for he would recognize it, smell it, and act upon it. Now she moved edgewise away from Madame De Rogiet's "ladies," her body agued with a cold sweat. Stupidly she looked down at their ribs, the bones of their long backs under the shining brindled coats, and with great effort declared: "They are very beautiful, Madame." She understood that she was undergoing some sort of trial and childishly tried to flatter her judge. Somehow she began the interminable distance to the gate.

Madame De Rogiet moved easily with her, a hand in each dog's collar, and looked critically down at them. "Yes, they are truly beautiful. Perhaps a little *maigre*, but then it is an aristocratic trait. Noble thinness is always becoming." She shrugged her mobile, bony shoulders.

Under the last arch of trees they stopped for a moment, and the dogs pricked up their tulip-shaped ears, moaning in their bulging throats. Madame De Rogiet gave her a last appraising measure of a look and for an instant let go one of the dogs' collars, thrusting out her hand as she had done in greeting. The released dog started forward, baring yellow teeth. Then Madame De Rogiet said with half-closed eyes: "*Au revoir, Mademoiselle*, it was a most enjoyable afternoon with you." She clucked chidingly at the free dog, who stopped growling but did not take its eyes from Madelaine. "You must come and see us again before your departure from Chartres."

Madelaine blinked rapidly, saying yes, she would love to come again. "It was a privilege to be here," she concluded, relaxing a little as she saw the woman slide her hand back through the dog's collar. When she was sure the slender fingers had a firm grasp on the leather, she turned her back and strolled with great effort across the small space to the gate, her feet slipping in the moccasins. She turned the gate handle, calling out a final farewell, her voice ringing falsely hearty, her eyes so moist with fear and rage they did not see the snapping release of the long pale fingers. She slipped out the gate, crashing the grillwork door behind her. The bell on the top pealed ceaselessly, trembling.

But in the seconds it took her to reach her bicycle, the dogs were already rattling against the door as they tried first to hurtle it, barking, then snarling as they worked themselves up to a frenzy of howling disappointment. And Madelaine knew that they had been discharged after her retreating back, that Madame De Rogiet, still cool, still smiling, had let them loose before the final clicking of the lock upon the gate.

The Master

Carefully Roger locked his door on the prize possessions in his suitcase: two letters of introduction to internationally known artists and a bottle of Scotch. His fine hair still held the ridges of water combing and he wore a clean nubby bright-blue linen shirt, cut like a Basque sailor's, that he had bought in Avignon. Though he had hardly slept, he made himself get up early and set out into the hot morning in the direction of Juan-les-Pins. The whole day was his, he planned to relax, to sketch a little, to nap under a big tree on the grass and drink plenty of cognac after dinner that night so he would get a good night's rest. Tomorrow Jim Norton arrived, and for that he had to be in good form.

But the determined stride slackened on the long walk to Juan, and he had to stop occasionally by the roadside under a splayed palm and revive himself with a cigarette. The heat wore him out, weakened as he was by the dysentery he had contracted in Avignon. And to make matters worse, the water closet on his floor had broken down, and several times a night he had groped down two flights of cold marble stairs, the only soul awake in that damp hotel where the mistral banged the shutters and made the palms clack their leaves like clappers. Oh, he was sick all right, he could tell from that ache behind his eyeballs. But he refused to stay alone, isolated in that room.

He cheered up again once he got into Juan, where in the early sunlight the shop windows were opaque mirrors that reflected the passers-by, clogging along in sandals, displaying leathery tanned legs, aging paunches in immaculate British shorts. It made him feel happy, seeing all these tanned idlers; perhaps if he sat in a café that afternoon he could strike up a conversation with a local character. To get in out of the sun, he ducked under an awning and caught a glimpse of himself in the shadowed glass that was startling: he looked so exceptionally weak, his fine arching nose thrust out so from the hollow cheeks, and he looked smaller than ever. He straightened his spine as though that might make him feel better and walked along snappily, smiling faintly at everything from behind his enormous horse-blinker goggles.

Across the street, the window of a gaudy shop set out with brilliant pottery bowls and mats caught his eye. He loved colors, and these were of the purest, glazes and weaves in primitive dyes. He thought how there was always money in this sort of thing—these artsy-craftsy wares that caught the tourist eye—and he wondered if perhaps he could interest the dealer in some of the bright watercolors he had done in Avignon. To size up the dealer, he peered into the shop and saw there, at a table of knotty pine, Jim Norton leafing through a large folio of prints which he held up to the light as the shop-owner stood at his shoulder, running a suave monologue about the pictures. Their backs were to him, he could easily pass up the street unnoticed—obviously Jim hadn't wanted to meet him until tomorrow—but he pushed on into the shop, which reeked pungently of raffia mats and wet clay.

For the first moment Jim was visibly startled, then he let the big folio fall shut and came forward to shake his hand. Roger first noticed the clothes: a blue flannel blazer with some sort of school crest, a starched white shirt with a red silk tie. Boyish, debonair as always, Jim made him feel grotesque in the gaudy linen shirt and thick gum-soled shoes. A sheepish smile broke out across Jim's long narrow face, as though implying that it was all a game, a big joke, he had planted himself there a day ahead of time just to be found this way. "I was coming over to Antibes this afternoon," he said in an ingratiating voice. Then casually, coolly, "This folio of Picasso prints is signed in pencil. The great man's doodled all over the margins. The owner here says he knows him."

So *that* was it, he had come a day early merely to size the place up and see what his chances of meeting Picasso on his own were, in case his other plan failed. By now Roger had totally forgotten the shop, his idea of making some money by selling sketches. "Maybe he does," he said, trying to sound cryptic. "Does he have any originals?" He made no comment on the day-early arrival; he too would be casual. After all, he had been deliberately followed —Jim had only come because of the letter.

He had known Jim was also abroad for the summer but never dreamed of an encounter. But by freakish chance they had met in the large dry garden of the Popes' Palace in Avignon. Traveling alone as always, Roger had been sitting silently on a bench overlooking the rushing muddy water, surrounded by chattering Spanish-looking women out for an afternoon promenade. A cracking stage laugh, that imitation Britishy voice saying something glib about the Pont d'Avignon, and he had turned to see Jim leaning over the parapet with an older man. Immaculately dressed in linen, Jim then, as now, had immediately made him feel uncouth, almost dirty, and he had even seen Jim hesitate unpleasantly before introducing him to his companion, a Frenchman with some sort of title. Only Jim Norton could manage to know this sort of person. He was a past master at the art of making the right friends.

Introduced in the dusty garden as "a fellow artist from New York" by Jim, he had tried desperately to find the remark which might strike Jim, or more, his disdainful friend. So when he was asked out of surface politeness, "And where are you going from Avignon?" he had answered coldly. "Antibes, I guess. Then I might try Cannes . . . though I first ought to use my letter of introduction to Picasso." Jim had looked down from his great height, his narrow blue eyes widened to ovals, the manner immediately thawing. After a moment they parted with good-by-until-New-York-next-winter, but Roger had known all along that Jim would follow him. And sure enough, his second day in Antibes he had gotten Jim's card saying he would see him Friday.

Yesterday he had decided that Jim would not be included on the visit to the master, that the whole thing would be brought off with a touch of sadism; let Jim think he had a chance of coming in on it, but he would privately complete his visit, then head back to Paris without a word to him. Slightly diabolic, this, but he hated being used by anyone, and since Jim obviously thought he was this gullible, he would prove finally he was not to be stepped on.

The shopkeeper could speak English. He drew together wiry eyebrows and said indignantly to Roger, "I have two signed studies locked in my safe. They are not for sale," he added haughtily.

"Is he actually here in Juan-les-Pins?" asked Jim, all innocence, in a voice so ingenuous it made Roger wince. Jim held up a large cubist study that hid his face. "Someone told me he sits around in the cafés sometimes and talks to people who look interesting to him."

The dealer said he had not been about at all that year, then softly asked Jim, "Are you an artist, Monsieur?"

"Oh, I do some painting," said Jim in that self-deprecatory way that he had, the manner that endeared him to older men and women. Whenever he talked he had an air of forestalled importance that made one listen to what he said, no matter how trivial the subject. A way of shooting out the words a little breathlessly, the eyes vacant, so that it seemed that his mind, not present, was trained on something far more important.

"Then you must by all means try to meet the master," said the dealer, straightening a rainbow-striped ascot. "These things are important for the young artist."

Ignored up by the window, Roger coughed as he put down an orange pottery bowl, but the dealer glanced with a quick disapproving look at his linen shirt open pirate-style to deep in the chest, and the soiled white ducks and sneakers, and did not ask him whether he were an artist or not, Monsieur.

With great tact they finally managed to get out of the shop without buying a thing. Roger suggested a place for lunch, so they walked back over to Antibes, Jim striding easily, while Roger had to stop to mop his face and sit down by the side of the road. The little restaurant was set up in a shaded open courtyard, a Spanish patio, with lanterns and vines hanging from overhead crossbeams. The tables were nearly all filled, mostly with Belgian and English tourists. Jim chose a table against the wall, and as Roger drew out the chairs like a waiter he felt that he was going to be monumentally magnanimous. Oh, he would invite Jim back to his hotel room to drink some of the Scotch, would treat him to several meals. He would be distant, disinterested as he had never been in New York, and he would never bring up the letter of introduction, the projected visit to the master—the only thing that Jim would want to hear. One morning, mission accomplished, he would quietly slip off and get on a train, while Jim slept the sleep of the innocent in his hotel, dreaming of the meeting with Picasso.

"I thought you were going directly to Nice," he said as he poured Jim some cool white wine.

"Oh, I'll go on to Nice next week," Jim said. "I'm joining the Baron there at his villa, so I sent my luggage ahead with him. Like an ass"—he ran his finger over a smooth bony jaw—"I put my razor in the trunk."

"Well, don't buy a new one. Come over to my room any time you want," said Roger with what he felt was magnificent generosity. "Here is a key, I can get an extra. Any time from now on when you want to come over and take a shave, come ahead. Don't go out and buy a new one, they cost a fortune in francs."

For the first time, Jim gave a genuine smile and looked surprised at this kindness. "By the way, how is your work coming along?" he asked, pocketing the key.

"Oh, its stronger, stronger," said Roger, working at the fish with a knife.

"Still painting those birds and trees?"

"No," said Roger angrily. He had heard how Jim made fun of his work, calling his delicate leaf drawings and splashy watercolor birds "Rorschach Ink Tests." Jim himself painted massive black-outlined pyramids in green and earthy browns which, Jim would explain in outrageous pretension, "had all the solidarity of Cézanne, the emotional emphasis of Rouault . . ." In New York they both saw the same people, went to the same parties, but Jim belonged to a tight cliquy inner-circle of writers and painters who were all having some sort of small success. Seven years out of college, Jim had been spending all his time since the Army painting and getting to know the people who would be of use to him. Success, even if small, was the password. He lived frugally on the Government checks and the slight income from some capital that his father had invested for him. But he lived well, always being taken out to dinner, given choice seats at the theater and ballet. Every Christmas he went back out to Grand Rapids for a visit, carrying glossy photostats of his latest paintings so that he might prove to his father he had been working, that his life in New York was sound, sober and industrious.

One night, in the corner at a party, Jim told Roger confidentially that he looked "arty" (did he mean suspect?) and ought to try toning himself down. It was ironic that Roger got along in much the same way: unemployment insurance, the sale of a few "clever" things to interior decorators, checks from his mother . . . their lives ran parallel in many ways. But *something* in his unmistakable Ohio voice, his bright blond hair that fell back in a deep wave from a delicate brow, his eagerness, antagonized and alienated. The telephone calls he had made to Jim went unreturned, and they merely nodded at parties. Names were the only thing, Roger began to see; Jim liked to be able to use them in his offhand-manner anecdotes.

"Thank God, you're not still painting all that plumage and foliage," said Jim, lifting his wineglass with a witty little laugh. "I think you once told me you resembled Tchelitchew."

"Berman," said Roger dryly. He tried to seem nonchalant as he ate his fish, spitting out the bones with an ineffectual attempt at delicacy. Trying to think of a way to hit back at Jim's mockery, he found that he could not resist temptation and reached into his shirt pocket, pulling out the letter which crackled between his thumbs. "A friend, no one we know mutually, gave it to me," he said quite easily as he put the big envelope on the table between them. A beautifully untidy hand had scrawled the great painter's name across the envelope. "This man once lived in France, knew Picasso quite well, knew a lot of the others too. I've got two other letters back in my suitcase, under a bottle of Scotch." (There, the eyes widened again.) "To Braque and someone . . ." Jim had put his fork carefully along the edge of the plate and now picked up the letter gingerly between two fingers. "When are you going to use this? Are you going to his house? Do you know where he lives here?" His eyes narrowed as he put down the letter, sizing Roger up. "What could you say to a man like that?"

"I will simply shut up and say nothing at all," said Roger, infuriated by the suggestion that he would make a fool of himself, talking, perhaps, about watercolor birds. Jim began to eat again, thinking intently as he cleaned off the plate.

After lunch Jim suggested that they walk up to the museum at the top of Antibes. He had heard, he said, that the great man's paintings were on exhibit. "You might as well have something to compliment him on. I hear that the things up there are some of the best he's done."

Roger explained that he did not intend to flatter; such tactics were not his sort. "If I talk at all, I will ask about development. A master always likes to advise the novice."

They mounted slowly the steep hill to the museum, and though the sun was out in full noon heat there was a dry hot wind coming in from across the blue water. "That's the mistral," said Jim, wiping an eye that had been filled with the chalky dust. "They say it bodes good luck when it blows." At the top of the climb they had a perfect view of the Cap d'Antibes, the violet water, the burning tan rocks of the shore. Roger found it almost unbearable to look at, and though that summer he had stood at the precipice of many inspiring views, the ever-willing tourist viewing the spectacle, he looked out now across the perfect, curving inlet and quickly turned his back.

While waiting for the museum to open, they watched two workers smooth cement between repair bricks in the lower part of the museum wall. There was a large sign tacked to the door announcing a pottery exhibit for the end of the month, and from inside they heard the sound of hammers putting the place in order for the new exhibit. Roger went down to watch the man smooth cement expertly between the cracks, then offered an American cigarette to the one who stood resting. The man wiped a dark sweaty face and thanked him, shrewdly taking Roger's measure. In a strange garbled French he asked if they had come to see the paintings in the museum or the master himself.

Roger scowled, hoping that he had not heard correctly, and glanced at Jim, who suddenly looked tense and alert.

"The paintings, of course," Roger said.

"Well . . ." shrugged the bricklayer with a wry irony. "He is inside. Every afternoon he comes here to do work on a panel. He is in there now." And again shrugging, as if this were no concern of his whatsoever, he moved off back to the foot of the wall, giving the other worker the cigarette, now half-finished.

"I don't believe him," said Roger, turning to Jim. He wanted to leave.

"Why not?" asked Jim a little too eagerly. And he moved to the door, which someone was unbolting from the inside and swinging out with a creak of old hinges. Roger reluctantly followed into the dark inner courtyard lined with bosky little prickly plants. Jim put a hand on his arm. "Listen." From around a stucco corner came laughing and the sound of footsteps descending dusty stone steps. They both instinctively pressed back into a corner and waited.

Picasso, followed by Sabartès, followed by a graceful girl in dark blue slacks, followed by three laughing women, moved out into the courtyard to the far exposed section, where a stone wall shielded a sheer drop to the rocky shore below. Another Napoleon surveying his Elba, Picasso stood at the parapet edge of the garden and looked out at the view of the bay, the wind flattening his linen shorts against tendoned brown legs, shaking the flaps of his open blue collar.

Hoarsely, Jim said to Roger, "In a second he'll see us. The letter, the *letter!*" And Roger, mesmerized, involuntarily lurched forward until he stood mutely before the great man, holding out his letter like a chalice, while the entourage regarded him, regarded Jim, with the civilized hostility of people whose privacy has been grossly intruded upon. But the great man was by far more graceful. "Monsieur?" he asked from an insurmountable height, as Sabartès stepped menacingly toward Roger, suspecting an assassin. He opened the proffered letter which billowed and flapped, puffing out in the mistral so that he had to move into the inner court to better read the message. Finally he looked up and smiled, and for a moment the dark and shining eyes fixed Roger, then Jim, who hung back by the wall, and he seemed to see everything in that instant. There was an inquisitive murmur about the letter writer, and Roger answered in faltering French. There was another murmur that held the word "pleased." Pale and trembling, Roger turned to Jim and told him they were invited to make a tour of the museum. They followed a large woman in pearls and pale blue sharkskin, who spoke French like a true Parisian but was unmistakably American; she ignored them completely as compatriots.

"What did he say?" Jim demanded in a hoarse whisper. "Was he nice to you?"

"He said he would be pleased if we came along and saw the paintings," replied Roger, and hurried ahead.

The first room was big, a pale soft green, and every painting in the room had a key tonality of green or yellow; all seemed created just to hang there: chartreuse, gray blue, thick brown, terra cotta, olive—all of which was picked up by the Antibes sun on the walls of the room. Roger looked about stiffly, his hands in his pockets, not daring to show any sort of reaction in the master's presence. But he was not watching Roger at all, he stood with the woman in the pearls and said something which must have been very funny, because the woman showed every tooth in her mouth as she laughed. Roger recovered from his stage fright, thinking that one should be more self-contained and that when the master again talked to him, this time he would respond with intelligence. Two shiny reproduction marbles, of the Farnese Hercules and an archer, stood at opposite ends of the room; a crystal chandelier hung heavily from the ceiling's center. Jim moved from the Hercules over to Roger, who noticed that there was a moustache of perspiration along the usually clean upper lip. Jim said to him in a tight excited voice, "That one is Françoise . . . looking at the statues, the one gesturing and smiling, see the one I mean?"

Roger looked at a perfect oval face, colored a warm rose along the high cheekbones and the arch of the fine thin nose. Her hair was looped into a shiny Degas knot and several strands tendriled down on her neck. "She looks just like her portraits," said Jim in a reverential little voice. "Though they're only the line drawings, you can see the resemblance . . . She's really lovely, isn't she?"

Roger wasn't sure he thought so at all and followed the great man who had moved on to the next room, with not so much as a backward look at his guests. He wandered from canvas to canvas in this new room, examining his own work as though he had never set eyes on it before. Roger longed to approach him, to win one word, something that would made the occasion *his*. Jim had wandered off to a far corner and stood looking intently at a picture, his hands folded in a Germanic scholarly pose behind his back, a trick Roger had seen him often use in the Fifty-seventh Street galleries when he wished to appear the serious critic. Now he stood in front of a round fat blue satyr's face, seemingly studying it, his head tilted philosophically to one side, his hand on his chin. Holding his breath, Roger watched Picasso cross over to where he stood, saw Jim's lips move, then the great man's, smiling at something Jim had said. In an agony of resentment he turned away, just as the group of women came up, all smiles and half-finished sentences. It was only a second, the whole incident, but Jim was glowing, his thin face was brilliant as he lounged toward Roger, his crisp brown hair falling over his brow.

Roger hissed, "What were you saying?" but Jim hurried on to the next room, where the master had gone, so Roger followed again, trying to compose himself. In this last gallery only the women and Jim remained, all chattering brightly in front of the pictures. Just as Roger came in, Françoise announced in a charming cool Oxford voice that the master had gone off to work on his panel. She raised her perfect oval eyebrows, her eyes shone at Roger; he was pleased to meet the American messieurs, she said. He was interested in young artists. Crushed at this schoolboy dismissal, Roger stared dully at the shut door at the end of the gallery. Jim was now edging near the group of women, still looking at the pictures as though he were trying to memorize their composition but sidling up to the American in pearls.

Without a moment's hesitation Roger turned on his heel and left the museum, alone. The bricklayers were gone, the strong hot wind had died, the afternoon was strangely silent and calm. He walked with long furious blind strides until he reached a bakeshop, hung in front with a curtain of beaded tassels that rattled like dice as he pushed through. He ordered tea and some squashy rum cakes, then paid and left without eating a mouthful. Useless, fooled, he felt himself to be terribly weak, as though all the attempts he had ever made had come to this failure. Raging, he stalked impotently up and down back streets, then finally went down to the rocky beach under his hotel where he sat and threw pebbles into the water and let them slip, round and smooth, through his fingers. When he felt calmer, he wearily rose and started back to his room. Then he remembered that he had given Jim his key at lunch . . .

With trembling fingers he turned the concierge's key in his door, a strange hope arising as the handle swung to. He longed, as one might long for the lash, to discover the real coup, the most masterful stroke of all . . . but the Scotch was untouched and the two precious letters still lay under the bottle. The only vestiges of intrusion lay on the sink edge, where a tiny chain of bubbles encircled the shaving cream tube, the safety-razor lay wet with recent work, and "Thanks" was scrawled in soap across the bottom of the mirror.

Accomplice

He wanted only to have her think him this new person he felt he had become, and as he sat down on the edge of the unmade, soft-springed bed, making the mattress dip under his heavy body, he was especially careful to sit with his spine straight for a look of alertness. But it was all lost on Isabelle. She was still fussing deep in the closet, sliding hangers in an impatience of vanity over what to wear. He tensely tap-tapped a cigarette against his morocco case, clearing his throat like a prayer. "You've changed and I'm glad to see it. When I last saw you in October you had great circles under your eyes, your fingers shook when you lit a cigarette . . . I really thought you would have a breakdown. Everyone did. But even your voice is quieter now."

He hoped that by passing comment on *her* appearance, *her* changes, she would in turn observe the ones wrought in him, but instead she said in her soft Southern voice that muffled as she stooped for shoes: "Breakdown? *Who* said? I never got it. Did you really expect me to or did you want me to? . . . You've gotten heavier, haven't you, Brady?"

His hopelessness got caught up in the welter of leather picture frames that stood in a semicircle on the desk, frames that set off the face of a tanned, handsome man who flashed variegated smiles for Isabelle. No, he had not gotten fatter. He had actually *lost* weight but she had not even taken the pains to ascertain this by a really fair look at him (the room was darkened by the pulled rattan blinds), and now her indifferent back arched fluidly forward as she selected shoes. "Damn!" she muttered from the closet bottom, rattling shoe trees and tissue paper in her search for footgear.

The same Isabelle . . . and would he have her changed? Brady smiled sadly to himself as he took off his jacket and lay back on the bed, gazing at the room that she had already made hers, spiting the standard equipment of brass bed, black desk and dresser. Her big trunks were pushed against the wall, blistering with peeling labels, the open drawers bulging and foaming with hand-knit sweaters and woolen things she'd bought in England. A closet door stood open opposite and on its shelves he could see stacks of new kid gloves, dotted swathes of veiling, bottles of cologne and nail polish. It was clear that she had already been out on the town. Isabelle had been a motherless child for years, and since her father's death two years before her only loving occupation had been to spend the inheritance. From the looks of things France seemed the best market she'd found yet.

"These are ugly," she said, emerging with sandals dangling straps, "but they're perfect for walking. I walked all over Rome in them. *You*'ve got to show me Paris since you've already had a week on me." The long line of her spine moved under her silk robe as she backed out of the closet and faced him, a dark tailored shadow in the airless quiet. She stared for the first time that afternoon at his rumply yellow hair and flat-planed pink face. "No, you haven't changed a bit in the last year . . . just that wee bit fatter. How did you know I was in Paris?" she asked as she disappeared into the bathroom with a bundle of lacy white things over one arm. Her voice reverberated in the tiny glass-enclosed room. "It's funny that I should meet you of all people because not a *soul* I know is in town!"

How did she mean that? "Hell, I didn't expect to see you," he said heartily, hoping that from here on in they would override last year by letting foreign territory mean a new footing for them. "If I had, I would have come to Paris a week sooner. I got in from Dijon on Thursday and every day since then I've made trips to American Express just to see who's put their name in the big books. Just *hoped* I'd see a familiar name." He lay all the way back and stared at the ceiling. "Your handwriting is one in a million, so when I saw it I came right over in a cab . . . God, it's *good* to see you, Isabelle! It's been lonely as hell traveling my way."

Immediately he hated himself for letting her know that. "I haven't met anyone I know all summer." *Brrrsssk-snap, brrrsssk-snap* went her electric hair under the brushing. He raised his voice: "But I met some marvelous new people just by being aggressive as you said . . . remember? Even though you don't think so, I've changed. At the drop of a hat I talked to perfect strangers —it was awfully easy after the first time—and once in Biarritz I actually had my bills paid by a rich old harpy who just wanted a restaurant escort. Then there was an Englishman you would have loved—"

"Who's paying for the summer?" she asked through a mouthful of bobby pins.

He could imagine her purposely directing this at him as she took down her hair, making a face at herself in the mirror. "Father," he admitted. "It's a sort of last fling before I enter the firm this fall."

The disaster between them had come the fall before, a time when Brady had had only great expectations and he had brought Isabelle home to meet his father, much like a hunter returning with prize game. But his father had found her vulgar and ambitious and had plainly told Brady that she was only after their money. He might have anticipated the whole little drama, since his father had never approved of any of his friends or the girls he had liked (few as both had been) and slowly had made Brady drop them. His only ambition was to see Brady a brilliant lawyer, though in his heart he knew the hope would fall short.

Brady said loudly: "He and I are on a much better footing now. The old man can be quite amiable when he wants to, it was only that picture of us in the paper; he's always thought that kind of thing cheap and claims it can only hurt a dignified career in law. And he didn't *snub* you as you thought, Isabelle. He even told me that he'd once met some uncle of yours from Savannah."

A sharp rapping report on the outer door cut his bungling explanations short.

Would he please see who that was? Isabelle shut the bathroom door completely.

Obediently he rose from the bed and opened the outer-room door on a valet who stood scowling down at a freshly pressed skirt hung over one arm and at the tea tray he carried. When he saw Brady his eyes narrowed with surprise; then he smiled and smiled. They stared at each other for a long moment, until Brady quickly stepped aside, instinctively repelled by the seallike head with oiled flat hair, the sallow skin, the shrewd black eyes.

"If it's my tea, tell him to put it on the desk inside," called Isabelle from the bathroom.

The valet understood her English and went right on into the bedroom, clearing a space on the littered desk, pushing papers and old prints (Isabelle was collecting them from the Seine bookstalls) to the floor as he set down the tray. While hanging the skirt on the doorknob he furtively glanced about the room, his darting lizard eyes not missing a thing: Brady's jacket folded on the turned-back quilt, Isabelle's discarded clothes in a wilted heap by the bureau. In the outer room he paused before the bathroom door, a tense silence communicating his intrepid presence to Isabelle performing her toilette inside. When he finally realized that there was to be no tip he went out with a spinning release of the doorknob.

"Creep," said Brady to himself, looking at the well-filled tray.

"Has he gone?"

"Yes."

"Thank God," she said, laughing. "I swore to myself I wouldn't give him any tips today. That worked out very nicely!"

"May I take some of the tea?"

"Take it all. I always forget I've ordered it. It comes every day and I never want it."

Typically Isabelle. He lifted the covers off the two dishes of patisserie and toasted muffin strips, poured out a big cup of tea and took great stuffing bites of the pastry. So here she was, living in the same style she had in New York, taking her pleasures and little luxuries wherever she was—the room with its expensive disarray, the exacting services she commanded several times a day from maids, valets, the oversize tips she felt compelled to hand out in payment for them. He hated to think of how much she had spent that summer.

Hastily he swallowed two of the small doughy muffins before she came out so that she would not have cause to remind him he had gained weight and therefore ought to be strict with himself. He had *not* gained—he had just weighed himself in Pigalle the night before—but it was one of those odd psychological things that he *did* seem to feel bigger when she was around and he supposed he communicated this feeling in some way in his bearing. What was the old saying: Feel ugly, look ugly? It was a sad puzzle to him how anyone could, by her mere presence, make one feel gross (a sense of ballooning), but that was precisely what happened when they came together; as soon as she was there to examine him with her cool, round green eyes, he could feel his nose thickening, his tongue become inarticulate in his mouth, his hands sprout spatula fingers.

"Phoufff . . . it's like a steam-room in there!" She finally emerged from the bathroom, her face powdered down and carefully put on but giving a soft, pretty effect, her whole person exuding a compound scent of soap, cologne, powder, ointments. "Give me a shiny-tiled American bathroom any day—these French are a *riot* with all these basins and bidets!" He noticed, now that it was out of the pins, that her dark hair was cut very smartly short and that she had a completely new way of smiling with her head tilted provocatively to one side, a trick she had probably learned from watching her idol, Garbo, in revivals. Now she looked at herself in the full-length pier glass, binding her bathrobe sash about her thin flat waist, saying as much as: Look at me—could I be more desirable?

"Did you get a look at the terrible man who was just in here?"

"Yes," confessed Brady, glad that it had not just been his usual hypersensitivity that had made the valet seem sinister. "He was rather spooky . . . Considering the fact that I've never been here before, he gave me a really peculiar look, as though I ought to feel guilty about something. Lord knows, I haven't done a thing I should be ashamed of."

"That's the point: *you* haven't. If I'd been in my bathrobe, it would have been perfect for him."

When Brady merely looked puzzled, Isabelle frowned impatiently at him standing there with his feet planted wide apart, the half-light glinting off the lenses of his horn-rimmed glasses; then she kicked off her red leather mules and sat down on the bed, opening the night-table drawer filled up with jars and boxes. She drew out American cigarettes. When Brady lit one it tasted like face powder and hand cream.

"One afternoon," she began, obviously launching herself with relish into a story, "I came back here sooner than I usually do with my arms piled high with things I'd bought at the Flea Market. The cab driver wouldn't help me carry the bundles upstairs because he thought I hadn't tipped him enough for the long ride from Clignancourt, so I had to open the lock very, very slowly . . . or I'd have dropped some of the lovely Bohemian glass. Just imagine the shock I had when I got to the doorway of this room and *he* was standing over my bed! The valet, of course. He'd dumped the big carryall purse where I keep my reserve money all over the bedspread and he was counting fistfuls of franc notes and stuffing them inside his vest."

Brady's eyes had been steadily widening behind the glasses.

"Somehow I knew that the most important thing was not to let him see I was frightened—to get control of the situation. If I'd gone for help he would have disappeared. So I looked as outraged as I could and shouted something like: '*Qu'est-ce que vous faites là?*' but that monster didn't even flicker an eyelash. He looked rather annoyed and then smiled—the smile of the devil—you can't imagine such a smile. And then, just as cool as a little clerk in the bank, he went right on counting the money, only he put it *back* into the carryall as he counted it off, making it into a sort of burlesque . . . as though he'd just been taking inventory for me."

Brady tilted forward on the edge of his chair as Isabelle made a high sweep with her thin, articulate hands. "I still had all those plates and glasses in my hands, so I must have looked pretty damn foolish trying to be ominous, but I yelled something like: 'Take the rest of that money out of your vest and put it on the bed and get the hell out of here before I call a gendarme!'

"Well," she said breathessly, turning her hands up in a helpless gesture of futility, "he only *smiled* again—that ghastly smile—so I thought up the most dire and terrible threats involving the American Embassy, and he finally backed out, baring his nicotined teeth as though he would like to tear me limb from limb, but he knew that he had been beaten." She smiled. "Of course I should have gone to see the manager the moment he walked out of here, but I had the strangest intuition that he would retaliate by telling the manager perfectly horrible lies about me, ones that would get me put out of the hotel. He hovers around the stairs all day—he makes it his business to know about everyone in the hotel and I wouldn't be a bit surprised to learn that he runs a high-powered blackmail mill on the side—but, after all, as a paying guest it is my business to have people visiting me at whatever time of day or night I choose!"

With mounting concern Brady had watched her pretty face grow more and more distraught. Ignoring the sordid implications of her story, he lumbered over to the bed and put a hand on her shoulder. "Get him fired. That's all there is to it. It's absurd to put up with this kind of thing. What harm could *he* do *you?*"

"Oh, Brady . . ." She shook her shoulder rudely free of his hand and took out her key ring. "It's stupid to make such a big fuss when it's much simpler my way. This way I give him fat tips, lock up my purse, and pretend as best I can that nothing ever happened. Since there's something in it for him, he pretends too. A reciprocal agreement."

Isabelle quickly stood up and showed that she was ready to leave and didn't want to talk any more about it. Together they went silently out into the hot afternoon.

That was the way he started to see her again, and he marveled that it had happened to him at all, he'd been so alone all summer. She let him see her every day (her explanation being that no one she knew was in Paris) and they spent long afternoons touring the quiet city, which was drained of its true Parisians. He saw and absorbed more in her company during those few days than he had by traveling alone all summer. Her arm through his, he virtually floated down streets, buoyed up by his pride in her.

On a dry, hot Sunday afternoon they planned a trip out to Versailles. In a travel-bureau brochure they had read that *les Dimanches* at four o'clock there was a spectacle of playing fountains not to be missed. Brady had been an avid student of French literature and history in college and he felt inordinately excited at the idea of seeing such a famous and venerated landmark. He invested the whole day ahead of them with a holiday spirit, despite the fact that he and Isabelle had had an unpleasant quarrel the night before, and he felt a boyish abandon and happiness he hadn't experienced in a long time.

On the train out they sat facing an interesting couple—an older woman, faintly Spanish-looking, with smooth, cool white skin, dark, rustling clothes, and a racily handsome boy with delicate, pointed blond features, certainly an expense to the woman. Brady looked at them once without curiosity, then turned to view the outskirts of Paris through the window. But Isabelle could not keep her avid eyes off the striking pair, and without attempting any ruse for her behavior she openly watched the woman talk and twist finely gloved hands in a black silk lap, watched her passionate-madonna smiles at the faintly epicene young man. "She's *somebody*," Isabelle finally whispered fiercely in English. "Just watch the way she moves . . . there's such manner, such presence!"

Embarrassed that they might hear and understand her, Brady looked and nodded agreeably, but her preoccupation with them made him uncomfortable. Feeling his innocent elation about the day and the excursion ebb away, he thought of foolish Isabelle and the things she so admired in people: beauty, eccentricities, cleverness, social brilliance . . . even sexual deviation. Would she never grow up? She hadn't changed much in a year; she had only resolved what had once been half-formed and her expectation of things to come her way had only grown. Out of all this had come his crushing unhappiness of the previous year.

Brady had met Isabelle at a party after a Princeton game, a reunion party given by one of his old classmates. Each year Brady went to these parties without interest or real enjoyment, but merely to reassure himself of a connection with a group. Isabelle was there. Fresh up from Savannah, she had been staying with an aunt, new to all of the New York she wished to crash. In the crowded, noisy room that afternoon at the party she had been easy to find, to see, obscuring all the other girls there, not by anything remarkable in her looks but simply because about her face and whole gracile figure there was an indefinable light. She looked dangerous. She looked a cruel type. (He was quite qualified to say now that Isabelle was everything she looked. After only a two-week affair in which he suffered, she had summarily told him off.) At another party—there had been many of them—after spending most of the evening avoiding him she had gravitated back and

pulled him off to a corner where they could watch unobserved all
the guests in the noisy room. "Brady," she had said after pointing
out celebrities, people who were lovers, "beautiful things and
beautiful people—they're the only things I consider worth-while."
Then, "Brady," she'd repeated with utter simplicity, "you're really
a dreadful bore. I want us to stop. Here and *now!*"

He watched the steel meshes of the Eiffel Tower disappear, ob-
scured by the suburban shrubberies, feeling all that humility revive,
begin its cruel rondo again. For just the night before, after several
fine cognac under the scalloped awning of a café, the scene had
been played again when she'd said quietly that she had tried to
see him in the all-too-flattering light of Paris but it didn't quite
come off and she still thought him stuffy, thought he lacked imagination as well as grace . . . so wasn't it silly, she'd said, shrugging
lightly, for them to even *try* to get along? He hadn't answered since
he did not take it as a question, and he would not let her see that
he took her seriously. *Hadn't* they "gotten along"?—what about
the days when just walking in sunny parks and down broad boule-
vards had been amusement enough? No, he couldn't believe that
she meant it this time, it was more in the nature of a come-on; he
didn't let her see that her words had even remotely touched him,
but before going to bed that night he had looked into the mirror
above the basin, not very certain whether he would break the mercurized glass that reflected or the fleshy face that confronted its
reflection. It was *that* face, with its placid, stolid surface, which
had always put the distance between him and things desired.

What was it about his face? His father called it looking "sub-
stantial" and said that a good honest face like that was an asset in
a lawyer's career. But it was not the safeness or the conven-
tionality of his face—there was something else. He had very dilate
blue eyes, which behind the thick convexity of his glasses looked
rather enlarged and weakly harmless. But once this deception of
lens was gone the eyes were startling: one saw immediately an unusual talent for discovering and observing *all*, for marking down
people precisely with those eyes. Friends requested only once:

"Brady, take off your glasses and let's see how you are without them." For it was disarming, almost frightening, to see a completely *other* Brady once the glasses were gone.

At Versailles they began a systematic tramp down graveled garden paths, they stood at the parapet and looked into the spiky palm fronds of the Orangerie. They drank Swiss beer at a kiosk and took funny snapshots of each other in front of a marble nymph. As the brochure promised, the spraying waters did not begin until four, and the basins and wide pools stayed quiet, their stone fishes leaping above tranquil eddies. He walked her up, down, up and down the bosky paths, knowing that she had long ago become bored and that it was only her projection that suddenly made this historic monument, with its Sunday tourists, seem to him like one of those huge picnic parks back in the States where families excursioned warm spring Sundays to play baseball and eat sandwiches under the trees . . .

Finally he managed to find them canvas campstools at the top level of the garden tiers and they sat gazing out, stupefied by the immensity of the box-row perspective that fell away beneath them, bored by the monarchal splendor of the horticulture. Then at last at four, with theatrical precision, after a few tentative squirts arced across the pools, the fountains started up with fizzing jets into the air. When this happened Isabelle gave a loud laugh and in her most Southern drawl said: "God, just *look!* It's like the World's Fair!"

That was Versailles.

So it was unbelievable, after all the day's events, that it was this evening that Isabelle chose to come back to his hotel with him, precedent to a series of such evenings, with the gaudy lights of the Gare du Nord across from his hotel shining in on them and summer footsteps falling echoing beneath the window. He could not believe it but he took it as a reprieve. Days they made tours of the far, quiet galleries of the Louvre, of antique shops, and in one of these he bought her a fine old carved ivory cat, saying that it was her talisman—she was just like that cat: long, slender, evil, and tense. For a week the dream lasted and she let him build up these trite symbols of an intimacy and a closeness that never existed for her, while he knew that it was all soon to end.

Thursday evening he hurried to her hotel through the Paris dusk, full of plans for dinner. Instead of waiting for him up in her room she had already come downstairs to the hotel courtyard and was drinking at one of the round wooden tables with a preoccupation that should have warned him. Her greeting was wan. In a distracted voice she announced that they would have to meet some friends of hers after dinner; she had run into them that morning at American Express and had promised to meet them at a café at quarter to ten. Would he mind? In his present state of ascendancy concessions like this seemed easy enough to make, so he said no, he wouldn't mind, and at a quarter to ten they arrived at the appointed café for their coffee.

The two friends were men, one tall and angular, with a stubby Vandyke beard, a sensuous mouth and a frigid stare, the other also tall and angular, with thinning red hair and fine freckling, Isabelle's sort of "beautiful people"—overbred, overly clever, witty. They had taken a table near the edge of the sidewalk and, since it was the hour in the evening when all Parisians were promenading, they were watching the steady back-and-forth of couples. As Brady came up squiring Isabelle, the two men carefully measured him and found him wanting in some table of their own measures: after introductions had been accomplished and extra chairs had been drawn up, they began to talk exclusively and intimately to Isabelle about people he'd never heard of. They could all have been back in New York.

"I saw an old friend of yours in San Sebastian," said the one with the brown beard. "At the bullfights." He smiled in delighted complicity at the name he brought forth, a name certainly evocative for it made Isabelle blush. Brady immediately thought of the handsome man framed many times over on her desk at the hotel.

"I haven't seen him for months. Didn't he tell you we weren't seeing each other?"

The Beard shook his head and tried to look disinterested.

Isabelle looked at him shrewdly, then pulled her chair closer and urgently began to tell him about it. The Redhead sat back nursing his drink, and after sizing Brady up as a passive listener he launched on a long and intensive monologue about the advances made by France and Italy over America in "civilization." Winters, he told Brady, he was a professor at a boys' college in the States. Teaching was the only way to keep intellectually alive and still have the summers free for travel, he confided. Brady listened. After a while the other two had exhausted the topic of the mutual friend and drew the Redhead's attention away from Brady, asking him to verify a piece of gossip. Brady stopped listening altogether and their conversation fell around him and passed him by. He watched the people parading past their table and wondered was there nowhere to go to avoid this sort? Tonight the promenading crowds afforded little contrast to his company, there being almost no Parisians or even Left Bank poseurs. Instead there seemed to be only Americans relentlessly parading up and down, American boys who linked arms with each other, American college girls looking for adventure, filing along in cotton dresses, glancing with furtive, predatory stares into the faces at the tables.

As the other three rudely continued to drink and talk without attempting to draw him in, he began drinking two glasses to every one of theirs, a neat little tower of saucers accumulating in front of him. He tried to think of what he had said to his father about the trip, about wanting to get away from the sort of people he'd known all his life and the plans he'd made accordingly: to visit remote provincial hamlets, to travel third class and meet Real People, to cycle with a knapsack along the Côte. His European plan of action! In his wallet, still folded into the neat creases he'd put in them, were slips bearing the addresses of bicycle hostels, a complete Spanish itinerary that now seemed a Hemingway parody . . . Because of his loneliness it had not seemed worth-while and he had gone from town to city not caring much. Needing an Isabelle, he could see sights only through another's eyes. Strangers were not the wonderful "characters" that he had tried to make them, and he was *sick* of the second-rate measure of making friends on wagon-lits and in hotel dining rooms. Paris had come alive only since they'd been together; by letting him love her she'd given him back his self-respect.

"Just another year," he overheard Isabelle. "By then I'll have really had all I want and then I'll go home and marry. Live like landed gentry in Savannah." Brady turned to see if she could possibly be serious in saying something like that, but what he saw concerned him more than what he'd heard. She was smiling at the Beard, he back at her, the eyes and mouths of both filled with understated promise. And the Redhead sat close to all this muted passion, pretending to contemplate the color of his cognac, playing entrepreneur.

Very neatly and quietly then Brady took up his burning cigarette. For a speculative moment he looked from its glowing ash to the three heads together: concordant, conspiring, all of a kind—then he turned down the fiery cigarette tip into his flesh, stubbing, ruthlessly grinding it out on the back of his hand as one might do in an ashtray of impregnable china. His eyes brimmed, the pupils violate and distended; but for him physical pain had set in well before the burn. None of the others saw him actually perform this feat, but all of a sudden there was a funny smell in the air and they looked up to see Brady biting his lip, staring fixedly down at the smoldering cigarette. They looked, and when they had comprehended what he'd done they turned to each other to confirm what they saw, their faces blank with amazement and horror—for who in the world would *do* such a thing? Their thinned lips and deliberate avoidance of comment showed Brady that they thought him quite insane. So there was nothing for him to do but get up and leave, winding his hand in his pocket handkerchief as he went, sensing without actually hearing the remarks of outrage that followed his back.

By the next morning a big bubble of blister had mushroomed up on the back of the hand, which now felt as though part of the glowing ash had become imbedded in the skin. He daubed it with iodine and left it unbandaged, setting about the day as he'd planned: to meet Isabelle at eleven and take her to lunch. She would undoubtedly be piqued about the night before but it would be nothing that she would not get over, nothing serious. There he was wrong.

Isabelle had left an explicit message that she was not in to Brady. There was the same message again that night, the next day —and all the weekend. There was nothing for him to do but own up and face the facts: it had been coming anyway and he had only hastened it by the scene in the café. Perhaps, though . . . if he let the weekend go by Monday she might just see him in her room for a moment because he felt that he had to have a chance to at least talk sensibly about things between them and what had happened. About what he had done wrong . . . though he could answer this himself. They had made a special appointment for lunch on Monday and he began to count on her fidelity in at least keeping that; he decided that she would be there and went to wait at the Trois Marrons with confidence.

After waiting an hour, turning up his wrist at ten-minute intervals to glance at his watch and putting off the angry waiter with his most officious stare, he gave it up. The finality of her failure to come, added to all the insults she had dealt him, afforded him a perverse and not unpleasant pleasure, and he ate his omelet with the bitter, galling appetite of someone who has put off hunger in anticipation of greater rewards. For a half hour he had watched the boulevard from behind the clipped hedge, tricking himself into believing that at any moment he would have the intimate satisfaction of being able to recognize her a full block away, of seeing her swing around the corner and pad quickly along in those soft, flat, catlike shoes of hers. As the waiter whisked away the little cone of napkin and the place setting opposite, he tucked his own napkin up under his chin and ate with the vengeance of gluttony, thinking that if she had been there now to see him fold those big wads of the nutty French bread into his mouth, to see him put away the huge omelet and cheese, the fruit, she would have been repelled, told him he was too fat for such behavior—and perhaps have left. And the unhappy knowledge that he could always disgust her in that or in infinitely more subtle ways became now to his eyes a source of power.

After lunch he wandered aimlessly about the network of streets near her hotel until four o'clock, when he was sure that she would be back in her room taking a bath and lying down with pads over her eyes, that tiny portable radio playing anything, droning into the silence of the afternoon. It was a ritual she performed each day, the only thing, she said, that "kept her going."

He knocked once and when there was no answer concluded that she must have the inner door to the bedroom shut. He knocked very loudly with the sharp knobs of his knuckles then, and finally the inner door was pulled open. "What *is* it?" she asked in a furious, muffled voice. "Who is it? What do you want?" When she heard Brady's voice she gave an exasperated gasp, "Oh, for God's sake, Brady . . . go *away!*" and slammed the inner door, the springs of the bed groaning as she threw herself down.

Then he heard low laughter.

Under his eyes the dull pattern of roses on the carpet blurred, the new healing scar on the back of his hand twinged faintly, remembering. Quickly he went down into the hotel court, where he paused and from behind a screen of trelliswork looked up at the window barred against inquisitive eyes, against the hot, airless afternoon.

Without a destination he took a Métro to the other side of the city, but much as he despised himself decided that the only thing to do was to go back an hour and a half later. He would surprise them if they were still in there (Isabelle had given him a key), and no matter how sordid he would at least have a scene to give him some significance, to end squarely what he'd had with her.

This way he was cheated of the doubtful privilege of finding her guilty; it was as though nothing at all had happened between them to *bring* to a significant end. He had been rejected with the rude and final shut-door callousness shown to a suburban salesman.

Did he imagine it or did the ugly Frenchwoman presiding over the front desk and mail cubbyholes look at him with pity? He crossed the quiet inner court and climbed the stairs with the suppressed stealth of a long-practiced thief, pausing outside her door to adjust his cuffs and catch his breath, shortened by the hammer-beats of his heart.

The door to her room was slightly ajar, oddly enough, so he stepped in noiselessly on the balls of his feet, thankful for rubber-soled shoes. Silence. Not a sound from inside. Would his embarrassment ruin it or could he make this his triumph? *Chink, chink, chink* went the sound of keys being jingled or metal objects being tumbled. With bravura he pushed open the inner door.

Over the bed stood the valet, methodically filling his pockets, weighing objects with a curving palm. At the moment he held Isabelle's gold cigarette case (from which he had just selected and lit a cigarette) between thumb and forefinger, considering it for some private scheme. He could not possibly have heard Brady, yet he swung around abruptly and silently faced him, while someone in the courtyard chose that moment to throatily call: "*Eh, Paul . . . Paul . . . on vous demande!*"

Brady faced him, probing the soft black pupils that shone from the pleasure of the crime with his own cold blue ones, virtually holding him at bay in this way.

The background was a rumpled bed, an ashtray on the night table brimming with stubs, a whole room still warm with Isabelle's scent. The valet seemed to guess what Brady was thinking, and taking pleasure in it he broke their interlocked stare to survey the rowdy room, a suggestive and vulgar smile breaking widely out. Warily he put down the gold cigarette case, shifting his eyes so quickly that the whites flashed in the shuttered dark room, obliquely facing Brady like a panther switching its tail. But as he planned to make the violent escape that seemed his only solution, shove Brady sprawling back against the trunk, Brady took off his glasses and began the smile . . .

The valet looked and blinked. He looked into dilated cold eyes and found himself helpless, impaled there. Never such eyes. And that smile besides. There was something in those refracting eyes that made him breathe with difficulty and heave his shoulders in a monumental shrug; such a thing he could not understand, such a *type* as this American, this formidable monsieur who seemed to approve of what he saw taking place in the room of his mistress. He did not seem angered or alarmed to find someone stealing from this lady. What is more . . . the look in those eyes gave cause to think that the American saw far more than was there, that something in the room appealed to what he thought he could see. It was not safe. But . . . *alors!* Before he himself could even speak or raise a hand, the American was gone out down the stairs, his senseless whistling reverberating up the hotel courtyard.

On the way to the Métro he would take to get back to Concord, Brady had to pass the café where they had all met the other night. He got out his pocket guide to make sure he was taking the right train, then sauntered slowly down Saint-Germain with his hands in his pockets, stopping to peer in a window at some lovely Chinese plates, then stopping again at another to look at the paper-backed books ranged row on row: *Le Grand Meaulnes*, Gide, Proust, Balzac. Paris—a cache to pillage for a loved one. Too bad, too bad there was no one now whom he might please with a gift from such a window.

Of course they were there in the café (he had seen them as he turned the corner) in the front row of tables right under the scalloped awning. He could feel them watch his maundering progress up the block, could practically hear Isabelle say: "Here he comes . . . oh, *dear* God! Let's be so nice he'll have to go away!" He knew she would say something like this because when she'd been with him he had often heard her say the same sort of thing about other people she spied across theater lobbies or met by chance, like this, in the street.

He waited until he was well in front of the café before he chose to recognize them. The sun seemed to be in his eyes—he squinted, then smiled and advanced toward them, casually borrowing a rattly cane-backed chair from the adjacent table and swinging himself easily into it.

"Hello there, Brady," said the Beard heartily, and Brady smiled, knowing for sure who it had been in the room with Isabelle.

"Well," said Brady, settling down after ordering a vermouth cassis, "how nice to run into you all again."

There was an awkward silence. Amenities? And since when did Brady practice the lighter amenities? Where did this sudden urbanity find its source? Isabelle kept a surveillant eye on Brady.

Charming, easy, light-paced, sure. He talked amiably, blinking into the late sunlight glancing off the marble-topped table and shining through burnished glasses of Cinzano. The Redhead watched him all the while. The Beard nudged Isabelle under the table: *Get* this, was the message, just listen to our friend here!

But Brady was not disconcerted by their obvious discomfort; he kept on talking and finally succeeded in drawing the Redhead into an extensive conversation. He did not talk to Isabelle at all since, in his mind's eye, he already saw the sad drama that would drag her down. Some afternoon soon, very soon, Isabelle and her bearded friend would be back in the shade-drawn room and unknown to either of them the outer door would crick open and, confident of other successes such as he'd had that afternoon, the marauder would steal in softly, his black and white valet's vest gleaming in the dusk. Then the scene that Brady had not brought off would have its rightful effectuation, and this time there would not just be the question of a jealous lover. The repercussions from such a scene, involving management, gendarmes, desk clerks, and chambermaids, would be endless. And the chambermaids would be loyal and testify for the valet. Poor Isabelle.

She was still as he looked at her profile turned against the sunlight, the features near him quiet in shadow; he looked a long while at the lips so greedily taking the wine, at the sweet curve where her fine chin met the long throat. Lovely. Treacherous. "O thou weed! Who art so lovely fair and smell'st so sweet . . ." Funny that he, Brady the Philistine, should remember any lines from *Othello*. Weren't there some better ones by Iago? "Put money in thy purse!"

"Did you say something, Brady?"

"No," said Brady almost wistfully. "No, Isabelle." He rose then and pushed back the chair rather clumsily so that it jogged the table and all the glasses sloshed over a little. He fumbled in his jacket and drew out a thick pigskin wallet and selecting a large franc note from it put the note by his half-empty glass and saucer. "Good-by," he said, giving a funny little stiff bow and looking as though he might kiss someone's hand. "A *bientôt!*" he said with an odd smile, as though the joke were on him—*his* talking French! He headed quickly back up Saint-Germain toward the Métro.

"Ass!" hissed Isabelle, watching him go. "He *must* be drunk. Why else would he get up and go off like that? Or come over in the *first* place?"

"He's *your* friend," said the Beard, giving her hand an affectionate, patronizing pat. "He's just a harmless eccentric." His smile savored the whole situation, the superior position he thought himself in. "And you've got to take into account the fact that he might be tired of our company. After all, we *did* give him a hard time!"

Isabelle still fumed.

"He was actually quoting Shakespeare." The Redhead asserted his pedagogical side: "I'll swear he was mumbling something from *Othello*."

"Fool!"

"No, he's not that, Isabelle," said the Redhead, looking somewhat critically at her. "I was just beginning to see that he *wasn't* such a fool." Troubled, he stared at Brady's unfinished vermouth. "Actually I was beginning to take to him. He opens up as you—"

"I don't want to hear another word about him!" burst out Isabelle as she set down her glass with a final crash. "Anyone who would show up after the scene he made at the hotel this afternoon . . . is stupid."

At mention of the hotel the Beard smiled possessively, reminiscently. "Marvelous Isabelle," he murmured soothingly. "Marvelous darling."

"Marvelous," echoed the Redhead irresolutely, not having his friend's ardent cause for conviction.

Here Again

The Jewish Cemetery

It was a day at the end of November. Thanksgiving was just five days past, and the weather had turned overnight from freakish mildness to a bitter cold that smelled of snow. The sky was hung with festoons of clouds, dark bluegray, pulled thin by a wind which, nearer the ground, roared unimpeded across the cemetery's vast and open space. The hearse, followed by one limousine, rolled between the gates and proceeded past an ugly tan brick building on the left, finally stopping a hundred feet beyond it on the road. With a slam of the door that rocked the curtains and made the flowers tremble on the coffin top, the driver of the hearse got out and, ducking his head against the wind, rushed past the limousine, up the building's steps. Beset by questions which he could not answer, the driver of the limousine announced, "I'll be back as soon as I find out something, folks," and got out and followed the driver of the hearse.

Most of the questions had been about the eight other cars which had once been behind the limousine, but had become disconnected by staggered red lights and ruthless drivers cutting in. Now the passengers in the limousine stirred. There were just four of them—Eden Werner, his mother Mrs. Werner, his sister Janet and her husband Harold Block. Eden was sitting by choice on the jump seat. The other three shared the broad dovegray rear seat.

The car was overheated and smelled of fur (Janet's seal coat), dry-cleaned clothes, and mints discreetly sucked against bad breath.

Janet, a tense-looking woman who had Eden's sandy coloring but not his good looks, sighed and said crossly, "*Now* what, for god's sake. Do you suppose they'll ever find this place?"

She said it because she could not keep still, but Harold, who was not overly bright, took her literally and said, "Maybe not. There are four other cemeteries here they could pick."

Eden laughed. Janet glared. "Of course they'll find it," Mrs. Werner said. "Most of them have relatives buried here. Besides, we're early," she added and, lifting her veil, calmly began to powder her nose. She was a handsome well-dressed woman in her sixties, with beautifully groomed short white hair and a cool even-featured face that had the same graygreen eyes both children had. In fact, when the white hair had been sandy, mother and children had looked remarkably alike; of the dark-haired father, long dead, long forgotten, there had never been a trace.

"What time is it, Eden?" Janet aggressively demanded, ignoring the heavily jeweled watch she wore, and Eden, his back turned on the jump seat, smiled as he glanced down at his wrist. He was perfectly aware of the fact that his sister merely wished to get a look at him: skeptical about the motives that had brought him to the funeral, she had searched all morning long for signs of the condescension that she was certain was there.

"Eleven-fifteen," he said turning and smiling quickly at Janet, then the others, immediately turning back. He did not much like to look at his sister, whom he had not seen in several years. Though she was just thirty-one and had a husband and two children and all the material things she had always craved, she had acquired, in the time since he had last seen her, the waspish deeply soured look of some embittered old maid.

For several minutes there was silence. Then the relentless Janet brightly asked: "Would you like to use the facilities, Mother dear?"

"Oh for god's *sake*, Janet!" snapped Mrs. Werner and both Eden and Janet's husband laughed. But poor Janet, the only one among them to seem affected by the morning's events, had expressed her agitation by compulsively chattering and by treating her mother like a senile idiot. This, when Mrs. Werner, the sort of woman who would never be senile, was completely composed—in fact far too composed, Eden had privately thought. So far she had only wept once and that had been, Eden felt, from sheer galling irony, when the rabbi (who had not known Morris Halpern at all) had unctuously eulogized about his "wonderfully rich and full and productive life." While it was true that the dead man, his mother's only brother, had been sick for years, dying for months, and his death had been expected, even hoped-for a long time, his mother's self-restraint angered Eden, irrational as he knew it to be. He was hardly in a position to be critical, for there *he* was feeling nothing at all but an acute discomfort and astonishment at finding himself where he was. Aside from a brief time when he had been a child, his uncle had meant nothing to him; he did not believe in family gatherings of any sort, and he did not believe in weddings, funerals, rabbis, in short any kind of organized religious show, and the life he lived was as remote from these things as it would have been had he lived on the moon. Yet the morning he had read the notice of his uncle's death in the *Times*, he had put down the paper and like someone in a trance had gone to the phone and called his mother, whom he had not talked to in over a year. After some rather awkward conversation ("Why didn't you come to my opening?" . . . "Oh Eden, you know I never liked those things.") he had asked directions to the funeral chapel on Long Island where the services were to be held. "That's very sweet and thoughtful of you, Eden," his mother had said, clearly taken aback, "but it isn't necessary. At *all*. Just knowing you had the thought is enough. As I told you, I'm really all right. He suffered so, I can only be relieved at this point. It's such a long ride from the city, and I know the mornings are the best time for your work . . ." Growing strangely more angry and upset by the minute, Eden had patiently waited until she was done, then calmly: "But you see, I want to come. Won't you tell me how to get there?" And of course she had, describing today's arrangements.

Now their liveried driver came back and, opening the door, stuck his head in the limousine, letting in a blast of fresh cold air that made the sleepy Eden feel better at once. "There's going to be a twenty-minute delay," he announced. "It's not the other cars. Another funeral is blocking the road up ahead. If you folks want to go inside where you'll be more comfortable, you have plenny of time." As he shut the door and went back to the building, the two women conferred and decided to stay where they were. Eden and Harold got out of the car and were immediately struck by the knifing wind. "I feel like getting some air and stretching my legs," Eden said to his plump brother-in-law, adding after a pause, "You want to come along?" but looking predictably insulted, Harold shook his head. "You must be nuts, it's about eighteen degrees," said Harold with intense disgust, and went scuffing away on his shiny black shoes to the building down the road. Just as disgusted, if not even more so, Eden turned up the collar on his heavy new coat, and started up the macadam road: Why had he let himself in for all of this? Though his sister and her husband made endless noises about his being a patronizing snob, *they*, on the blessedly rare occasions that they met, were the ones to patronize *him*. Particularly Harold, who called him "Mister Paintner," and never failed to leeringly ask about how he was making out with his models, and if he had sold any paintings, which, until recent years, Eden had not.

Coming from behind him, the wind stung his ears, and the aching cold of the ground came right through his shoes, but Eden didn't mind—he welcomed it after the sickening stuffiness of the car. For the first time in years he was properly equipped for winter, and though the brand-new flannels and tweeds were hardly appropriate for a funeral, Eden had never owned a dark suit in his life and, furthermore, didn't give a damn. Several yards past the hearse, he saw on the left, built out almost flush with the road, a huge massive mausoleum with the name FROYNE carved above the coffered door. Ignoring any profanation that might be involved, Eden stepped off the road over looping iron chains onto the frozen turf on the far side of the tomb. There, finding himself out of the reach of the wind, he moved back against the thick marble wall, and with his back almost resting on the barred stained-glass window with its chromatic view of the tomb's murky interior, he pulled out a crumpled pack of cigarettes. He lit one, greedily inhaling, and relaxed at once, relaxed for the first time really in hours, and looked about him with bright clinical interest: he had never been in a cemetery before in his life. He had been only four when his father had died, and his mother had never taken him or Janet to the grave, which, for all he knew, might be there, in that huge, dreary place. In front of him, over more looping chains, lay more of what was obviously a plot for a whole generation of Froynes: "Tessie Froyne, Beloved Sister . . ." "Regina Froyne, Our Dearest Mother . . ." "Nathan Froyne, My Beloved Husband . . ." All in all, about thirteen Froynes were here laid to rest. Contentedly smoking, Eden wondered why the headstones were so crudely hewn and ugly, and why several had strange rows of pebbles lined up on their tops. He also wondered how the Froyne or Froynes who lay behind the mausoleum wall on which he leaned had managed to win such stony privacy above the ground.

As car doors slammed like pistol reports, Eden stuck his head around the corner of the tomb. Through tears the wind brought to his eyes, he saw that five of the lost eight cars had arrived, and that their occupants were getting out and going up the steps to use the building's "facilities." Relieved—he was not at all ready to go back to the limousine—he stepped back out of the wind and surveyed the panorama unfolding in front of him. With an expert eye he took it all in—the frozen knolls and dipping hollows abristle with slabs, with shrouded marble figures, funerary urns and strangely Byzantinesque balls, and here and there the monolithic mausoleums like Druid structures upon the hills. Above it all was a threatening sky, so low the mournful trees seemed to scrape it with their tips . . . cypresses, official symbols of mourning, bareboughed willows, a few maples and elms, and cedars cut in peculiar mushroom topiary shapes. It all reminded him of something, and he stood for a moment pondering, perplexed, until he suddenly realized it was a painting of one such actual scene—Jacob Van Ruisdael's *The Jewish Cemetery*. Pleased with himself, Eden smiled: He often sought to see life in terms of Art, and though he sensed there was some serious weakness in this, he went about doing it all the same. Now in his mind he went over the Ruisdael, which he remembered in complete detail, a typical moody Seventeenth Century landscape of the Romantic School with the inevitable props of crumbling classic ruins, a melancholy waterfall trickling over rocks, a stormy sky dramatically moiling with clouds; the novel additions were the squat and ugly tombs, carved with Hebrew letters and some falling apart, and a dead bare tree in the foreground—an inspired touch—a jagged white tree which looked like some retributive lightning bolt from the heavens above. But his self-congratulatory smile began to fade, as Eden stared out at the bleak winter scene: Aside from the shapes of the tombs and the threatening sky, where was any similarity? Was it just the overall mood, the brooding sense of doom and death and decay? Or was it simply that they were Jewish cemeteries both? Probably just that, thought Eden, beginning to laugh, his laughter falling amid the chains and stones. And what the hell did it matter?—it wasn't a picture *he* would ever paint!

Though Eden painted strange precise pictures (landscapes, interiors with figures, still lifes), they were not considered Representational by the art critics, who gave them all sorts of fancy names. It was just in the last two years that these critics had finally begun to consider him at all, and there were still some with reservations who said that Werner undoubtedly had great talent, but that his pictures revealed the lack of a certain "emotional development" he must go through before he ever could be considered really first-rate. Eden didn't care what they said either way, and though, at thirty-three, after struggling many years, he was grateful for the money success brought, it had made little change in his quiet life. Almost fanatically disciplined and dedicated, and enormously productive as a result, Eden was a source of great irritation to many of his painter friends, but Eden took their hostile jibes quite calmly, for he knew they secretly envied him. He also knew, without going about consciously acknowledging a debt, that it was his mother who had made him as strong and single-minded as he was. Though many people found her a strange and cold woman (sometimes even Eden himself), Eden mostly thought her remarkable considering the middle-class-Jewish background from which she had come. Left a penniless young widow with two tiny children—Eden had been four, Janet two—she had picked herself up and gone out to work to make a life for her children and herself. And just as she had been unlike so many Jewish women of her generation and class, by not collapsing and sinking into a quagmire of self-pitying helplessness when her husband died, she had been unlike them in her treatment of her children, most particularly a son. She had never pushed or pulled at Eden, never tried to imprison or smother him with love: Hands Off had been her policy, sometimes almost too rigorously carried out. Tough, self-made, self-reliant, she had tried to teach her children to be the same. With Eden she had succeeded, but with Janet she had mysteriously failed: poor frightened Janet had married stupid rich Harold Block first chance she got.

Eden, however, beginning as a boy of nine delivering drugstore prescriptions on his bike, had always fended and provided for himself. Though there were times he ought have, he had never since his boyhood asked his mother for a cent. This had made for many hardships, but he knew without bitterness it had made him strong, and when the time had come to decide whether or not to be a painter, he had only had to answer to himself. He had technically left home at seventeen (to go to a college he had put himself through) and had never gone back, but he had always kept in touch with his mother and tried to see her from time to time. He had done this because he guessed that her lifelong policy of Hands Off aside, she still would have a few pretty classic maternal worries about him: Was he getting enough to eat? Did he have warm clothes? A roof of some sort over his head? Would he ever stop living with a succession of sluts and settle down with some Nice if not Nice Jewish girl? But in the last two years Eden had been so buried in his work and so deeply involved with a crazy brilliant girl, he had not kept in touch with his mother at all. Apparently it was guilt about his silence, a guilt he hadn't dreamt he felt, that had brought him to the funeral in an attempt to make amends: No matter how calmly reconciled to her brother's death she might claim to be, his mother could not help but be touched by some sign of respect for that sad luckless man. Poor Morris had been one of those people who are dogged by failure all their lives, and who, no matter how golden the opportunity, invariably manage to botch it up. In his wretched lifetime he had owned five businesses each of which had failed in turn, his marriage had been childless, and his wife had died of leukemia at thirty-two. As far as Eden knew there had only been one time when things had gone well for him, and that had been the same brief time that Eden had loved him—fiercely—as only a boy of six can love a man. All Eden could remember of that time was that his gentle uncle had suddenly been around a lot, and had taught him things—how to swim, to throw a ball, how to ride a two-wheeler bike. Whenever he looked back, which was almost never, Eden could see that it had been a natural—the fatherless boy, the childless man—and could see that his love for his uncle had filled a terrible void. The love had ceased because of a series of incidents, and while he was not sure of the time-lapse involved, the incidents made for one of the only bad memories that Eden had. What happened was that the frail bubble of poor Morris's prosperity had burst, and within the space of two Job-like years, his business failed, he went bankrupt, his wife died and he had a nervous breakdown which landed him in a sanitarium for seven months. When he got out Morris came to live with them (was it for several weeks or months?) and it was the one time that Eden had ever hated his mother, violently: Why had she done this to them? Why had she been the one to take him in? Couldn't she have let some of his wife's family take care of him, or paid a trained nurse-companion to take care of him in his own apartment (which she was later to do)? Of course later he saw that she had had to do it, just as she'd had to support him for the rest of his life. But at the time, frightened, unable to understand, he had spent all his time in their house hiding from the ashen man, who shuffled about in a bathrobe and slippers, eyes glassy, mumbling to himself, or sometimes calling loudly, plaintive, "Eden? Eden, where *are* you? . . . Eden come and sit with Uncle Morris on the porch." Forgetting that those shaking hands had once gripped him firmly as the giant breakers came surging in, or that those obscenely white and hairless legs had once moved with speed across the lawn in pursuit of a ball, Eden had not been able to overcome the deep revulsion and fear that his uncle inspired. Without his knowing what it was, some terrible emanation came from the broken man to the boy of eight, striking terror in his heart, warning without instructing: Look! Just look at what can happen to a man!

A long irritable blast on a car horn brought a startled Eden around the corner of the tomb. The hearse was gone, having proceeded on ahead to the site of the grave, and all the lost cars had arrived. Stepping back over chains, Eden hurried to the waiting limousine. After the clean icy air the smells and heat of the car were sickening. He was greeted by a faintly amused smile from his mother, an aggrieved look from his brother-in-law. "What were you doing—painting a picture?" jeered Janet.

"No, taking a pee," Eden said.

"Oh for god's sake, have some respect!" cried Mrs. Werner, showing some emotion at last, and the brother and sister meekly subsided as though they had become children again. With a lurch the procession started up, their limousine in the lead, moving at a crawling pace down the gently rising and falling road. As they penetrated the vast cemetery, which seemed to Eden to stretch for miles on either side, he dully stared out at the names on the tombstones, fighting a growing nausea which he decided came from the heat of the car.

At last, to break the smoldering silence, Eden's mother cleared her throat and brightly said: "I still can't get over Mrs. Shallit's coming. It's wonderful of her."

"What's so wonderful," said Janet disagreeably. "They were next-door neighbors for fifteen years. And he was the one who found her and took care of her when she had that stroke."

"She's in her seventies. And she's a very sick woman," said Mrs. Werner with a dogged reasonableness that made Eden grit his teeth: he himself was barely able to keep from turning and belting Janet in the mouth.

"She certainly doesn't *look* that old," returned the perverse Janet almost comically. "I never understood why Morris didn't marry her. Maybe it was because she was older . . . he was funny about that sort of thing."

"He didn't marry her because they were perfectly content with the arrangement they had. They were happy just to be companions, going out together to sit on a bench in the sun, running next door to visit and watch TV."

"How *depressing*," said Janet, and for once, Eden had to agree with her. Worse than depressing, a vegetable existence, a kind of death-in-life. And to his consternation his mother's description of his uncle's life—particularly his uncle's habit of going out to "sit on a bench in the sun"—made him remember a day he had forgotten until now, a day well over ten years past, when, just back from Vietnam, he was resettling in New York. It had been an unnaturally balmy March day, as hot as June, and he had decided to take the day off from his work and go and see the El Grecos up at the Hispanic Museum. He lived way down in Saint Mark's Place, and a subway would have been the wise choice, but he took a bus and rode in a rear seat with the window wide open and the miraculous air blowing in on his face. On Broadway in the Sixties the bus had stopped for a light, and moonily blinking out Eden had found himself confronted by the big ugly building where his uncle Morris had lived for ten years. As he stared at the turreted building a violent impulse to get off the bus and visit the sick and lonely old man had almost propelled him from his seat, but then the light had changed, the bus had rolled on, and looking out at the crowded traffic-island benches, Eden had come to his senses at once. Taking in the old men and women on the benches, warming themselves like rusty crows in the sun, Eden told himself that his uncle would not be home in his apartment on such a day, but would be out there among his cronies enjoying the premature spring. It was certainly idiotic, he had reasoned, to consider walking around for blocks and searching all the benches for the old man and, sitting back, Eden had tried to resume his simple pleasure in the ride. But the ride was spoiled, the whole outing was spoiled, and he did not recapture any of his original mood until he stood, lost, before an El Greco, thinking, Yes, the hands, yes *that's* how it's done . . .

Suddenly they were at the grave site. The limousine stopped and Harold jumped out, reaching in to help his mother-in-law out, but, spurning his hand, she climbed out herself and briskly started off for the grave. Behind the limousine the other cars came to a stop, there was a slamming of doors, and people stiff from sitting so long got out and wobbled across the frozen turf. The last one out of the limousine, Eden softly closed the door, then stood by the car, his breath taken away by a fierce gust of wind. Finally, with a strange reluctance, he joined the other three at the open grave. Janet, almost childlike, stood pressed against their mother's side, her arm hooked through the older woman's in a clear need to take rather than give support. Harold, out of some ritualistic sense of what was fitting (which Eden could not comprehend), stood slightly off, behind the women, leaving a space for Eden on his mother's left side. As he took this designated place, Eden gave his mother's profile a furtive glance and saw, with something oddly like relief, that she looked much paler and her features seemed pinched with what could be strain. Violently shivering—he was feeling the cold as he hadn't when he'd stood by the mausoleum—he watched the other mourners assemble on the far side of the grave. He wondered why they didn't come and stand on his side, and wondered as he had at the services, who they all were, these old men and women who, for all he knew, might be related to him. As they had left the chapel to get into the cars, his mother had nodded and murmured to some of them, but had made no attempt to introduce Eden, which he had found somewhat rude and strange. Well, whoever they were, he thought as he pulled his collar higher for warmth—old cronies of Morris, or remote relatives that he, Eden, would never know existed—the main thing was that they all had managed to get there and help give poor Morris a decent last show.

Growing colder and more impatient and nervous by the minute —when would they put this show on?—Eden once again glanced sideways at his mother, whom he now found staring at the coffin straight ahead. Curious (What could she be thinking?), he followed her glance and was soon marveling at the pure ugliness of everything—the metal casket with its vulgar mahogany veneer, poised above the crude hole in shiny supports that looked like plumber's pipes, the stiff spray of salmon-colored gladioli (which he thought the ugliest of flowers), the brilliant mat of green plastic grass that was supposed to hide the waiting mound of dug-up earth. Then several yards away, to the left behind some tombstones, he noticed three gravediggers huddled together for warmth, and with interest and pity took in their thin earth-stained clothes, their watering eyes and raw red faces and hands. When he saw they were stealthily passing round a flask, Eden, that hooker-upper of Life and Art, stepped in and with an indulgent smile thought proudly: The gravediggers in Hamlet . . . that's what they're like!

To Eden's relief, the rabbi finally appeared, coming to take his place at the foot of the grave, a thin, professionally sorrowful-looking man in a broad-brimmed black hat that almost rested on his ears. For a moment he stood there, adjusting his white silk prayer shawl, fingering his prayer book with big chapped hands; then he turned to Eden's mother, elaborately closed his eyes, and, rocking slightly, gave three long and mournful nods. After this he opened his eyes and cleared his throat, and without any further ceremony began to read the Hebrew Prayer for the Dead. All the mourners bowed their heads, shuffling closer together for warmth, for protection against the wind which cut like a scythe across the marble-sprouting wasteland. Eden, taller than everyone there by inches, also respectfully bowed his head, the Hebrew chanting falling, meaningless, on his ears which painfully ached from the cold. To combat a growing agitation, he focused on the coffin's shiny back, and in place of the responsive chanting of the others, tried to think something meaningful about the man inside; but try as he would all he saw was a stooped thin back in a tan-and-maroon striped robe, and clopping slippers, shuffling along, carrying their wearer down a long dim hall, round a corner, out of sight.

In a burst of exasperation—What the hell was he trying to do? Trying to make himself feel?—Eden brought his head up and almost defiantly looked around. His eyes fell on the gravediggers, who apparently knew all the clues in the Hebrew prayer, and had moved a little closer in readiness for their chore. Unaware of Eden in turn watching them, they stood watching the rabbi, the rocking chanting Jews, nastily smiling, their narrowed eyes filled with contempt. Stunned, Eden looked hard to be certain he was not mistaken in what he saw and, when he saw he was not, began to tremble with uncontrollable rage. The bastards, the *bastards* he thought, and to keep himself from making an outrageous scene— from laying all three flat on the ground—Eden bowed his head again, all the while cursing the bigoted men. Hands clenched into fists, he struggled to get control of himself, desperately trying to understand the intensity of his rage. What was he so excited about? What sort of scum did he think dug graves? Who and what did he want to defend? It was all so unlikely and had him so muddled that it was several seconds before he saw that the gravediggers had come forward and were lowering the coffin into the grave on leather straps. As he watched them straining, grunting, finish their job, then retire to one side, shovels in readiness, his rage subsided and he dismissed them, ashamed: Poor wretches —what did he want from *them*?

Across the trench that now held the coffin a stout white-haired woman—Mrs. Shallit?—now began to sob and cry out "Morris? Morris!" in a wailing voice that made Eden's flesh begin to crawl. At his side his mother stirred, opening her purse to take something out. With a racing heart Eden turned to examine her, but whatever he had hoped to find was not there. Her profile was cold and composed, the one eye he could see was completely dry, and the handkerchief was applied to a nose made pink and runny by the wind alone. Why doesn't she cry? *Why doesn't she cry?* Eden wondered as the terrible rage, displaced from the gravediggers, now found its rightful place. He stood there, wildly staring at his self-possessed mother, and asked himself had he come for this, had he only come to see if she would cry? Then he became aware that the rabbi was holding something out to him. Dimly perceiving that he, Eden, had been singled out and was to scatter that trowelful of earth in the grave, he stepped forward and did so; the clods fell like hailstones on the coffin top.

As he stepped back into place Eden was aware, without looking directly anywhere, of many things—his mother's complacent look of pride, his sister's glare of sheer animus, the stir he had caused in the group across the grave: Who? The nephew? Ah so *that's* who. The rabbi's voice was droning in conclusion, when the exhausted Eden, who had decided nothing worse could happen that day, felt his throat tighten on a pit-like lump which threatened to cut off his breath, felt his chest ache in all its ribs while, despite all his efforts, his eyes filled with tears. For god's sake, it's too much! he protested, blinking, staring out across the bowed heads opposite him and wondering was he losing his mind. What's happening? What's *happening*? What does it all mean? he asked the wind-swept landscape beyond the bowed heads, but of course there was no answer there. Out there was only the crude slabs of tombstones, the statues, the tombs, the trees, the bleak and ugly stretches of a Jewish cemetery in Queens.

Icarus

She couldn't sleep. The corridor noises had stopped long ago; the luminous hands of her traveling clock stood at ten-twelve, making it over an hour since she had laughingly washed down the sleeping pill with *brut* champagne. Alcohol and Seconal—an overpowering combination, one would think, yet obviously not powerful enough for the terrible state of her nerves.

She decided against ringing for another pill—ashamed, she didn't want the nurse to know—and instead lit a cigarette. When she snapped on the gooseneck lamp, the room that sprang out of shadow looked like a stateroom for some improbably luxurious voyage: flowers everywhere, a jungle of bottles on the bureau, a gold-paper chest with little drawers full of melting Belgian chocolates, a box of cigars (cigars, she'd learned, were not just handed out in cartoons), telegrams stuck in the mirror frame, and on a chair a teetering pile of gift boxes trailing ribbons to the floor. The door was wedged open with a rubber stop and both windows were as high as they could go, but there was not even the faintest hint of a crosscurrent to stir the hot air.

Giving a racking sigh, she dangled her legs over the side of the bed—pretty legs, bared to ruffled little bloomers that coyly peeped from beneath the short nightgown. It was the sort of thing she hated and never wore, but she had been endlessly warned about the discomforts of a July "confinement" and been told to buy cool nightwear, and, as usual, her sensible friends had been proved right. After finding her mules with her toes, she turned off the light and headed for the door with slow and careful steps, keeping hidden until she saw that the room opposite was dark and there was no one to see her in the silly batiste tutu she was wearing.

The corridor was darkened for the night. The only lights came from a desk halfway down, where the chief night nurse sat bathed in blue fluorescence, and from a room two doors down and across, where a sliver of light and the glittery sounds of ice and glasses and laughter spilled out. The room of someone privileged, undoubtedly, she thought with rancor—the one belonging to the senator's daughter, whom the morning nurse had talked about. She too had had her first child the night before. "A gor-r-geous nine-pound gel. Now, fancy that!" the nurse had crowed, indirectly disparaging six pounds and two ounces—or perhaps not indirectly at all.

Like her own threshold, the one for this room was bare. In front of all the others stood baskets, vases, bowls, and plastic baby boots filled with flowers, which gave the austere reflecting linoleum the poetic look of a woodland stream. "Put the flowers out for the night? But why? Do they poison the air or use it all up?" she had laughingly asked the maid who'd come in. The poor overworked soul had not been amused, just as she herself was not at all amused now when she left the cool doorway and turned back into the hothouse of her room.

Going to the river window, she moved a pot of African violets and a basket of daisies dyed blue and leaned far out, breathing in deeply. The night smelled of dust and tar and grass and the river. All was still, still. The gelid river surface was broken with jumping reflections of lights on the drive and bridge; a few cars thrummed beneath the window. On the strip of pavement edging the water a tall young man was airing a splendid boxer. A hot, becalmed July night, but its very essence of repose, of peace, made her nerves tighten, tighten, finally made her shoulders heave with the weeping she had tried so hard to hold back.

And why? she wondered, bewildered, ashamed, as she rubbed at her filling eyes. Why weep and weep at such a time in one's life? It was unnatural, horrible. Didn't it mean that something was wrong with her, that she was in some way monstrous? And what, oh, what—this was most incomprehensible of all—*what* had happened to the dazzling burst of glory in which the day had begun?

Breakfast over, she had lain back languidly against the cranked-up head of the bed, resplendent in pearls and a blue silk bed jacket, her heavy pale hair bound back with a blue ribbon (she had not been clairvoyant; she just looked dreadful in pink), feeling ridiculously like an Eighteenth Century courtesan decked out for a levée, but happy—happier than she had ever been in her life. She slowly waved the delicately painted Japanese fan that her husband's best friend had sent over, engagingly tied to a basket of flowers; and as she stared out at the brilliant morning she wondered if this feeling of enchantment might not be just a hangover from some kind of "happy gas" she had whiffed the night before. But the moment she heard the rattling of carts in the corridor, she knew it was really much simpler: she was about to see her son for the first time.

Last night's look didn't count. Dazed from something they had given her at the very end, she had stared about at shiny tables and instruments, tiled walls, unknown, smiling faces (who *were* all those people?), finally coming to a disbelieving focus on a red face folded up like an angry fist, a face from which an impossibly big mouth was discharging a barrage of squalls. Her son? Never. Her eyes had run up the tiled wall to a clock; a half hour had passed since she last asked the time in that tiny, stark room somewhere down the hall. Thirty minutes, and the fact was irrevocably accomplished. Her eyes had slipped back down the wall to the bundle being prodded by a stethoscope . . .

Now a small canvas cart alive with throaty sounds was wheeled into her room. After trying to absorb an impossible number of instructions, she was helped by the nurse to a chair next to the courtyard window (closed against "nasty breezes and horrid soot"), where she propped one elbow on a pillow, as she'd been told, and cautiously opened her arms. Trembling, she stared: tiny, curling fists waved like sea anemones beneath her chin; enormous, light, unfocused eyes moved and moved; a mouth opened mutely, a diagram of helplessness—which it turned out to be. He could not suck. At first she would not believe this. Surely . . . nature? Or instinct? she stammered to the nurse. But no. He simply did not know what to do with the rubber object placed in his open mouth; and so, with much clucking and hissing, the nurse showed a way to pinch in the flat little cheeks, making the mouth first learn to pucker and finally to draw in.

He took only one third of the tiny bottle. When she tried to prop him up and "bubble" him as she had been shown, his fuzzy head bobbled so alarmingly she gave up. She contented herself with cradling him in the crook of her arm, staring down into those bottomless eyes, which seemed to see her—but couldn't really, she guessed—and then, before she knew what had happened, she was laughing and crying at the same time, the big, foolish tears oozing down her smiling face.

"Ah, now!" said the returning nurse, her brogue as astringent as rubbing alcohol, "what have we here?"

"I don't know," she blubbered. "Isn't it stupid?"

"Not really," said this cool individual, who took the bundle and threw it casually against her sturdy shoulder, immediately raising a loud and startling belch. She set him down in the portable cart. "Just a little postpar-r-rtum depression, that's all 'tis."

She stopped weeping at once. "When will you bring him back?"

"Dinnertime," said the nurse, who was holding the bottle up against the light, counting the number of ounces that had been taken. "I think this first day it's best he be fed in the nursery."

Suppressing her anger and the conviction that she was being criticized for not nursing her child in the manner nature had intended, she acknowledged that he was, after all, a tiny sparrow of a thing—it really was wisest to let experienced hands take over the first day. You'll have time enough, she told herself, and peacefully relaxed against the pillows, listening to the carts clattering away, feeling the happiness begin to percolate again.

After the doctor's visit ("Don't worry about those tears; they're a perfectly natural thing. And my goodness, you're in splendid shape! Are you *sure* you don't want any visitors until tonight?"), the phone began ringing and did not stop all morning long. It was only after her lunch tray was removed that she realized she was exhausted, and she unplugged the phone and stretched out for a nap. But the heat, the relentlessly echoing page-system, the rich, bloomy smell of flowers and the shuffling slippers of exercising young mothers in the hall would not let her sleep. Finally she gave a huge sigh—the day's first—and after reaching out to replug the phone, she threw on a thin robe and went to sit by the front window.

It was an unusually humid day, with the outline of every object diffused by a trembling heat nimbus. Just across the river, Welfare Island lay gently steaming in the sun. Bemused, she stared. She had always thought of it vaguely as a place that must harbor either a prison or a hospital for the criminally insane, but the neat, pink, unsinister buildings sat among lollipop trees with such a pastoral air that it was absurd to think of its being anything but a charming illustration in a child's picture book. She blinked happily, drowsily, about to rise and stumble for the bed, when her mind's soothing fuzziness cleared and took sharp focus on a vivid scene whose backdrop was a remote French town, visited once for three days, nine years before. Perplexed, startled, she remained where she was, frowning with consternation as sleep slipped away. A part of her longed for that nap, but she was not a person given to looking back, either with nostalgia or regret, and she knew that she couldn't possibly lie down and rest until she discovered why Blois, of all places and at all times, should have come back.

Was it simply the perspective of the strand across the water? No. Though Blois did sit on the Loire, and she could vaguely remember a smoky, panoramic riverscape, the piece of Blois conjured up by memory was a grand-manner spill of marble steps, blinding in early-afternoon sunlight. She could not even remember just where in the town the steps were situated, except to know that they were not near the Loire, or the château they had gone there to see. In fact, though she had always remembered the château, little else about the visit to Blois had remained except the fact of it—and yet here, after nine long years, one moment was delivered up in such detail that she could smell that peculiar mixture of old stone and dust, could see the oil beads on the nose of the vendor selling them leaky cups of lemon ice, could feel the August stupefaction that had made them blink at the chalky steps, too lazy to climb them, too lazy even to find a shaded bench to sit on while eating the ices. Strange. How strange. For as all her senses relived these things the static scene in her mind began to creak and move. The vendor went away, pushing his cart with a gritty sound; she began to fan her face with an unmarked sketch pad; and he threw down his squashy cup with disgust, swore and scrubbed his handsome mouth with the back of his hand.

"What is important, really important? That damned question that plagues us all. This morning, when you went out for the *croissants* and papers, I lay on the bed so paralyzed by it, I couldn't get up and get dressed. And now all of a sudden, I know. And it's so simple. [He was talking not to her but to those steps, leading up to where?] What is important, the only things that really matter, are one's work and the people one loves."

Hardly a world-shaking maxim, that, but how for a moment her skin had drawn, her eyes had filled, as the words struck a small knell of portent in her heart! It had been a terribly painful moment, too, for she had stared at him—tanned, debonair, sun glancing jauntily off the gay clothes they had bought in Provence—and she had wondered what on earth he was doing, bringing up such things. Was he trying to make them question what they were? What they were, at that moment, were two young people who "painted" and were traveling together for the summer months—two lucky people (they had often agreed) who understood each other perfectly, and doing so, understood that there can be a brief shining time, if one is young, when freedom and a pure delight in living can be adequate substitutes for love.

With a short, derisive laugh she had broken the spell; taking one of his hands from the pocket where he'd plunged it, clenched tensely into a fist, she began to tug like a forlorn child begging a playmate to return to the abandoned game. And of course he had. His eyes had cleared; he had looked at her and really seen her again. Then he had laughed at himself—he certainly had been laying it on!—and hand in hand, like truants, they raced up the silent, burning streets . . .

The phone, she finally realized, was ringing in the hospital room she now sat in—in the present. Relieved, she went and answered it, so relieved that she deliberately prolonged the silly conversation that ensued, and afterward, to stave off further thoughts of Blois, she left it plugged in, and it rang at short intervals throughout the afternoon. When it did not, she willed herself not to think of that French town and that young man not thought of in years. *Years.*

During one of the longer lulls between calls, she was lying on the bed, drowsily fanning herself, no longer having to will herself not to think, when she began to have the uncomfortable feeling that she was being watched. And yes, sure enough, she turned her head toward the courtyard window and there, in the wing across the way, small, pale faces were peering at her from behind glass. The moment she looked directly at them, they burst into excited laughter. At first she was caught up in their joy, in their game, returning the tireless waves, the smiles. But soon she began considering why they must be there, in pajamas and bathrobes, on such a hot summer's day, their wan little faces pressed against the sooty glass, and the game palled. She was grateful when someone in the room behind them finally called them away. Good-by! they cried soundlessly, sadly waving. Good-by, good-by . . .

Her blurring eyes moved slowly away down the yellow brick wall of the building, then stopped at an open window two flights down. Inside was what seemed to be some sort of white-tiled treatment room, with an examining table stupidly (she thought) close to the open window, a table where a starched young man was just setting down a frail little boy of four or five. Knowing she ought to look away at once, she continued to watch, hypnotized, while the muscular young orderly unbuttoned the child's pajama top, then stepped aside to let a white-coated doctor, a stethoscope in his ears, come forward to listen to the sparrow chest. Then two new, bulky white shapes stepped forward and cut off her view of the child—and frightful, tortured screams began to rend the summer air.

Trembling, she assured herself that they couldn't be doing anything worse than changing a dressing or administering an injection. If it were anything more serious, they would have him in a surgically sterile, sealed-up room. But the sheer anguish and terror in those animal yelps of *Aeiye aeiye aeiye-e-e-e mama ma-ma-a-a-a!* undid her. Her heart began to race and scalding tears poured down her cheeks. She stumbled out of bed, crossed the room and locked herself in the tiny bathroom, where she turned on both taps full force to drown out all sounds.

When she finally ventured out, the cries had stopped. Still trembling, she marched to the courtyard window and blindly yanked down the opaque green shade. Then she turned and went to the front window, where, bracing her elbows on the sill, she leaned dangerously far out. Three-thirty on a Friday in July—the weekend exodus had already begun. Below on the East River Drive cars beetled along mere inches apart, their bumpers gently colliding with little thumps whenever the procession unexpectedly stopped. Beyond the burning metal of the cars she saw a group of boys in swimming trunks standing on the parklike strip at the river's edge, glistening from a recent swim. Trying not to consider the polluted water they'd been swimming in, she watched three of them jostle, shove, kick, in a snickery game that ended with all three of them tumbling back into the river. They're like pale, spindly frogs, she thought; the look of one whose legs disappeared last in a bandy white flash particularly struck her, provoking a strange shudder, making her heart contract with foolish, unwarranted fear and dread. But perhaps not so foolish, she thought, seeing the huge, flat-bellied barge piled with coal come bearing blindly down: it was pulled by a tug on the far side, where the pilot could not see them. Then, just as it seemed about to mow them down, it slipped laboriously past their seal heads with a berth of yards, leaving them gloriously rocking and splashing and laughing in the waves of its wake.

She flew to the phone that had been ringing (how long?), and the old friend at the other end was immediately concerned. "Are you crying? You *are!* What's wrong?" Ashamed and distressed (was she sick in some way?), she mumbled that she did not know, then unexpectedly giggled and added: "Just a little postpartum depression, I guess."

At four-thirty her husband came in, carrying some books and magazines she had asked for, a huge, fuzzy toy lion with a ferocious face, and an insulated bag holding a quart of ice cream.

"I'm such a wreck they made me leave the office early," he cheerfully announced, dumping everything down on the end of her bed, then kissing her forehead and seating himself in the middle of the clutter. "It's the damnedest thing, but I seem to be jumping out of my skin. I mean—what are you supposed to do or say? And how are you supposed to *be?*" Then he saw all the flowers, the telegrams, the bottles and boxes, and of course she had to tell him just who had sent what and who had called and what they had said.

"Visitors are not permitted on the beds!"

They peered around through their cigarette smoke at the nurse standing stolidly in the doorway—strong-boned and handsome, with shining, blond, bunned hair and tanned skin that smoothly covered high cheekbones—apparently German, judging by the voice. Implacable, she just stood there waiting, a Prussian martinet, until he sheepishly slipped off the bed.

"The babies come now," she continued, her powerful, silent directive having been obeyed, "so all the visitors must take their leave." Cold blue eyes swept the litter on the bed, the ashtray glutted with their cigarettes, the empty ice-cream container (they had taken turns sipping the melted ice cream), and the untouched dinner tray on a chair. "And the mother will please wash her hands."

Hands in pockets, slouched back against the bed, he said as she was leaving, "Are you from Lucerne?"

A squeak of gum soles, a rustle of starch. "What is that?"

"I asked—just a sort of bet with myself—if you were Swiss, if you came from Lucerne."

"So?" the voice affirmed and demanded all at once.

"So." He grinned, turning on the powerhouse of his homely but infallible charm. "So nothing, really. I saw your name on that little plastic badge you wear. When I was a kid we once stopped at a small hotel in Lucerne owned by a family named Langendal." Pointedly not checking on any connection, he quickly pressed on. "Look, Miss Langendal, I'm confused. I thought this was an ultraprogressive-type hospital. I mean, I've heard you sometimes have that rooming-in business, one big happy family, and yet here I am and I've only seen this guy once. And that was so late they had the nursery lights dimmed for the night—I could hardly see —and the joker who held him up stood three feet back from the glass. Now, I believe in antisepsis, but—oh, hell. Can't I just hide in the john until he comes?"

Formidable as ever, the nurse raised her arm and consulted her watch. But when she looked up, a wan ray of chalet sunshine flickered across her face. "Return at six-thirty and we will see what we can do."

At six-thirty-five he stood by the bureau, tied into a sterile gown amusingly like the smocks she wore at the hairdresser's, looking quite frightened as he gingerly cradled the bundle he'd been given to hold—the bundle that had gratifyingly taken four ounces of milk and burped three times. She was watching from high on her pillows, unaware of Miss Langendal poised in the doorway, seeing only those two heads so foolishly alike: thin, pale hair receding (or, rather, one coming, one going) from knobbly foreheads, huge light eyes, noses too long and mouths too big, and large and strangely vulnerable-looking ears.

"It's because I'm so happy!" she wailed when she found them staring at her wet face, and she indignantly snatched at a tissue and blew her nose. Not looking at them—the bewildered husband, the seasoned nurse—she took up her compact, powdered her cheeks and made a fresh face for the visiting hour.

Now she looked down at the river walk. Lighted by street lamps that cast spotlight pools of brilliance, it seemed a small stage; and, indeed, a little drama was just taking place. The young man with the splendid boxer (a young man who was equally splendid and handsome in kind, she saw now) was giving a newcomer a light for his cigarette. The newcomer was another young man, slighter but also strikingly handsome, with a huge white French poodle straining on a leash. She watched the mute tableau that needed no words, then rose and went to her bed, where she lay staring into the darkness, wondering what on earth was the matter with her. Life was life, as she had always known. All sorts of things could happen to men—to women too, all sorts of things. And as if to prove one facet of this, a muffled moan came from somewhere —either through the bathroom register connecting to a room upstairs or from a room down the hall. But wherever, she knew what it meant and what was happening to the woman, who moaned again.

She brought down lids over eyes that were grainy and dry, and lay there rigid, thoroughly miserable, for a long time. Then slyly, insinuatingly, against the black backdrop of lowered lids an image flickered, faintly at first, then brighter and clearer. Again and again she saw those skinny, flailing legs disappearing into the scummy water of the East River until it was no longer really that at all, until the image was part of a larger canvas—an actual painting, in fact. A painting so beloved that ten years before, the acolyte, the brand-new student of art, had kept a colored postcard reproduction of it taped to her closet door. Brueghel's *Fall of Icarus*. A boat sailed up a narrow strait; a foreground farmer tilled the soil; a shepherd tended his sheep, his moony face turned toward the sky. The boat charged ahead with bellying sails; the farmer guided the plow in the earth; the shepherd dreamed his doltish dreams—no one noticed the drowning boy. There was actually not much to notice, just splayed white legs disappearing into frills of waves, which, even if seen, would have seemed preposterous. What was a boy *doing*, falling like a meteor out of the sky?

According to the myth, this boy Icarus was flying on wings his father, Daedalus, had made of wax and feathers—when, made wild by the sensation of flying, he ignored his father's repeated warnings and soared nearer the dazzling sun. The wax melted, and amid eddying feathers and flapping strings poor Icarus dropped like a stone to his death—the fate, the somber myth instructed, of all rash and headstrong sons.

For a moment she lay there, frowning, unable to believe what she already knew. Then all at once she was laughing in the dark—laughing at herself, at the comic, labored workings of her mind. All day long a quavering voice in her head had been trying to make itself heard; all day long she had not understood. Now, in desperation, here was Brueghel, sublime Brueghel, trotted out not because of any beauty involved but simply because the painting posed the same question her mind had been asking all day long.

First brought up by the sick waifs in the neighboring wing, then again by the boys in the river outside, then this graphic illustration of Icarus tumbling out of the sky, the question asked by monomania was: Where were the *mothers* of all those children— the waifs, the boys . . . and Icarus?

It was really so ludicrous that she smiled ironically as the mysteries of the day unraveled themselves—the maudlin tears, the memory of Blois, the sun-struck figure of that young man whom she had never really loved. From somewhere the woman moaned again, but she no longer heard. "The only things that really matter are one's work and the people one loves," she said softly into the dark, seeing for the first time ever how her life stretched away from that day in Blois to this. Filled with quiet wonder, she saw how she had taken that statement, deceptively simple, almost banal, and used it as a yardstick with which she measured all that took place in her life.

Starting from that golden day in Blois, she had moved slowly and painfully forward through the years, checking, then rejecting ("No, that is not love" . . . "That is not my work"), until today, when—without knowing it at first—she had arrived at the end of her long journey, her long search. It had been a baffling day, she saw as she lay still in the darkness, simply because it was so hard to believe that things tallied, that the exacting yardstick could be put away at last—that she finally knew what she loved and what her work was to be. Stirring, she turned her cheek on rough hospital linen and gave the day's last tremulous sigh, a sigh of complete release. Then she closed her eyes and dropped off at once into her first night of liable maternal sleep.

The Perfect Day

They lurched to a stop on the level sand, and stood blinking through the early light at the violent change their beach had undergone overnight. To the left and right, as always, the white sand caroomed away to the hazy vee-shaped points where it met with ocean and sky, but dead ahead, instead of gently grading into crashing surf, it suddenly stopped: there was an edge or ledge, a line drawn by the precipice to an indeterminate drop, beyond which glittered the strangely silent harp of the sea.

For a few seconds they just stood there, rooted, dazzled, Cynthia, a cumbersome figure in hat, sungoggles, shirt, sandals, carrying an umbrella and the two huge straw bags that held all the equipment needed for her ceaseless battle with sun and sand, Davy, free as air in faded blue trunks, a plastic pail and shovel in each hand. Then, without warning, Davy took off, running across the flattened sand to the mysterious ledge, where, dropping pails and shovels, he simply stepped into space and disappeared. Frantically calling his name, Cynthia started after him, impeded by her heavy load, only to find, feeling foolish, that it was a drop of less than five feet to the wet sand below. She watched Davy angrily try to get a toe-hold in the sheer crumbling wall, then set her burdens on the sand. "No. *I* can," he said, scorning her hand, and sighing (the pride of four was a trial), she straightened up and looked all about, marveling at what had occurred. Sometime, during a night which had sounded windless (she could say, for she had tossed, sleepless, for hours), a sea of violent tides and waves had gone as far as the base of the dunes; in withdrawing to its usual place, it had left the sand yellowed, beaten flat, marked in scalloped patterns with broken shells, oily clumps of seaweed, tarry sticks and logs, and then, in some final giant whorling spasm, had sucked out tons of sand, leaving this cliff, not quite high as man, at the water's edge. But perhaps the oddest thing of all was the present state of the sea—gelid, still, still, making only the faintest tissuey plash as it plucked inshore.

"Watch. Watch *me!*" shouted Davy, having regained the higher sand, and she turned and watched him throw himself down again. Seeing this was to be a game he would play until he tired (a miniature Tensing, impelled to scale insurmountable heights), she sat down where she stood, not bothering to put the usual towel between herself and the sand. Each time he came up, breathless, triumphant, he found she had taken something off. First came the large and foolish floppy hat, next the long-sleeved shirt that buttoned to the chin, then the intricate Italian sandals, then the impenetrable goggles, until at last, for the first time that summer (just two weeks old), she sat with her eyes peacefully closed, her thin limbs exposed to the sun and cleansed morning air.

Finally weary of his game, Davy dropped, panting and perspiring, at her side. "Do you think we could take a swim?" he asked, but in the flat halfhearted tone children use when they expect their requests to be denied. Pained—how long had he been asking for things in that way?—Cynthia looked about: with the exception of an adolescent surfcaster fifty yards down the sand, they were still the only ones on the beach. For the past two weeks, she, a onetime fearless (and expert) swimmer, had not ventured into the water until she had made sure that several capable-looking swimmers stood on the shore. Yet now, miraculously transformed, restored, she said as casually as she could, "I don't see why not," and got to her feet. Taking care not to look at his shining astonished face, she took his hand, and pulled him to his feet; together they jumped down, and walked, hand in hand, into the glassy morning sea.

When at last they came out, pearly, dripping, they began to walk along the beach in wordless content, the little cliff to their right, the sea to their left, the climbing sun drying them off, tightening their faces, encaking their limbs with salt. "Look Davy," she said when they had not gone very far, pointing out the shallow trench at the base of the cliff, a furrow filled with a glittering harvest reaped by the sea. Going closer they saw there were shells, whorled and fanning, blunted or scissor-sharp, in orange, purple, gold and blue, and stones, plump and round as moons, lucid ovals, narrow as seeds, all scrubbed to cream or white and turned to perfection on the lathe of the sea, and last, bits of glass, blunted, undangerous, crude jewels of brilliant amber and green. But perhaps the most remarkable thing was the absolute immaculateness of these heaped treasures, the absence of buzzing sand flies and swarming gnats; clearly, whatever living had once dwelt in the shells, had either been knocked out by the sea, or picked out by the dawnlight scavengers, the gulls and pipers now strangely missing from the beach.

Cynthia was suddenly inspired. "I'll go back and get the pails, then we can each fill one with things we like best," she said, and Davy dropped to his knees and started stuffing his fists. She returned with the pails and they began, half-crouching, half-stooping, poking rifling fingers through the shining heaps, each hunting out their fancy's choice. Cynthia only looked for the smallest whitest stones, the ones that looked like seeds, and scallop shells in strange autumnal colors—grapey mauve, the gold of Indian maize, the rusted red of fallen leaves; Davy seized on any scrap of shell or stone or glass tinted with purple, his favorite color as of midwinter. As they slowly labored down the sand, the sun moved higher, the beach began to fill. Finally feeling the pull of muscles slackened by illness, long unused, Cynthia sat down on the wet sand, feet stretched out in front of her. Happily wiggling her sandy toes, she idly watched Davy, moving up the beach away from her, watching the vertebrae of his spine, as delicately articulate as the locked cogs in a fine timepiece, flex and arch under the brown skin. She found the sight so pleasing, so rewarding, it took her the longest time to mark the difference, to realize it was the first time in months she had contemplated him without experiencing that painful contraction and trip-up of the heart—to realize, more simply, that it was the first time in months that she was happy and at peace.

In the late spring she had been stricken by hepatitis, which had kept her bedridden for weeks, and left her weak, yellowed, and so unhinged a cross or ill-chosen word was enough to send her off into tears. Though the doctor repeatedly assured her and Clifford that this was often an aftermath of the disease, that she would be her old self in no time at all, this just didn't prove to be so. She quickly regained some weight and normal color, but some deep disorder that couldn't conceivably be pinned on the disease remained. She was simply another person. She had changed, during those weeks in bed, from a rational, active, sociable human being, into a creature of depressions and sudden fears, fears which ultimately came to focus on what she now saw as the world's certain doom.

For Clifford (and herself) she had an explanation: as a convalescent, she had read and read, not her usual books, but newspapers, magazines; at the end of a day her bed had always been adrift on a paper sea. She was simply someone who'd never before had the time (she insisted) to keep up, to keep informed, become someone too well informed all at once. For it seemed to her that when you put it all together, all those pieces gleaned here and there, the conclusive whole you found yourself staring at was the terrible one she saw. She was simply being realistic, she said to poor Clifford (who had to comfort her when she was awakened by her dreams of toppling landscapes, flickery fires), and even then, did not go to extremes. *She* didn't beg him to pull up stakes and run, run to a "safer" part of the world, she did not ask him to build a shelter in their own backyard. "I'd feel better if you did," he finally came back one day, his exasperated face a statement that he'd had enough. "For God's sake, don't you see that you can't go on, can't live like this. Oh, I see what you're going to say, and yes, it *might* happen some day. But the odds are against it. If everyone took your line the whole world would fall apart. You've got to get hold of yourself. Be brave and sensible like you were." She had shakily sighed: "I can't." And he'd snapped: "You can. And must."

Since they could not deal with it on this level, and since he was more distressed than he wished her to know, he harked back to the recent illness: she still wasn't fully recovered, that was all— the summer, their two months on the island, would do the trick. To her great irritation he talked of sun, sea, salt air, the best "medicines" of all, and without consulting her, bribed Lucy, their winter maid (who always went home summers), to come to the island for a month. Of course it had all been a horrible failure. Even the island, once beloved, was changed for her too, the very sun, sea, salt air become irritants instead of tonics. But the really terrible thing were those endless hours at her disposal, hours spent with Davy, hours in which she gave all away. Before they had arrived on the island, he had treated her with almost heartbreaking patience and trust: she had been sick, she was strange, but that was all right, she'd soon be back. But once on the island, the shortest time in her company was enough to inform him things were grave, worse than he'd dreamed, that she was stranger than he'd thought; too strange, for she now hated this place, this island he loved, his Ariel, his all, and that being so, she must be watched and treated with cunning—an enemy.

Now, magically, it was all over and done. She, Davy, the island, the world, were reunited, at peace, at one. And with the uncanny perception of children, having known her restored from their first moments on the beach that morning, Davy now came up and squatted beside her, proudly displaying the purple treasures in his pail. When he had inspected the contents of hers, they carried the full pails back to the piles of paraphernalia she'd left on the top of the cliff, and joined the latecomers now gathered at the water's edge. Or rather Davy did. For a while she hung back by the little cliff, shyly regarding the clumps of chattering women standing in back of the splashing children, those Watchers, those (as she had maliciously called them) Niobes of the Sea. Afflicted as she'd been by strange misanthropy, she had avoided them and of course had made them hostile. And now as she finally stepped forward, timorous, hoping to undo wrong, she read in their cold eyes the great damage done. But, miraculous as the day itself, it was not irrevocable; ignored or snubbed by most, she was instantly accepted and taken up by one, the mother of a boy named Robbie, a five-year-old redhead who lived on their street.

Robbie and Davy played in the shallows, she and Robbie's mother sat on the damp sand, smoking, talking with ease. Then suddenly, the powerful old longing—the one she had not felt all that summer—to throw herself, abandoned, into the sea, came over her. Leaving a totally oblivious Davy under Robbie's mother's eye, she ran, released, into the flat shining ocean, breaking surface in a shower of watery sparks, then slowly and steadily heading out to sea, going so far that someone finally shouted from shore. Coming to a stop, she did a furling turn, and after impudently signalling all was well, flipped over and floated on her back, her closed face turned up to the sun, her mind empty, free of the frightening thoughts that had kept her shorebound for two weeks. She saw no murky looming shapes, obscenely cruising through the greengold deeps into which her limbs dangled pallid, inviting; she felt no swirling secret tides, coming, hidden beneath the water's placid surface, to rip her, helpless, beyond the reach of any human aid. No, nothing, nothing crossed her mind as she floated, a thing made of air, and dreamily listened to the carrying voices from shore, except the one thought: What a perfect day.

And it was.

She and Davy returned to the cottage only long enough to eat the sandwiches that Lucy had fixed for them. Though she announced he did not have to take his usual nap in his shade-drawn room, once they were back down on the deserted beach, it was he who asked her to raise the despised umbrella (he had always refused to join her under it), and crawling under its spokey circle of shade, took up another one of her detested objects—one of the huge striped towels she always sat on—and rolling himself up in it, Indian fashion, lay down and dozed for an hour.

When he opened his eyes, Robbie and his mother were coming down the dune. The afternoon passed, perfect as the morning, so quickly that it was long past four when she at last began to wonder at the time. She and Davy had temporarily deserted the large sprawling group that had slowly assembled on the upper sand, and were building a sand castle by the water's edge. She had always been able to tell the time, with remarkable accuracy, from shadows cast by the sun, but now, sitting back on her heels in front of their sugary towers and pinnacles, she was astonished to see that there no longer *were* any sharply defined shadows cast by the sun. Getting to her feet, she squinted seaward, until, like someone pricklingly aware of a malevolent gaze directed at their back, she turned, and saw that in the other half of the sky giant clumps of blueblack clouds had piled into bulby heaps so high, so full of shifting movements, they seemed about to topple on over into the vapid grayness still left overhead. Going strangely cold, she peered over the little cliff, to find that this stretch of sand level with her eyes was deserted, but for a few stragglers gathering up belongings and preparing to scuttle home. From the heart of all that darkness (which would be suspended directly above mainland fields, far across water, miles away) came the mutter and spit of thunder, while here, like an echo, the dune grass shuddered then swooped under a spasm of answering wind. Shivering by now, she still turned back and managed to say, quite matter of fact: "Davy darling, it's going to rain. We'd better start for home." Without so much as a glance at the sky, he jumped up, stamped their lacy towers flat, and scampered happily up the little cliff.

The clothesline back of the cottage was empty, its flapping burden already taken in by Lucy. As they came up the walk, Coddle, their poodle (who, fastidious as Cynthia, detested sand), jumped off a canvas deck couch and came to meet them, barking at Davy, her one and true love. "Don't forget to wash off the sand at the back faucet," she called, but hating pure cold water, he pretended not to hear and, scooping up Coddle, rushed inside to use the bathroom sink. Sighing, not looking up at the purple-blackness now stretching far out to sea, she vigorously shook sand out of all the things she carried, then went inside herself. Because she was shivering violently now, she went into her bedroom and put on a robe; there, looking out the window over her bed, she studied the direction of the wind, then methodically went about the cottage, closing all the windows on the side that would be exposed. As she hurried back toward the little storeroom that housed bicycles, luggage, a tiny washing machine, she glimpsed Lucy sitting hunched over on her sagging cot, squinting down through the fast-failing light at a pair of undershorts she was darning. Caught short by guilt (poor Lucy hated the island, and remained only because of a deep devotion to herself) she paused, wondering why Lucy ignored the comfortable armchair and floorlamp across the room. "You'd better shut that window over your bed," she said gently, "It's going to rain in on that side, I think," only to be taken aback by the blunted look of fear on the dark face that now turned her way. Disturbed, unreasonably annoyed (why?), she said hastily, "It's just going to be a little thundershower," and rushed into the storeroom, bumping her shins on an old camp trunk.

The windows all closed, she went into the kitchen to make some tea. Standing on a chair pulled up to the sink, Davy was carefully washing the sand off his precious purple bits and pieces, and setting them on a dishtowel to dry. She put on the kettle, set things out; the water hummed, preparing to sing, the shells in the sink clicked like dice. When the tea was ready, they sat down, side by side, at the little kitchen table, and drank it, fiercely hot and milky-sweet, from thick pottery mugs, and ate ginger snaps from the box. From the little table they had a view of the living room, where, through the windows flanking the fireplace, they could see the wind rush wildly up the walk, angrily blowing up sand in floury clouds, whipping bordering grasses and rushes flat, making bushes dip and nod in a palsied dance. They also heard it making the eeriest whistling in their chimney, and despite the thick terrycloth robe she had buttoned over her bathing suit, Cynthia began to shiver again. "I'll go and close the rest of the windows—I think the wind has changed—and I'll bring you something warm to put on." She pushed back her chair, then saw Davy's face, gone milky as his tea, saw the suspended panic blackening his eyes.

Pulling back her chair, she called out, loud as she could above the wind, asking Lucy to close the rest of the windows, please. For a moment there was only the keening of the wind. Then at last there was the gritty tread of Lucy's city shoes on sandy floors, the tug and slam of warped window-frames. Remembering that mute mask of fear, she was about to ask Lucy to come in and join them, but another glance at Davy made her reject this—Lucy's fear would only increase his—for the louder the wind grew, the darker it became, the quieter, paler he got. And yet, reluctantly, she understood: though he had gone through two other thunderstorms since their arrival on the island without much fuss (he had merely asked her to sit on his bed when the thunder and lightning were at their height), there was something different gathering itself up here. She could not say just what it was, but she felt it, and against her will felt herself slowly filling with an unreasonable dread.

"Here. You put this on," she said, preparing to give him the warm robe she wore.

"*I'm* not cold," he came back with such fury, she retied the robe and let it go. For a long moment he stared fixedly ahead, through the living room windows, at the strip of walk and their neighbor's roof, both turning white as chalk in the purple light. "Why's it getting so dark?"

"Because it's going to rain," she said inanely, adding: "We're just going to have a little summer shower, that's all." Ashamed of this glaring falsehood, she reached out and tousled his hair, her discomfort turning to sheer dismay when he passively submitted to the sort of caress he despised.

Within seconds it had grown dark as twilight. Knowing the poodle was somewhere in the house, Cynthia fleetingly wondered where she was hiding—in a closet? under Davy's bed? From the back of the cottage came the singing of bedsprings as Lucy reseated herself on her cot; it was perfectly audible for it was suddenly, ominously still, the worrying wind had stopped. I suppose, thought Cynthia, in her frightened heart attempting to be wry, this is the famous lull before the storm. "Lucy? . . ." she began, having suddenly decided she could not possibly let her be alone, but her invitation was lost in a detonating crack of thunder, which was immediately followed by a raw pink lightning flare.

With a small convulsive movement, Davy clapped his hands to his ears and screwed his eyes tightly shut. "Davy. Davy darling," she said, but this time was drowned out by the sound of the rain, which, slanting at the sharpest of angles, was making a small thunder all its own on the roof over their heads. With a sudden decisive gesture, she set down her mug, and standing up, lifted him, unresisting, face streaming with tears, into her arms. Though his bones were covered with the sparest layer of flesh and fledgling muscle, he was tall for his age, and seemed inordinately heavy. Still she managed to carry him, with peculiar ease and grace, to a large armchair in the living room, where, seating herself amid the smells of mildewed wicker and cretonne, she held him cradled in her lap, the attitude of their limbs—the long knobbly legs, the delicate bony feet splayed out over her terrycloth drapery—creating a bizarre and moving tableau, a picture filled with strange symbols and portents, like some Renaissance Madonna and Child.

A primitive comfort settled in. The rain thrummed steadily on the roof, there was no thunder or lightning. His eyes, dry once again, opened, his thumb stole, regressive, into his mouth. Then suddenly without warning it was darker, dark as night, the pitch of the wind increased. Still filled with the placid air of sunny early afternoon, the little cottage ticked and cricked; with inner and outer pressures at such odds, it literally bulged, and Cynthia thought she could actually make out the whiny pull of nails, the groaning and straining of piney boards. Beyond the streaming windows there was a tinny clapping roar and a cylindrical gray blur, as someone's garbage can was sent spinning down the path. Numb with unreasoning terror, she tightened her arms about Davy, who wept into the lapels of her robe without any movement or sound. As she sat desperately trying to maintain an outer calm, she was assailed by fantastic visions in which roofs, chimneys, telephone poles, and then at last the cottage itself, were uprooted by that giant wind and sent flying and whirling into upper space, to be finally set down, rocking gently, like the Ark, upon the sea. It's just a freak storm, she told herself; if it were anything more serious the Coast Guard would have warned us hours ago. But as the packets and gobbets of thunder ceaselessly exploded over their heads (like huge inflated paper bags, gleefully punched by giant hands), and the afternoon was lit again and again by unearthly violet flares, her terror grew and grew, the largest part of her fear being that Davy might discover just how deeply frightened she was.

They could no longer see outside. In fact, opaque with moving water, sheetily coated, the window panes gave the impression that the whole little cottage was already submerged, sunk deep underwater. Slowly, hypnotically, she turned her head and looked at the doorway, where Lucy, looming like some enigmatic Gauguin figure, stood hesitant, her frightened eyes flashing in the gloom. "Hello, Lucy. Do come in," she said, mild and arch as a hostess at tea. Moving crabwise, Lucy approached the couch, and with head bowed, hands loosely clasped, seated herself like someone taking a pew in church. Then too came Coddle, reduced to feline behavior by fear: with curly pink tongue lolling crazily, belly almost touching the floor, she crawled under their fascinated gaze to the fireplace, where she feebly began scratching on the firescreen, pitifully trying to gain access to the ashy cave within. For a moment they all hovered on the brink of laughter, cruel, but promising relief. "Here, Coddle. Here, girl," called Cynthia, and, blindly turning, the poodle made for the chair where she sat holding Davy on her lap. Ignoring her dangling, comforting fingers, the dog frantically tried to burrow its way into the four-inch space between the chair's sagging bottom and the floor. As it finally settled down, quivering, nose wedged into this space, Davy, peering over her shoulder, began to laugh. But then a fresh relay of thunder broke out overhead, and lightning, clear as a zigzag on a graph, forked into the bushes just across the walk.

It was just too close, too much. Drawing back, Davy began to pummel her chest with puny fists, shrieking, "You make it stop. Right now. You *hear?*" In her distress, Cynthia wildly threw a look of appeal across the room, but Lucy sat on, chin tucked down into her ample breast, looking like some large huddled seabird, resignedly taking the beating of rain and wind. "It's just a summer storm, a little thundershower," she desperately crooned, knowing even as she spoke that it was unlike any summer storm she had ever known. Over and over she endured his appeal, his terrible belief in her omnipotence, her eyes filling with tears, her heart with rage at her helplessness. "Make it stop. You make it stop. Right now. You hear. You *hear?*"

She couldn't. But of course it did. At first the wind slackened, lost its angled force. Then the impenetrable wash on the window panes became runnels and streams; within seconds they could see out again, could see the leveled grasses springing upright, the bushes cease their antic dance. As the thunder moved rumbling out to sea, the light changed with dazzling rapidity from violet to gray, to white, to gold. For as the rain played a splattering coda on the roof, the sun broke through once again, restoring the room and the day to the sane light-and-shade of a summer's late afternoon.

"There, you see. It's all over," she said foolishly, superfluously. Already off her lap, he stood, quivering with fury, in the middle of the sunny room. Small, bellicose, he looked from one to the other woman, enraged at them, himself, and the storm which had reduced him to such a state of shame.

"Why did it do that?" he demanded. "Why?"

Sighing, Cynthia prepared to say what she could about hot-and-cold currents of air, but before she could speak, Lucy rose from the couch, smoothing out the wrinkles in her skirt. "Because the farmers needs the rain," she said with slow dignity, not looking at Cynthia. "They needs the rain for things they grow."

"Things. What things?"

"Oh. Lettuce. Carrots. Beans. And corn. Kinds of things you like and needs to eat."

"There aren't any farmers here," he cried. "They don't grow things like that on this island. So why do we need it here?" With a contemptuous turn of his back he dismissed Lucy, wheeling on Cynthia: "You tell me why."

Discreetly coughing into the silence, Lucy moved from the room.

"Will it do that again?" Becoming impatient, enraged, he now switched his focus to this: "I don't want it to do that ever again."

All textbook explanations done in, she speechlessly stared at him.

"Will it do that again?" he shouted.

"Yes," she said at last. "Yes, it will. But it will probably never be as bad as that."

Betrayed, the fists dropped from his hips. "But . . . I don't like it."

"I know," she said. "But when it does happen again, you'll be brave. You must. You will."

For a long moment he stood there, hating her, hating the unacceptable import of her news. Beyond the water-dotted windows there was the chrome flash of tricycle fenders struck by sun. Without moving his head he looked out, taking in tricycle and rider. Then his glance came, merciless, back to her. "Will you?" he said softly, with a flare of his small nostrils handing it over, passing it on, repeating the challenge: "Will *you?*" Then he slammed out the door, crying loudly as he went, "Hey, Robbie . . . wait for *me!*"

Why Do You Look
So Beautiful?

"Speak to you Tuesday?" she called for the second time, but the revving taxi motor drowned her out. Giving up, she returned the final wave he gave her from the rear window of the cab, her hand furtively dropping to slip the bolt on the screen-door latch as the taxi lurched away. Then, remaining there (it was important she give the impression of not being in any kind of rush), she impatiently watched it cruise down the street—barefoot, tan, too tan for a blond, wearing a faded blue Indian cotton caftan. Setting sun made burning-glasses of all the windows in the house across the dirt road; beyond, the sea lay quiet, already a darkening evening blue. The moment the taxi turned out of the street she was off, lightly taking the stairs two-at-a-time and going into the tiny bathroom at the top of the stairs, walled with sheets of cheap plastic printed and pressed to look like tiles. Breathless from her sprint, she fitted a worn old rubber stopper in the tub drain, threw on both taps, took a fat bottle of amber bath-crystals off a shelf, unscrewed the top, lavishly poured; a tingling astringent smell, like uncorked Rhine wine, filled the little room. The water made a tinny roaring in the old-fashioned tub, but the door was still open, and she finally heard the call—imperious, angry at having to try again: ". . . *Mom*mee!"

Instantly angry herself, she stepped into the hall and turned toward a room at the hall's end, orange with setting-sunlight. "Diana. I thought you were asleep."

"Did Daddy go?"

"Just left." Then, again, lamely: "I thought you were asleep."

"How long's his plane take?"

"Half an hour. He'll be in the city by eight-thirty." Reminded by this talk of time, she unstrapped the expensive imported watch on her wrist, and hurried back into the bathroom to put it on the shelf above the sink. Then, picking up speed, making up for lost time, she turned off the water, yanked off the caftan, and tucked her blond hair into a bubble-printed plastic shower cap. She then opened the medicine cabinet and took down a jar, and swiftly began smearing thick white cream on her freshly sunburned face.

". . . Mommy?"

She frowned at the open door but her hands kept going. "Diana. Go to sleep. I'm not fooling."

A silence considered then dismissed this for what it was worth. "Why do you have to go out tonight?"

Slowing, the fingers made a pearly whorl of cream along the jawbone. "I don't *have* to. Mommy and Daddy were in all weekend. We had all those people here last night—Mommy just needs to get out of the house for a bit."

"To a movie?"

"Yes. A movie."

"Who's coming to stay with me?"

"Sally Sinclair." Finished, she pulled a Kleenex from a wall-dispenser and wiped her hands.

"But I don't *know* Sally Sinclair."

"You know her sister, Julia Sinclair. She's just as nice as Julia. Nicer, in fact. Now go to *sleep*."

"How do you know she is. Nicer."

She stepped, naked, into the hall, right in front of a window overlooking the road. "Diana. I'm going to shut the bathroom door and take my bath now. You did everything you like today.

The night light's on in your room. Now *you* do something nice and go to sleep . . . you hear?"

When this was met with a silence, a possibly conceding silence, she slipped back into the bathroom and closed the door. Ten minutes later she reopened it, and rushed down the hall to a large, ugly bedroom with ivy-printed wallpaper, where she snapped on a glaring overhead light; during the ten minutes torchy sunset had given way to dusk. For one second she stood poised on the threshold, calculating ways to save steps, one hand holding the billowing French-hotel terrycloth robe modestly closed, the other holding the balled-up caftan. Then she crossed the room, tossed the caftan on the big double bed, and, going to a chipped green bureau, began rapidly opening and shutting drawers. When she had collected a neat pile of clothes, she set them on a chair and flew around the room, first pulling down all four rain-stained window-shades, then throwing off the robe and starting to dress—a hasty brown-and-flesh-colored flawless shape in the harsh overhead light.

Minutes later, fully dressed in a lemon-colored shirt, white duck slacks, sandals, she went to a small mahogany table and snapped on the two pimply milk-glass lamps flanking an oval mirror. Pulling a kidney-shaped stool out from under the table, she sat down, and after taking things from a large, canvas shoulder-bag, set to work on her face. Finishing all but her lips, which she momentarily left pale and strangely numb-looking, she took a hairbrush from the purse and vigorously began sweeping it around her head, making the thick—slightly too thick—long yellow hair crack and snap and, finally, shine. She was following the progress of this in the mirror, when the mercurized glass suddenly reflected another face just over her left shoulder, a face considerably smaller than her own and bearing no resemblance to it whatsoever. More weary than angry, she finished drawing the brush down a long strand of hair before she turned. "Now *listen*, Diana dear . . ."

Diana stood very still in her thin pink cotton nightdress, staring.

"What on earth's gotten into you?"

A blink. "Why do you look so beautiful?"

"Do I?" The hairbrush was carefully set down on the tabletop.

"You do. Very."

"Diana, sweetie. Come here, love."

Diana reluctantly went and let herself be embraced, coolly stepping free of the encircling brown arms as soon as possible, but staying close enough to watch the goings-on in the mirror, lightly leaning against the dressing table. With critically narrowed eyes she watched the nimble brown fingers unscrew the top on a pot of glossy rusty-rose pomade, watched them work a brush into the color, then bring the delicately loaded brush to the pale mouth, then pause. "Darling," said the mirror-mouth. "*Please* go to bed. I don't want things to get awful, don't want to have to threaten you."

The unmistakable change in tone—the voice was now begging something, but not that she go to bed—kept Diana deaf. Still lolling against the table, she half-turned and carefully took in the room's disarray—the wild jumble of the day's discarded clothes on the bed, the drawers standing open in the chest; joggled by her twisting movement, the rickety table tilted, the elbow braced for support on its surface dislodged and the brush missed its mark, leaving a shining snail-trail of rusty rose on the curve of the smooth chin. Startled by the choked exclamation, Diana turned and watched the chin get scrubbed with a Kleenex. Then, as chin and lips got recoated in a cloud of toast-colored powder, she bent her head and thoughtfully picked at the frayed pink ribbon threaded through the *broderie anglaise* trimming on the yoke of her nightgown. "You know," she said weighingly, "I don't really even like *Julia* Sinclair." When there was no response to this—the brush was deftly bringing the pale mouth to brilliant life—she picked a purse-sized phial of perfume up off the table, and, unscrewing the cap absently inhaled. "I said," she doggedly repeated, "that I don't really even like *Julia* Sinclair, so why would I like her sister."

"I happen to know that you do like her, so don't lie," came the acidly incisive reply. Alerted to danger, Diana watched the nimble fingers knot a batik scarf into the open neck of the shirt with dispatch: the tone of voice and rapid gestures signaled the arrival of a decision, of steps, postponed, about to be taken. "From what I hear, Sally's even nicer than Julia. As I told you before."

"But I don't *know* her," wailed Diana, and petulantly slammed down the little phial of perfume, which immediately keeled over on its tiny base and emptied itself on the dressing table top.

The open-fingered hand, a layer of batiste notwithstanding, made a report like a cap pistol. A second of hovering silence. Then: "I *told* you to go to bed. I told you fifty million times!"

Diana clapped hands over her face; an eery trickle of sound leaked out through the laced fingers.

"My God," she whispered. Then in a very loud and rational voice: "Diana. Diana. I'm sorry—I didn't mean to hurt you or frighten you. The only reason I slapped you was because you wouldn't listen. You understand? I asked and asked you to go to sleep, but you just wouldn't *lis*ten to me. And now on top of everything, you've gone and ruined Mrs. Morrison's lovely table. Just look." Belying her words, growing uncontrollably righteous in her wrath, she agitatedly wadded some Kleenex into a ball, swabbing and mopping, bringing away a bunched tissue dark with varnish—and leaving a cloudy white blotch on the tabletop. "Just look at what you've done!"

The terrible high thin sound stopped. Diana took her hands from her face and looked, terrified, from the reeky wad of Kleenex being waved beneath her nose, to her mother's face. Then ran squealing from the room. Just as the front doorchime gave an insanely sprightly peal from downstairs.

Muttering, she went into the hall, first distractedly peering at the room down the far end, then turning to the nearer stairway and clacketing down steps splatter-painted with red and blue enamel in her loose sandals. Beyond the locked screen door, under a porch lamp furry with moths, a homely, dark-haired girl in her early teens stood waiting, a pile of magazines under one sweatered arm. "Good evening, Sally . . . won't you come in," she said in a voice as artificially musical and merry as the doorchime, and, opening the door, led the way into the dark living room. The sound of weeping—wild, uncontrolled—poured down the stairwell. She briskly stepped to an end table and switched on a lamp shaped like a Spanish galleon, then turned and said cheerily: "We've just been having a bit of a fuss. Diana's always edgy Sunday nights. When her father goes back to town for the week, that is. If you come on upstairs and let me introduce you, she'll stop. The sight of a stranger will shame her into snapping right out of it."

But the girl remained in the middle of the hall, face tilted toward the stairs, unwilling to move.

"Goodness, Sally," she said, deliberately cruel. "I'm sure you've had to cope with weepy little girls lots of times."

Sally silently followed her up the stairs.

On the far wall of Diana's bedroom were two brass sconces; replacing the parchment shade and bulb of the fixture on the right, was a night-light shaped like a lamb. The room was a sickly ghostly blue, but Diana was plainly visible, lying face-down on the bed, her nightgown twisted above the strangely vulnerable-looking hollows at the backs of her knees. Leaving Sally Sinclair standing woodenly on the threshold, she went and sat down on the bed. The soft-springed mattress sloped, gently rolling the quivering body against her. "Diana," she said above the sobbing. "Diana. Stop that. At once. And sit up. Sally Sinclair is here."

With a convulsive heave, Diana twisted herself away from any contact with the duck-covered hips; lifting high in the air for impetus, the skinny legs began to violently, rhythmically kick.

"Diana. You *stop* that!" she cried harshly, but put a gentle hand on the small back all the same. With a convulsive rearing movement, the back immediately threw the hand off. "Diana," she said unsteadily. "I'm sorry I hit you before, but you wouldn't listen to me. Just like now. Now you stop that silly crying this minute—you hear?"

". . . *orrible*," came from the tangle of light brown hair on the pillow.

Shakily sighing, she stood up. "Okay, Diana. I'm going. You can either stop that foolishness and sit up and kiss me good-by, or you can cry yourself to sleep." When the weeping merely increased in volume, she motioned to Sally Sinclair to follow her down the hall to her own larger room. There, as the girl stood blinking at the room's disorder, she picked up the canvas shoulder-bag and began jamming it with things from the dressing table. "She's done this before, Sally," she said, businesslike. "It's all very calculated, all for effect. The minute I leave she'll stop. She's really a terribly *good* little girl, basically—a perfect angel. Sunday nights are just very hard for her, as I said before." A forced laugh. "Like all little girls her age, she's absolutely *mad* for her father."

Stony, not buying any of this, Sally Sinclair watched her check the contents of the shoulder-bag, and finally burst out: "How old *is* Diana, Mrs. Miller?"

"Seven. Just. I thought I'd told you over the phone. Anyway, I assure you," she began, giving the girl a wide berth as she moved toward the door, "that everything will be all right as soon as I go. I'll call from the movies to check. I'm only going because my staying would encourage her, would only make things worse."

". . . Mrs. Miller."

She grudgingly paused in the doorway. "Yes?"

But suddenly pale, the overhead light harshly striking her tense face, the girl couldn't speak.

"Look," she said wearily. "I'll pay you extra. Double what you usually make per hour. When I've gone ask her if she wants an ice cream soda. That never fails. Then maybe after that you can read to her. No matter what you do she'll be fast asleep in half an hour from now. I can swear to it. And when she *is* asleep there's a marvelous movie on TV. Carole Lombard and Cary Grant— you'll *love* Carole Lombard."

"Thank you," said the dry voice, following her out to the stairs, "but I've brought my own magazines."

The sound of weeping followed her out of the house and across the lawn, only growing fainter when she got into the small car parked halfway down the gravel driveway. She thrust one of a bunch of jingling keys into the ignition, but then, instead of turning it, left the whole bunch dangling and slowly wiped her slippery palms against each other. Above the driveway, from the bluish rear window, the sound of exhausted sobbing billowed out like limp net curtains. Flat with fright, Sally Sinclair's voice said something incoherent about ice cream. Gripping the steering wheel with both hands, she laid her right cheek on the back of her right hand and closed her eyes. Behind her the night sea rustled, a smell of baked-dry sand and clam shells drifted across the quiet road.

Finally raising her head, she pulled the key out of the ignition like someone withdrawing a knife, loudly slamming the car door, then the front screen door behind her. In the dim hall, in an alcove formed by stairs and wall, stood a cheap red lacquer table holding a telephone and lamp shaped like a Mandarin of the Ch'ing Dynasty. Snapping on the lamp, she stood blinking dazedly down into sixty-watt glare, then furiously threw back her head. "Diana!" she shouted up the megaphone of the stairwell. "I'm back, Diana. I'm not going to the movies. I'm coming upstairs in five minutes, and you'd better stop that crying before I do."

Not waiting to hear any upstairs reaction to this announcement, she picked up the receiver and jerkily dialed. Then, burying the earpiece under a spill of blond hair, she picked up the base of the phone with her free hand, and made for a closet just to the right of the front door. The extra-long cord let her stand in stale rubbery-smelling dark, but the closet door wouldn't close, and the sound of weeping still came through the crack.

She shut her eyes and jammed the receiver hard against her ear. "Listen, it's me," she said suddenly, her lips brushing the sticky perforated black mouthpiece. "I can't come. I can't explain now, but please oh please say you understand . . ." Straining to hear, she audibly swallowed, then whispered, "Oh God, yes. You know it. But I just *can't*, don't you see, absolutely can't. I mean, you're the one who's always saying we have to . . ." A sharp slamming sound from the phone at her ear cut her short. Frozen, she stood listening to the dial tone, then took the receiver out from under her hair, blinked at it with filling eyes and soundlessly replaced it in the cradle of the base she held in her other hand. Emerging from the closet like a swimmer from the deeps, her breathing as labored as a swimmer's, she set the phone back on the table and started trudging up the stairs—the weeping slowing, subsiding, and completely stopping by the time she reached the top step.

In the Woods
of Truro

Standing thigh deep, dotted here and there like conversational groups in some Eighteenth Century print of the Piazza San Marco, the analysts took an afternoon dip. It could not really be called a swim, since only upon squatting, gingerly lowering themselves into the bland and lukewarm pond, could they get wet all over, find water enough to paddle away. About them the pond stretched glinty, choppy from the faint west wind, while sunlight, strangely thin, poured down from a cloudless sky.

Outside of several teenage girls tending children, there were no women in the water. They, the women, the wives, sat in clumps of twos and threes like their husbands, disposed along the landspit dividing this pond from another, a strip mere yards wide, densely overrun with weeds and scrub, narrowly banded by sand. It was here that Laura Pepper sat with two other analysts' wives—her hostess for the afternoon, a flatchested young woman named Virginia Archman, and her hostess's neighbor-in-the-woods, a fattish homely creature named Martha Gunzendorfer. They sat in a sandpocket so shallow there was barely room for their spreadout towels; close, too close to their backs, shiny trifoliate leaves spiked from the undergrowth, brothy water lapped their toes. Utterly wretched, Laura Pepper could not sit still. Though her back was to the sun, her expression was that of someone trying to make out

objects in dazzling light. Prettyish, twenty-nine, she looked neither pretty nor quite that young; unhappiness, self-doubt, drew
some obscure veil over her whole person. Now, after blotting her
legs with a sandy towel—she had just finished wading to the tops
of her thighs—she stared with exasperation at her companions,
wondering just how much longer they were going to have to sit
there. They had already been at the pond two hours. Rooted to
their towels, the other two had steadily ignored the water. Blind
to her discomfort, but not really rude (bored, lying, Laura had declared herself a hopelessly incompetent cook), they now sat exchanging recipes for Beef Stroganoff; murmuring things like "sour
cream" and "tomato paste" and "never boil," they kept their eyes
turned on the shallows, where two Mother's Helpers pulled their
children about on miniature plastic-foam surfboards, inflated plastic rings.

The three husbands, theirs and Laura's, stood twenty yards
offshore, the tepid water not quite reaching their private parts,
their three heads nodding, close. Stocky, fat and thin in turn, they
were all strikingly young—that is, if one considered their profession. Of the three, Ellis Pepper looked youngest, in fact, necky,
ribby, strung out, he looked like a senior in college. He was thirty-
seven and had been a practicing psychoanalyst for six years. He
made forty thousand dollars a year without taxes. Standing there
in faded tan trunks, bobbing his sandy head and absent-mindedly
tapping cigarette ash into the water, he had a boyish look of vul-
nerability—a deception: new patients, misled by this look, foresee-
ing a possibly endless postponement of grave matters at hand,
soon found themselves wondering how they could have been so
mistaken; Laura, misled for two out of seven years (one of
courtship, one of marriage), now sat taking in this look with narrowed eyes, no longer wondering anything.

"Why, you're all *goose*bumps," cried Virginia Archman,
Laura's hostess, making Laura jump and look away from Ellis in
guilty confusion. "Here. Put this on," she added and, before

Laura could stop her, took a droopy blue terrycloth cape from her shoulders and draped it about Laura.

Hating the clammy feel of it, Laura murmured thanks and let it be. The two women were now closely examining her. "There's a funny chill in the air," offered Laura, but Virginia Archman doggedly went on staring out from under shaggy blond bangs. "Perhaps we ought to go," she said at last.

Laura, having waited two hours for this, said nothing.

Martha Gunzendorfer said: "Let us wait another ten minutes. It is just twenty past four." Sun in her eyes, she beamed waggishly at Laura, crinkling up the flat planes of her sallow face, looking like an Eskimo squaw: "You are not an Outdoor Girl."

For the first time in hours—weeks really—Laura laughed.

"That's no crime, Martha," said Virginia Archman, throwing Laura a wildly nervous look.

"Nobody said it was," came back Martha Gunzendorfer, complacent as ever: "I was merely making an observation."

"Accurate, too," said Laura subsiding, and, to reassure her poor jumpy hostess, took one of the terrible mentholated cigarettes she was offering round again. To Laura's surprise Martha Gunzendorfer took one this time, and as Laura watched her, fat limbs splayed out on the sand, sending up jetty little smoke-signal puffs, she almost began laughing again. Utterly at home with herself and her ugliness, as larded with self-esteem as she was with flesh, Martha Gunzendorfer was what Laura had long ago learned constituted the Perfect Analyst's Wife: not necessarily psychoanalyzed themselves, in fact strangely in most cases not, they simply took over their husbands' professional personalities and vocabularies, their perpetual air of inviolability, inscrutability. Once intimidated—she was so far from being or ever becoming the Perfect Analyst's Wife herself—Laura was now only amused. But faintly. She had gotten Martha Gunzendorfer's number the moment she arrived at the pond. She was therefore neither surprised nor disturbed when, five minutes after being introduced, she was aggressively crossexamined: Had she no children? Ah . . .

And how long had she been married? Ah. And what on earth did she do with all her time? Ironically, the one to be upset had been Virginia Archman who, blushing, looking guilty and distracted, had only shown that she'd longed to ask the same questions but hadn't had the nerve, had shown that as the Perfect Analyst's Wife *she* still had a way to go.

Having decided between them that they had had enough, the three husbands (Karen Horney, William Alanson White, New York Psychoanalytic) now came sploshing out of the water, their hairy wet-stuck legs making a forest about the women on the sand. One glance up at Ellis and Laura looked quickly away (instead of How are you? that concerned frown meant How is it going?), looked at Irwin Gunzendorfer, the spokesman. Fat, swarthy, even possessing a faint Viennese lisp, he was uncomfortably close to the cruel cartoon caricature of his profession. Now, wetting his lips, he said like an oracle: "Listen, ladies. It is growing windy. We think that now it is time to go."

"Yes?" said his wife, doubtfully considering their blue-lipped daughters in the shallows.

"Yes," he repeated, incisive, her match: "Yes, it is time. We have all had enough."

So they went. Slowly, men first, women, girls and children following, they returned, a motley crew, back along the narrow finger of land. After crossing through ankle-deep water, oozy on the bottom and stuck with razory reeds, they at last climbed onto dry ground and started up the path which wound steeply up the wooded hill. It was a dirt path, painfully full of exposed roots, small sharp rocks, nettly weeds, but the Peppers, the visitors, were the only ones without slippers or sandals. Deep in discussion with Irwin Gunzendorfer at the head of the line, Ellis picked up his big bony feet like a prancing horse; straggling alone at the line's end, talking to no one, Laura was too absorbed to feel any pain. In here it was suddenly all heat, the true, close, burry heat of a mid-August afternoon; moments after they had started up the densely wooded trail a locust, hidden by leaves and grass, had begun to parchily sing. All summer long Laura had waited for such a moment; in the past weeks, shivering on beaches and in forests farther north, she had decided that this year the summer had simply passed her by. Now she dawdled along, gratefully breathing in the rich pitchy smell of the pines, the sweet threshy scent of berried shrubs and tangled grasses, too happy to notice the Archman children, jostling at her back. Exasperated, they finally pushed out and cut rudely in front of her, trailed by their apologetic Mother's Helper, a shy pink girl from Marymount in a too-tight Rudi Gernreich suit.

At a sudden forking in the path, the Gunzendorfers took their leave. "Walk over for a drink," called Virginia Archman, but Irwin Gunzendorfer called back, "The Goodchucks are coming, we cannot," and with a flat wave of the hand disappeared behind a clump of firs. Then they were on top of the hill, coming out into the sunny clearing where the Archmans' house stood, a strange house to encounter in the woods, for though it was made of harmonizing redwood, all weathered, huge expanses of wall had been gouged out to make "picture windows," and beneath propped-open sheets of glass, through screens, the startling plastic whiteness of modernized rooms shone out.

Twenty feet from the side entrance Virginia Archman began giving directions: the two children, Moira first, would use the outside shower, with Betty Anne Mayberry to help them; Laura would use the inside shower first—she looked so *horribly* uncomfortable—and the rest would take their turns one by one. Uncomplaining in their clammy trunks, the two men wandered off on the hilltop. Virginia Archman led Laura into the house, where the white vinyl floor was blindingly alight with trembly refractions off the pond. "I'm awfully embarrassed," she said, bright, unembarrassed, "but I hope you've brought some towels. We have *such* a laundry problem." Saying yes, she'd brought towels, Laura went and gathered up her things from the tiny spare room where she and Ellis had changed. As she was shutting the bathroom door, Virginia Archman hurried past, her thin arms piled with towels and clean clothes for her children. "Use anything you need," she called, "*you* know . . . deodorant, talcum. Just go easy on the hot water. We have only one tank, if you see what I mean."

Laura saw. Eyes closed, she stood under a trickle of warm water, listening to the shrill voices of the children arguing with Betty Anne Mayberry, the faint amiable voices of the men wandering about on the hill. Leaving the jumble of bottles and jars on the toilet tank untouched, she dressed slowly and carefully, knowing she was taking too long, but not caring. When she finally came out her hostess was sitting bolt upright on the bright green foam rubber couch, a pile of neatly folded clothes in her lap. Jumping up, she said, gay, forever bright, "Feel better? Good. You *look* better too!" Then spoiled the effect by slamming the door.

Laura went outside, after a moment's hesitation, approaching the two men sitting on the edge of the slope. "Isn't this pretty?" said Ellis as she came up, turning on her a smile so warm and openly welcoming she was thrown into confusion.

Nodding, she gingerly sat down on the ledge which was brown and slippery with pine needles: though Ellis had advised something simpler—"not so damned chic" to be exact—she had insisted on wearing her best pale pink linen shorts and its shirt with matching flowers. Settled, she looked down through the switchy pines at the pond: "It looks like Maine."

"No, it looks like Truro," corrected Harold Archman. Coquettishly tilting his pudgy pink face, he "twinkled" at her from behind his hornrims. "Why do people always do that? Why does some place always have to look like some other place? Why can't it just be itself?"

Though it was all rhetorical, Laura felt compelled to answer. "I don't know," she said, shrugging. But within an instant her manner became as consciously arch as his, and she added: "I spent most summers in Maine when I was a child. Perhaps my saying that means something."

And there. She had done it. Next to her Ellis jerkily swept away inflammable needles, grinding his cigarette into the damp earth beneath. If she could only realize, he had patiently explained a hundred times, how utterly pathetic her childish snipes at psychoanalysts and psychoanalysis made her look: while they did more or less make public her deep hostility to him and all he was, they publicized need far more—it was the caviling of the so-called nonbeliever who really believes. Wearily, knowing what she would find, Laura met the sharp bright eyes of her host, intently studying her across Ellis's blond-furzy knees, and yes, there it was: Ellis Pepper? Ellis *Pepper?* What's he doing with such a wife?

With shouts of release, the Archman children came out onto the hill. Moira Archman had been put into smocked yellow cotton, all starchy, all wrong for the woods; Alan Archman, his dark hair stuck in wet points from the shower, had put himself into a Beethoven sweatshirt and olive-green corduroy shorts. Was Betty Anne Mayberry using the outside shower? asked Harold Archman. No, said the boy, Mother had finished with the inside shower, Betty Anne was using that one. Putting a stubby hand on Ellis's shoulder, Harold Archman urged him to use the shower next. Gladly, not needing persuasion, Ellis rose and brushed pine needles off his flat rear end, going quickly toward the house for his clothes. Restless, the two children wandered down into the gently sloping grove, where, dwarfed by soaring boles, lit by chinky sunlight, they took on the pretty unreality of an illustration in a child's picture book. Left alone with the small piercey-eyed analyst, Laura sat calmly while he stared at her, unabashed, his short pointy nose almost quizzically sniffing. When he at last portentously cleared his throat, she was certain he was about to say something extremely personal, but he merely said mildly: "You know it's really too bad you didn't rent a house here, even if just for one month. It would have been more rewarding than traveling all over— especially since Ellis knows everyone here."

Smiling, Laura spoke before she thought, one of the gravest of all her many faults, in Ellis's eyes: "But that's just it. Ellis always makes a great point of spending the summers in places where he doesn't know a soul."

"That so," said her host, and nodding almost gratefully—as though she had given him food for thought—he turned to stare down at the pond.

Her face burning, Laura's hand closed on some prickly needles: Now—had she done it again? If so, why, when she'd only told the truth, the particular truth here being that never, before this summer, had she and Ellis gone to a place where psychoanalysts gathered, in fact Ellis had always gone out of his way to avoid places where they were to be found. Childless, they'd never had the problems of other couples their age; not having to search out places rife with potential playmates, daycamps, juvenile distractions, they had always been free to suit themselves. In five summers they had been to Europe twice, Mexico twice, California once. This summer, their sixth, had been horrible, had perfectly mirrored the state of their marriage: after endless quarrels followed by long fumy silences where nothing could be decided, they had aimlessly started north in the car, spending two weeks roaming about Canada, two and a half in Maine. Ten days ago, when they had awakened in Ogunquit to another freezing foggy morning, Ellis had suggested they try the Cape. Though she didn't see why they couldn't just go back to New York where they could at least be wretched in warmth and comfort, she wanted to avert another quarrel at any price, and agreed. It was only when they had settled in the gimcrack motel outside of Truro, and Ellis feverishly began looking up people in Wellfleet, South Wellfleet, Truro, North Truro, that she saw they had come there for a reason. Combing the woods, he succeeded in routing out just about every young or not-so-young analyst he had ever met during his internship, residency, and time at the Institute. Though it would have comforted her to even read a sinister meaning into this—perhaps he was just finally dragging her toward what he saw as her only salvation—she'd had to face the crueler truth: he simply couldn't bear traveling alone with her one more day, and this was the nearest relief. Since their arrival ten days ago, not a day had gone by that they hadn't seen someone Ellis had dug up. Of all these people she had only met two or three before. She had never met Harold and Virginia Archman before today. She hoped never to meet them again.

With a slammy rattle of the pull-chain, the rush of the outside shower stopped. Harold Archman stood up. He had strangely girlish legs under his stocky torso. Sunlight made opaque yellow discs of his glasses, but Laura felt him studying her again. "I'm going to collect my clothes. Can I get you anything from the house? Would you like a drink now, or would you rather wait?"

"Oh, I'll wait," she said too quickly, too emphatically, touchily blushing. As he trundled toward the house she unsteadily lit a cigarette, making a face as the shrieks and shouts of the Archman children floated out of the high-roofed grove. "Oh shut *up*," she muttered, blowing out, wreathing herself in smoke, the moment she had spoken seeing proof of what she'd come to: tense and irritable around children, she was no longer sure she liked them, was just no longer sure she oughtn't be enormously grateful she'd been unable to bear a child. But just her thinking that was an indication of the state she was in. It was all, she often thought, like Angel Street. For there were times when she almost believed all that Ellis now continually said—that she rejected her Role as a Woman on every level, that she rejected Reality as well, that her steadfast refusal to accept a simple Reality like her sterility and her subsequent refusal to do something Realistic about it, in short, to now adopt a child as he wished, proved how much she longed to remain her doting parents' only child forever, proved how disturbed and neurotic she was, how deeply she needed "treatment." Luckily she never believed any of this for long, and, snapping back, knew that all that was the matter with her was her lifelong passivity, her total inability to wound, inflict pain. Since speaking up and out in her marriage meant hurting, not only Ellis but her parents, she had kept silent, but she knew that soon even she must speak. And speak. She must say (to her parents as well as Ellis) that like someone in one of those terrible repetitive dreams, who endlessly find themselves at the wrong party or wrong examination at the wrong time, she had somehow gotten into the Wrong Life. She must tell Ellis that, ironically enough, his initial judgment had been quite correct—she *was* just a simple, normal soul—and that all that was wrong with her was their being married: she was not the proper material, she would never become a Perfect Analyst's Wife or anything remotely resembling it, would never become what he wanted, and needed, and had expected. She must explain that though it would seem like just more "sickness" to him, she still, after everything, believed herself capable of bearing a child with another man if she wished, and that all she wished with all her heart was to be free to find out if that was what she wished. For she must say finally that they had to divorce, he must simply let her go, that surely he realized a divorce couldn't hurt him professionally, for the world would look at *her* and cast the stone.

Dousing her cigarette in the spot cleared by Ellis, Laura watched, like someone in a dream, the Archman children coming out of the wood. "Let me see, let me see," chanted Moira, her face ripe with excitement, doing a frantic two-step to her brother's one. "*I* found him," she added breathlessly, trying to pummel him on the arm, but as he strode on, relentless, gave up the blows to save her breath, changing her tune to, "What're you going to do with him? What you going to *do*?"

As they passed behind her, Laura turned. "What did you find? —a frog?" she asked, without knowing why.

"Nanh. A toad." The boy had stopped in his tracks. "Wanta see?"

"Yes," said Laura, feeling peculiar. Bursting with self-importance, the boy came and crouched down, his scarred knees grazing her bare upper arm; putting his cupped hands before her face, he moved his thumb a quarter of an inch, and between the finger-bars Laura glimpsed two eyes, black and beady with fear, which met her own and then were shudderingly hooded by crepy gray lids. Feeling something like a shudder herself, Laura asked: "What are you going to do with him?"

"Find something to keep him in," said the boy, standing up, and, trailed by his sister, strode toward the house.

Left alone once again, Laura turned to face the pond. Her heart was pounding, pounding, pumping away, she was short of breath —what on earth was wrong with her *now?* Behind her the jerky gush and rush of the shower stopped again. A solitary breeze passed up through the grove. Frowning, working, Laura stared down the falling slope of the hill, fanny-feathered with pines through whose branches the big pond stilly glittered, and when she suddenly, violently shivered, it was not from the balsam breeze, but from the impact of closure, of past and present power-fully hooking up.

With an enormous bemused sort of calm Laura faced the signal memory, detached enough to see the great irony of the situation, honest enough to wonder if she oughtn't acknowledge a debt— this was the sort of thing they worked hard to bring about, and perhaps it was their very presence, catalytic, that was helping her, making her see. For her childish gibe aside, her mentioning Maine *had* meant something, it had after all been the Maine of her childhood busily at work in her, Maine on a particularly greengold day when she was nine years old, and therefore old enough, her father thought, to be taken fishing on the lake. But how wrong she had proved him! One moment she had been a clean glossy little girl, sitting docile in the middle of the boat between her father and his friend, the next she had become (they said) a raving ma-niac. But suspended between had been nightmare seconds: the anchor dropped, she had idly watched her father pry the lid off the mysterious can he'd brought along and, thrusting in a hand, draw out one of the beautiful tiny green speckled frogs she had caught in the woods and trustingly brought to him to keep "safe" for her; mute with horror she had watched his friend do the same thing, had watched both men take the little creatures and put them, struggling, on the hooks, pushing the barbs into the delicate stippled backs until they came out curving, hideous, through the pulsing white softness of the underbellies. Her shrieks had ricocheted all over the lake. Quickly rowed ashore, she was carried, kicking, to the cabin, one of fifteen stretching in a row from the lodge. Told to stop, stop that at once! she did not and was fiercely slapped. Her sobs subsiding, they became gentle once again: Why that was Life, they assured her over and over, at the same time giving her a garbled version of Darwin's Law—why if it hadn't been her daddy who needed them for bait to catch the fish they all hoped to eat for dinner, it would have been owls or hawks or weasels who needed the frogs for *their* dinner, or would have even been some hiker innocently squashing them underfoot while trampling through the woods . . .

With a slam of the screen door, the children came back out. Alan Archman carried a shiny aluminum coffee pot. "Mommy will have a fit!" was Moira's protest now, but her brother hissed, "This is the old one, the filter's lost," and holding the pot against Beethoven's tormented face, stalked off toward a clump of scrub and grasses near the entrance to the grove.

Anxious to see what they would do next, Laura pivoted about and found that Ellis had just come out of the house where he'd clearly been combing his hair. Spruce, pink, he stood restrapping on his wristwatch, then came slowly to where she sat, inclining his head toward the children. "What on earth are they doing?"

"Torturing some poor toad that they caught."

A look of infinite exhaustion, infinite pain crossed his face. My god, she heard him think. My god, she thought herself and, with tears blurring her vision, watched Alan Archman rip off a handful of leaves and grasses and, lifting the lid of the pot, cram them in. "Whad'you do that for?" demanded Moira, asking precisely what Laura wanted to know.

"To make him feel at home."

"But he won't be able to *breathe*," wailed the little girl, uncannily echoing all in Laura's mind: "He'll *die* in there."

"Don't be a jerk—he's getting plenty of air through the spout holes." And so saying, her brother clasped the pot tightly to his chest and collapsed to sit crosslegged where he'd stood, looking like some small sallow Buddhist monk.

"Who'll die?" asked their father genially, coming fully dressed out of the high wooden shower stall. Smoothing down his rumply hair with a hand, he went over; listening, peering into the pot, he then came laughing to where the Peppers stood. "Kids," he said, forgetting the Peppers were childless, shaking his head. "Aren't they marvelous . . ." Suddenly remembering, he flushed.

Swiftly, determinedly cutting into his embarrassment, Laura coldly said: "I thought you would make them let it go."

"Really?" Harold Archman's small eyes widened. "Why?"

"Because it *will* die," said Laura, flat.

"Nonsense," cut in Ellis threateningly.

Ignoring him, she said to her host: "Children can be awfully sadistic."

"Not mine," said Harold Archman. Again heavily embarrassed, but only for Ellis this time, he turned to him with a forced chuckle, a complicit smile. "And even when kids are sadistic, it's an important part of development and shouldn't be inhibited, wouldn't you say? So they pull the wings off a couple of flies or butterflies, cut up a couple of worms or garter snakes just to watch them squirm. A few tries and they've learned and seen what they want, they're satisfied and stop. Of course, the ones that don't stop are simply disturbed children."

Speechless, Laura watched the two men gravely nod at each other, visibly recoiling when her host put out a hand and patted her bare upper arm. "They'll let it go at bedtime," he said soothingly, propelling her toward the house. "Don't you worry—I always make them turn things loose before they go to sleep."

The blender made a noise like a small monoplane warming up. Swirling about inside, knocking and frothing against the glass sides, was a purplish wash—cranberry juice, lime juice, orange juice, vodka, cracked ice. As if it might indeed take off at any minute, Harold Archman held one hand clamped down on its top. He and Ellis stood at the waist-high counter dividing the kitchen from the living room. "I call it a Whippoorwill," he loudly explained to Ellis; Ellis, who liked his whiskey straight, tried to look enthusiastic. Behind them in the narrow kitchen Virginia Archman had her head in the icebox. Backing out with a head of romaine lettuce in each hand, she noisily pushed the icebox door shut with one knee and dumped the lettuces into the stainless steel sink; with a distracted look she headed for the deep-freeze unit, out of sight around a corner, reappearing within seconds holding two long ramrods of frozen French bread.

All this bustle did not impress Laura, the only one sitting down. Longing to do something, she had asked to help, but Virginia Archman was one of those hostesses who love to make a great martyred show of doing everything themselves; "You just sit and *relax*," she'd said, shooing Laura from the kitchen with a harassed air. Far from relaxed, Laura now stirred on the cushioned window seat and, having nothing better to do, watched Betty Anne Mayberry set the big round white formica table down at the end of the room. A big girl, she went clumsily bumping round the table, making a great clatter as she set down the stainless steel forks and knives and spoons, her cheeks a blotchy red. Feeling Laura's eyes, she glanced up, turning a deeper shade. Pitying her, Laura quickly looked away—she could guess what kind of summer the girl had had in that house—and she could not help but remember how at Betty Anne Mayberry's age, which she placed at seventeen, she had spent the summer lying prone on a canvas-covered float, only sitting upright long enough to re-establish contact, to wildly flirt with the young lifeguard seated above. Though she and the almost too-handsome lifeguard had constituted a minor scandal that summer, though she had deeply grieved and shamed her parents, it had been the only time in her life she'd ever done so: that brief burst of wildness spent, she had immediately settled back down and become the model daughter she'd always been, their endlessly gratifying only child who did all they hoped—and expected. And for this she had ultimately been rewarded, in their eyes, she won herself the true prize: the brilliant young resident psychiatrist, the quiet and modest and handsome son of one of her father's oldest friends.

To Laura's astonishment, everyone seemed to be moving outside. Putting a plastic tumbler in her hand, her host importantly confided he was going to start the fire for their steak, wouldn't she join them? Tasting the grapy drink (it was surprisingly good), she followed him out the door and across thready new grass to a crude brick-lined pit fifty feet from the house, a pit already piled with plump black cushions of charcoal. Stationed at one end, Ellis and their hostess stood sipping their drinks, smiling inanely. Harold Archman busily unscrewed the cap on a giant can of fluid, glancing up and beaming at the two children who came, as though summoned, around the corner of the house. Waiting until they were at the pit, he then ceremoniously tilted the can, pouring amber liquid with a flourish. Everyone raptly watched.

"How long will it take?" asked Virginia Archman, nursing bony elbows.

"Oh, about twenty minutes," said her husband, now taking up a long dry stick and igniting the tip with a butane pocket lighter.

"Stand back, children!" cried Virginia Archman.

Edging away, they came close to where Laura stood.

"Normally we'd let the coals bed at least half an hour," Harold Archman explained to Ellis, waving the feebly burning stick to encourage the flame, "but we got a late start tonight."

Laura leaned down to the boy at her side. "What did you do with the toad?"

"Left him out back," he said vaguely, hypnotically watching his father wave the stick to a bright flame.

"Out back where?"

"Under a *tree*," he said irritably, giving her a swift contemptuous look.

The firebrand was touched to the coals. Smoke billowed out, pungent, charry-sweet. Ignoring warnings, the two fascinated children edged closer to the pit. "I'm going inside to toss the salad," announced Virginia Archman, on her way passing Betty Anne Mayberry who came out carrying a huge slab of bloody meat on a wooden cutting board. As the girl gingerly set the board on a canvas chair, the two men silently appraised the steak. "What a cow," said Alan Archman. "How'd you manage to find a sirloin like that around here?" asked Ellis. Making love to the steak with his eyes, Harold Archman mentioned the name of a local butcher, negligibly adding, ". . . we've been coming here so many years, I guess he treats us better than most." Simply, without any attempt at stealth, Laura turned away and walked around the corner of the house.

The coffee pot stood, Brillo-shiny, under a tree near the shower stall. Her heart beating powerfully, but steadily, Laura picked it up and lifted off the lid, hoping that a tiny springing form would fly out. When nothing happened she peered inside: beneath a blanket of pine needles, leaves, grass, bits of bread there was a general pulsing, a frantic expansion and contraction, and from under a hat of pumpernickel crust a solemn little face confronted her, the eyes bulging with fear and readiness for whatever horror was to come. Making a fussing clucking sound, she started to reach in with one careful stroking finger, then, realizing this would only terrify, withdrew it, crooning, "It's all right now, it's all right." Crouching low, straining the expensive seams of her Bermuda shorts, she held the pot out at arm's length, tilting it toward the underbrush. At first nothing happened. Then she felt a dislodging thump. Then, in a streaking blur, something shot out of the open mouth of the pot, something birdlike yet pliant, something striking out for freedom, for life.

She left the pot lying on its side, only turning the open top in a misleading direction; she did not replace the lid. When she went back the steak was being lowered in an iron grill onto the glowing coals. Only Ellis remarked her return with a glance, a glance that was all of weariness and exasperation: Couldn't she even *pretend* interest? Couldn't she ever just stand *still* like other people?

"Of course the coals aren't quite right," apologized Harold Archman. "As I said before, I'd normally wait at least half an hour. But it's Betty Anne Mayberry's night off, and she always does the washing up before she leaves."

"Who hates garlic?" shouted his wife through the kitchen window.

"Nobody," said Harold Archman, answering for them all.

Letting the screen door loudly bang behind her, Betty Anne Mayberry came out once again, silently retrieving the cutting board, putting a large white ironstone platter in its place. As she went inside the children stirred; jostling each other, they moved away, trailing around the corner of the house. With a thoughtful air, Laura sipped her drink. The air was thick with the rich smell of sizzling beef. "My god but I get hungry when I'm on vacation," Ellis confided to their host. "It's really strange, because at home I barely have any appetite, but the minute I get away I . . ."

The shrieks of the children drowned him out.

Harold Archman's face looked peeled, as though he'd yanked off his glasses; behind the kitchen window-screen a white blur swam up; his mouth still forming words, Ellis seemed to gape; only Laura stood unmoving, unmoved, watching the two children come flying around the corner of the house, Alan Archman first, brandishing the pot high in the air like a sword, his sister stumbling after.

The two men understood in an instant and both turned on

Laura, accusing, yet still hoping she might somehow prove them wrong. But Laura nodded, calm and sure as Fate. "I'm sorry," she said. "It *would* have died." And then, inexplicably, burst into tears.